YELLOW
MOON

YELLOW MOON

Jewell Parker Rhodes

ATRIA BOOKS

New York London Toronto Sydney

ATRIA BOOKS

A Division of Simon & Schuster, Inc.
1230 Avenue of the Americas
New York, NY 10020

First Atria Books hardcover edition August 2008

ATRIA BOOKS and colophon are trademarks of Simon & Schuster, Inc.

For information about special discounts for bulk purchases,
please contact Simon & Schuster Special Sales at 1-800-456-6798
or business @simonandschuster.com.

"Yellow Moon" by Aaron Neville and Joel Neville
©1988 Neville Music Publ. Co./Apache Red Music
All rights administered by Irving Music, Inc. (BMI)
Used By Permission. All Rights Reserved.

Designed by Jaime Putorti

Manufactured in the United States of America

10 9 8 7 6 5 4 3 2 1

Library of Congress Cataloging-in-Publication Data
Rhodes, Jewell Parker.
    Yellow moon : a novel / by Jewell Parker Rhodes.—1st Atria Books hardcover ed.
        p. cm.
ISBN-13: 978-1-4165-3710-6
ISBN-10:   1-4165-3710-4

1. African American women—Fiction. 2. Women physicians—Fiction. 3. New Orleans
(La.)—Fiction. 4. Voodooism—Fiction. I. Title.

PS3568.H63Y45 2008
813'.54—dc22

                                        2008015221

Dedicated to the Imani Readers of Atlanta
and to my husband, Brad

YELLOW MOON

PROLOGUE

Drifting in darkness, lost in the vast Atlantic, it woke. Where had it been? Where was home? No answer. Only longing as it drifted in icy water, among currents and tides, shipwrecks, and murdered slaves' brittle bones.

What was it? Who?

It couldn't remember.

The Port of New Orleans is never quiet. Like a good whorehouse, there's always activity. Needs being fulfilled.

Daylight, ship horns bellowed as longshoremen unpacked crates from China, India, the Americas and outfitted ships for the ride north, up the mighty Mississippi.

Nighttime, when the moon was shrouded, sounds muted, activity of another kind stirred—illegal shipments of drugs, alcohol, and people. Police were paid to look the other way while gang members, knives slipped in their boots, guns in their belts, trafficked in contraband, ensuring New Orleans's fame. The Crescent City. Named for the thin sliver of a moon with the devil's upturned horns. Sin City. Big Easy. Except nothing was easy.

It was in a watery grave, blending invisibly with water. Seeking comfort it couldn't find. It couldn't remember a beginning or an end.

JT wished he wasn't here. Blackjack called him like a lover, and he'd succumbed, hoping to score. Sometimes, he did; most times, he didn't. His day job, counting crates arriving and with what, didn't pay much. Union wages weren't for illegals; so, he hustled for a few dollars more. Played lookout in case some unsuspecting Joe got too curious or too close to the skiffs maneuvering between the stately cruise and merchant ships.

JT wasn't a bad man. He had scruples. He wouldn't watchdog if it involved kidnapped women or children. He wouldn't take pay in coke. Not even rum.

Tonight, he felt uneasy. There was a shipment of pirated electronics. Or so he'd been told. He was too old to be abroad at night. Too foolish not to give up the cards. Fifty-eight years old, and he knew he'd never find his pot of gold.

His luck had run out.

Below the sea, it flailed. Fish darted blindly. Crabs scuttled across the sea bottom. Incoherent memories. Triumph. A face? A serpent, then pain. Couldn't remember what, how. When.

He looked across the black Gulf dotted with ship lights, low-slung stars, and billowy clouds. His mother had sworn Agwé, the sea god, would protect him.

As a child, he'd sailed safe from Haiti in an overcrowded raft. Others had died from heatstroke, starvation, or were drowned after being tossed overboard by a rough sea or an angry hand.

It gathered itself. Fish darted. Crabs scuttled. Coalescing, it moved, surging against the current, the grainy sand. Growing stronger.

"JT—you on watch?"

"Here," he said, raising his arm at the thickset man.

"Better be."

JT scowled, then marched left, right, left, then right again. All he saw were cops waiting for their cut and wharf rats scavenging for crumbs.

His mother had had dreams for him; he wasn't living any of them.

"You," she'd said, kissing him farewell, "I dedicate to Agwé."

The local spell man had slipped a foul-smelling, leather bag about his neck. "Keep it safe," he'd told him. "Keep it safe."

But once in America, after the fourth boy, picking a fight, poked fun at his charm, JT threw the bag away.

Staring at his rough hands, his calloused feet, JT whispered, "Agwé." He lit a cigarette, the tip glowing, and savored the smoke curling through his lungs.

It soared toward a light. A bright circle, suspended. High. Higher. Bursting from water into air. To another world. Less ephemeral. Sky. It remembered the word. Sky. Sun and storms.

JT saw rippling on the water's surface. A fish? A miracle?

He tossed his cigarette into the lapping water, then lay on rough wood, his head hanging over the wharf edge, his fingers dangling in the warm water.

"Agwé, you there? Beloved god of my mama?"

Desire formed—an old desire. It remembered lungs filling with air. It used to walk on land.

Each of the Voodoo gods had their song. JT didn't remember Agwé's song, the singsong chant, but he remembered beats. Syncopated, luring.

JT, his hands tingling with power, slapped his chest and legs. Like a minstrel drummer, his hands pounded the rhythm—the signal for Agwé to come.

Sound—it remembered sound. Vibrations calling. It moved toward the shore, searching for the source. For who called it.

JT sat, legs crossed, the dirty Mississippi dripping from his fingers.

A shadow hovered on the horizon.

Sailors told of shadows that roiled and rolled, forecasting hurricanes. JT shifted uneasily, stretching out his hands as if he could touch the distant storm. Then, he patterned the rhythm again and again, his hands stinging skin, blood rising to the surface.

Becoming dense, coalescing above the water, the shadow slid toward him.

Tears filled JT's eyes. In the approaching darkness, he thought he saw his mother, ever so young, beautiful. "Mama," he shouted.

It grew, dimensional, tall, skimming the water's surface.

The darkness seemed to walk on water. It must be Agwé, his mother's favorite god, JT thought. If Agwé possessed him, he knew he'd be saved. Knew his luck would change.

A ragged shape, an outline of mist. Limbs, torso. Not itself—but a memory.

It understood desire. Need. Wanting.

Understood sound, rhythm—compelling, cajoling. Calling the gods. Before. What was before?

It remembered smells. Flesh. Blood. It desired blood.

"Save me," JT bellowed, frenetically pounding his chest. "Agwé, save me."

The swift darkness neared. A frigid breeze blew across the warm Mississippi. Across the wharf.

It slammed into him.

JT fell, his skull cracking, his body, writhing on the wharf, like a catfish, belly up.

It pinioned the body to the ground. Inhaling the sweet, fleshy smell; feeling the ebb and flow, the rhythm of the blood, hearing the heart pounding. Pressing sinews, muscles, and bone. Insatiable. Hungry.

Coiling about JT's hand, it bit, puncturing his wrist.

Encased in a dark cloud, JT could see his flesh rise; feel, rather than see, his blood draining, disappearing into air. He wanted to scream but the pressure on his chest robbed him of voice. He struggled, legs flailing, but couldn't break free.

He felt his soul tearing from his flesh. Felt some thing, someone stealing memories, feelings. Through the mist, he could see the moon, the star-cluttered sky. Helpless, he stopped struggling, trying to hold on to memories flowing from his wrist. Into cold air.

He remembered: coffee and packs of saltines for breakfast; hunting trash bins to resell pop bottles and cans; a woman laughing, scornfully, when he smiled at her; fat-bellied Darryl, cursing: "Get to work. Too damn slow." Hauling crates in the too-hot sun. Searching the dock and alleyways for cops. Sleeping on a stained mattress. Voices, angry and boastful, floating up from the street. An alarm clanging: 4:00 am. Work. Waking, dreamless, to another day.

JT mourned for all he hadn't done.

Light-headed, organs starved for oxygen, JT remembered his mother singing, holding him close.

JT tried to call to her, but his voice was a dry gurgle—a final exhale.

Satiated, it uncoiled from the body, tasting the salty blood and savoring JT's memories. It dove into the sea, wriggling into the cool depths. Remembering.

ONE

Marie could hear the music wailing, bleeding through the spray-painted windows and door. Her body responded—her fingers itching to snap, her feet to dance. It would be very nice, too, if she got laid. DuLac wouldn't mind. That was the nice thing about going club hopping with a boss who was also a mentor and friend.

"Safe sex, Marie."

She laughed. "Are you saying I'm a loose woman?"

DuLac, in a double-breasted suit, a diamond in his ear, his hair peppered gray, was elegance personified. He came from an old Creole family; his face fine boned, like his French ancestors. Outwardly, he was genteel, gracious. A perfect companion. Inwardly, he was more complex, his soul steeped in African rhythms, mystery, and healing.

"Be good," he said. "Tomorrow, you and I have a shift."

"Sure thing, boss. You want me to monitor your wine?"

"Don't sass."

"Just have a good time?"

"Oui. Bonne temps en Nouveau Orleans."

They grinned like conspirators. Work hard, play hard. Marie slipped her hand through his arm.

The bouncer, a wannabe pro wrestler, opened the door, waving them into the club. A cave smelling of sweat, musky perfumes, and tropical rum.

The music was uplifting. Marie stepped lightly, hips swaying as the waitress showed them to their table. Dead center, in front of the musicians' platform. A table, every Saturday night, reserved for her and DuLac. An indulgence. Reward for the shifts battling Charity Hospital's violence, disease, and trauma.

Marie looked around the hazy, smoke-filled room. Votive candles decorated the tables. Dried magnolias hung like ribbons from the ceiling. Candle sconces decorated the walls, shimmering with shadows and firelight.

Waitresses dressed in sleek black satin with bustiers uplifting brown, yellow, white, pink-tinged breasts, offered drinks, roses for couples—gay or straight. For five dollars you could have your picture taken, your face burrowing into soft, perfumed breasts.

All in good fun. Music with a little sex, decadence thrown in.

But it was the music that held the greatest allure. Rhythms that spoke to and about the spirit. Saxophones that sounded like cries; trumpets that wailed; drums that proclaimed; and piano scales that cascaded, calling for "mercy."

Music—all powerful, knowing. Human. Humane.

Marie had thought there was a rule—only handsome people were welcome at La Mer. But she'd come to realize that New

Orleanians were always beautiful listening to music. It was as if they let themselves be transformed, opening their souls and bodies so they seemed larger, more infused with life. That's why she loved La Mer—rarely was it filled with thrill-seeking tourists. Just music-loving locals. Who understood the mating sounds. The life-in-death sounds. The excruciating pleasure of being alive.

Marie swayed to the moaning sax, her body answering the sound. She searched the bar for interesting men. Most were already paired; some she'd already enjoyed.

DuLac murmured, "Night's still young."

She blushed. "If you were younger—"

"I'm your father figure."

"True." DuLac had taken her under his wing. She hadn't known her father, but she couldn't imagine one better than DuLac. Only in New Orleans did fathers party, encouraging their daughters to have a good time. In a city filled with so much sin, holding tight to passion was a requirement for survival. How else could a people outlast slavery; Spanish, French, and American invasions; yellow fever; and hurricanes?

Live life large. Let the good times roll. New Orleans—her adopted home. The city where she felt most herself.

The song ended. Climaxing in a vibrato that left the audience breathless, whistling, stomping their feet, demanding more.

Charlie, the piano man, stood, his mouth slyly upturned, shouting, "Everybody . . . everybody welcome doctors Louis DuLac and Marie Laveau. Visit Charity Hospital. They'll fix what ails you."

The drummer hit the bass.

DuLac bowed. Blushing, Marie slid down in her seat. Charlie always liked embarrassing her.

"Dr. Laveau—descendant of the great voodoo queen—yes, that Marie Laveau, buried in St. Louis Cemetery number one, some say number two. But regardless of where she's buried, this here"—he pointed at Marie—"this here is her great-great-granddaughter. The beautiful, badass, turn your world around, upside down, Marie Laveau."

The quintet launched into a ditty:

> *Marie Laveau, wicked as a snake, strong as a bear.*
> *Conjure woman, turn your life around. Upside down.*
> *She'll put an evil spell on you.*

Customers were on their feet, applauding. Even DuLac stood, smirking.

Reluctantly, Marie bowed, blowing a kiss at Charlie. She'd told him that one day she'd hex him if he didn't stop embarrassing her. But Charlie had just grinned, like he was doing now, his left hand rolling with the bass line.

Someone sent over a hurricane—dark rum mixed with sugar, grenadine, and passion juice, topped with a lime.

She gulped the drink down. "If a man had been interested in me—that surely would've turned him off."

"Tell me another lie," said DuLac.

Marie scanned the bar. Maybe one of the single men had sent over the drink? But none of the men caught her eye. They were all watching Charlie—as well they should. He'd launched into "King Porter Stomp" by Jelly Roll Morton. It was one of her favorites: a mixture of ragtime, blues, African and Caribbean rhythms.

She leaned back, enjoying her night off from the ER—its sutures, IVs, and multiple stab wounds.

DuLac ordered champagne.

No worries. She let the music carry her. The drum and snare tat-a-tat-tapping in three-quarter time; the sax punctuating the pulsing bass; Charlie's fingers flying across the ivories. The song was joyful, upbeat. She studied the musicians' faces. Ecstasy. Charlie, eyes closed, shook his head side to side. Big Ben played his upright bass, his body and arms curving, cradling the wood like a lover. Aaron blew his heart into his sax.

The drummer was new. She didn't know his name. Rail thin, sandy colored, he expertly kept the music from spinning into chaos. His drums restrained the sound, then pushed, encouraging the musicians to let loose in their solos; then his snare quieted them, unifying the sound until, once again, it was time for Charlie, Aaron, or Big Ben to improvise, making the song new again.

Drumsticks sliced the air. Every part of the drummer's body moved. Feet on the floor and the bass pedal; head nodding; hands and arms, swaying, teasing more sound from the drum skins; his body, rocking, leaning forward and back to emphasize or lighten the rhythm. Sweat beaded his face. His eyes followed his hands. He was speaking as drummers had from the dawn of time. Pounding out a story. What needed to be said.

The room erupted in applause as the drummer shifted the swing into a more urgent, insistent rhythm.

Marie caught her breath.

"You all right, Marie?"

She didn't answer. *The drums echoed the power of ceremonial drums. Calling on spirits from another world.*

She looked around—patrons were transfixed, even Billy, the bartender, had stopped making drinks, the waitresses in their thigh-slit skirts had paused. Everyone watched the drummer, including his band mates.

DuLac watched her. "What is it?"

She blinked. *The drummer was possessed. He was looking at her, his eyes unnaturally bright. He was communicating, telling her to pay attention, to bridge this world and the next.*

He pounded the bass pedal once, then twice. The rhythm changed. The melody was gone. But the beats were staccato, shifting into Agwé's song.

Never before had she witnessed a spirit possess without being called. Agwé, the sea god, or Ogun, the warrior, even the great Damballah, the serpent god, the god of creation, appeared after offerings, chants, after Legba, the guardian, opened the spirit gates. Then the spirit *loas* entered human bodies. But Agwé was here. *Now.* In the drummer, in his music; and everyone in La Mer sensed the magic.

The drumming stopped. One second, two. No sound, no motion. Workers, patrons, held their breath, expectant. The drums swung back into tune. The pianist pushed forward the melody of "King Porter Stomp," then dove into its famous riffs. Lightning chords celebrating the black presence in the New World.

Activity resumed. Waitresses took orders, placed drinks. Men snapped their fingers, tapped their feet. Two women left for the powder room. Billy was a blur, pouring Johnnie Walker and rum and coke.

Amazing, Marie thought, everyone seemed to have forgotten what they'd seen and heard.

Big Ben played his bass; Charlie, lovingly, stroked chords; Aaron blew softly, seducing his sax. The drummer grinned, urging his brother musicians to finish the tune. Charlie inhaled, letting his hands rise, then he pounded down, striking C-major chords, launching into "Moon River."

"Did you see it, DuLac?"

"You know I don't have your gifts."

"But you felt it?"

"More that I felt you. Saw the change in you."

Marie knew DuLac desperately desired her spiritual gifts. "They're yours to carry," he often said.

Times, like now, she felt unbearably alone.

"Agwé was here. Something in the world isn't right."

Why would Agwé appear? And so only she could see him? She knew it had to be a warning. About what?

"Take me home, DuLac."

She headed out of the club, knowing DuLac would whisper apologies, make their excuses. It was rude to leave in the middle of a set. But Marie felt dread settling in her bones.

She unbuckled her seat belt, kissed DuLac good night.

"Let me come up, Marie," said DuLac. "Make sure you're safe."

"I'm all right. Need sleep, that's all." She stepped out of the air-conditioned car, into the humid night.

Marie couldn't help turning toward the Mississippi, its water lapping hungrily for miles. *Something was stirring in the water.* She smelled brine. Oil staining the shore. And something else. Fetid. Ancient.

DuLac rolled down the car window. "Are you sure you're all right?"

Marie stooped, poking her head inside the car. "Fine."

"Call me, if you need me."

"I always do."

Reluctantly, DuLac shifted his car into Drive.

Marie forced a smile, waving her hand. When the car rounded the corner, she entered her apartment's courtyard—dreary, a few potted plants, a cracked fountain with a gargoyle spraying water from its mouth.

Marie focused on each step, climbing the stairs to her second-floor flat. All she wanted was some quiet. To hug Marie-Claire.

"That you, Miz Marie?"

"*Ici*, here."

Kind Dog barked a welcome, his whole body wagging.

Louise—a grandmother at forty—never minded babysitting Marie-Claire. "My children are too grown," she'd complain. "My grandchildren, hooligans. Now Marie-Claire is all that a child should be."

Marie knew Louise didn't mean it. Missing a few teeth, with strong arms and hands to cradle a child, Louise loved the toddler stage. Soon as Marie-Claire turned five or six, Louise would be calling her a "hooligan," too.

"Did she eat well?"

"*Bien*. Like a champ. Black beans, rice, applesauce. Mashed bananas."

Marie smiled. Sometimes she wondered if Louise didn't need the mashing more than Marie-Claire. "Thanks," she said, slipping her cash and a hug.

"Dog ate, too. Licked Marie-Claire's plate clean when I wasn't looking."

"Dog!" said Marie.

Dog laid down, his ears flat, his eyes droopy.

"See, he knows he's bad."

"'Night. *Bonsoir,*" Marie murmured, locking the door behind Louise.

Marie stooped, hugging Kind Dog. She scratched his ear. "Did you take care of Marie-Claire?"

He barked.

"Good dog."

Marie slipped off her heels, tiptoeing into Marie-Claire's room. Kind Dog padded behind her.

Wind lightly stirred the blackbird mobile. Only in the Deep South did folks believe blackbirds were good luck, carrying souls of slaves who'd escaped slavery by growing wings. Some went back to Africa and became people again; others, preferred being birds, flying through clouds, across seas, and into forests.

She looked down into the crib. She really needed to get Marie-Clarie a bed. Three years old. Her tiny feet touched the rail. Barely enough room for her curl-tousled head.

Tomorrow, she'd buy a bed with a partial railing.

Marie still remembered, as a child, waking up on the floor, her hips and arms bruised. "Nightmares," her mother had said. She knew it was always the same dream that pushed her over the edge. Awake, she never remembered what had frightened her.

Maybe Marie-Claire would have only sweet dreams? She stroked her downy black curls.

It never ceased to amaze her how much love she felt for her

child. Small amber fingernails; a hand tucked beneath her cheek; a fat baby belly rising and falling beneath the yellow blanket. There was nothing more beautiful.

She still remembered the chaotic ER, slicing through a girl's abdomen and womb to deliver Marie-Claire. She'd thought the mother was dead. But that was a horror she didn't want to think about—not tonight. She'd had enough trauma for one night.

She needed to hold Marie-Claire. But that would be selfish. Let her sleep. She should be asleep.

Marie tiptoed toward the door.

Dog whimpered.

She turned back.

Slats made shadow stripes across Marie-Claire's body. She was breathing evenly. *The blackbirds were jangling, as if someone was jerking the strings.*

"Who's there?" Marie hissed. "Agwé, is that you?"

The blackbirds stilled, no motion.

Marie opened the French doors, stepping onto the wrought-iron balcony, a perch from which she could see the cathedral and Cabildo, the alleys and cobblestone streets leading into the French Quarter. She should get a new apartment. A city walk-up with no yard wasn't a fit place to raise a child. She hadn't moved yet because she loved the water. Beyond the ancient buildings, she could see Riverwalk, see steamers lolling on the Mississippi, see clouds hanging low over the muddy water, and a moon rising, changing every twenty-eight days from a sliver to a full moon. Tonight, it was almost full. In a week, all the crazies would be out—including those convinced they were werewolves. She'd see the damage in the ER. Stabbings, gunshots, assaults.

Now all she saw beyond the merchant and cruise ships was a ripple of waves blending with an indigo horizon. The quiet before a storm? Agwé, warning her? Why? About what?

Kind Dog barked.

"Sssh."

He sat, ears perked high.

They both looked out across the skyline to the water. A whole world of water. "Mississippi"—derived from the Ojibwe "misi-ziibi," "great river." Water journeying from Minnesota. Freshwater mixing with salt. Seeping into the Gulf of Mexico.

To the southeast was Lake Pontchartrain. Brackish. Black with algae. Refuse and eels skimmed the surface. During hurricane season, the lake rose, menacing. Tonight, it was calm. A skein of glass. Agwé's kingdom was miles deep.

City levees kept water at bay. Spirits, too?

Marie smiled wryly. She knew better than anyone that mysteries always multiplied. Boundaries of time, space, were only imagined. Spirits were ever present.

She closed the French doors, padding softy by the crib, looking at Marie-Claire with longing. She started stripping her clothes before she got to her bedroom. She preferred sleeping naked. It felt good to shake off restraints, to have clean cotton rub against skin.

As her head lay on the pillow, she shuddered. Most days, she loved being who she was. But, tonight, she feared what tomorrow would bring.

She sighed, cupping a hand beneath her breast. Kind Dog hopped on the bed, laying his head on the second pillow. Silky black—a cross between a Labrador and a golden retriever, she blessed the day Kind Dog had come into her life.

Still, she couldn't help sighing. It would be wonderful if Dog were a man—if she could bury her body in flesh, connect, for a brief moment, and remind herself that she wasn't only Marie-Claire's mother, a doctor, a voodoo practitioner. She was also a woman. Longing for the essential pleasures of being a woman.

T W O

The automatic glass doors parted quietly. Bright, artificial light washed over Marie. Air-conditioned air. Bitter iodine and alcohol. Body sweat. Flesh, decayed and dying.

ER. Her second home. Be a doctor and heal.

Adrenaline kicked in. Pulse racing, breath shallow, face flushed, Marie felt needed. Here. In Charity. Hospital for the poor. The uninsured. Brown and black people from the African Diaspora and native tribes; brown and yellow people from Vietnam, Thailand, India, Mexico, and Guatemala. Rural whites—backwoods, bayou people stranded in the city, underfunded pensioners, Wal-Mart and custodial workers. Urbanites, of all colors, who'd lost their way in drugs, disability, chronic unemployment, or underemployment. A United Nations of the Poor.

"How you doing?" called El, the head nurse for the graveyard shift.

Marie kissed her cheek. El was her most outrageous friend.

"Got your pincushion popped?"

"I wish."

"Another Saturday night," EI cackled. "You'll come."

Marie grinned, kept walking toward her locker. El was sixty-seven but looked as handsome as a woman in her forties. "Magnolias," she said. "Keep me young." Marie thought it had to do with her soul—though her nails were painted bright red and curved inward like a witch's, EI was the sweetest woman. The best nurse. Marie-Claire's godmother.

DuLac, clean, elegant in his head doctor uniform, scowled. He looked as handsome as ever. No matter how late they'd been carousing, he always seemed alert, fresh. She was sure she had bags under her eyes. She shrugged.

Yes, she was running late. She couldn't help reading one last story to Marie-Claire.

DuLac shook his finger at her, scolding as if she were a child.

Marie stuck out her tongue.

"How's your daughter?" asked Huan.

"Daughter." Marie loved that word. "Fine, Huan."

Huan pressed her palms together, bowed, and smiled quickly before darting off to another patient.

Huan, gentle like a butterfly, had stayed on after her residency. She translated for shrimpers, Vietnamese who arrived with scarred hands or legs nearly severed from steel nets. K-Paul, the best diagnostician, was a hometown, St. Bernard's Parish boy. Poor white trash made good. It was rumored University Hospital had offered him a position. More money. Better conditions. A hospital, unlike state-funded Charity, favored with countless federal research grants and alumni dollars.

K-Paul had second sight when it came to diagnostics. Marie teased him, saying he had to be African, a *ju-ju* doctor's descendant. K-Paul blushed, his porcelain skin turning redder. He was Cajun. Descendant of Acadians, the French settlers of eastern Canada.

Marie admired K-Paul. He stayed in the trenches. His senses—touch, sight, smell—saved Charity thousands of dollars. More important, he saved lives.

Marie opened her locker, donning her white coat, slipping on her white loafers. Stethoscope, reflex hammer in her pocket. She was happy. Time to beat back the devil.

Be a doctor and heal.

Her hand slammed open the lounge door. She winked at EI. Nodded solemnly at DuLac. She stared at the board. Names; symptoms written in red, black, and blue markers.

"What shall it be?" she asked DuLac. "Curtain One?"

"Sure," he said, still scowling. "A colicky baby. Think you can handle it?"

"No problem. Eight years of schooling. Hundreds of thousands of dollars in debt. Real-life experience as a single mother. Sure. I can handle a cranky baby."

She kept her features straight; out of the corner of her eye, she watched DuLac suppress his smile. She plucked the baby's chart.

From far off, at least two miles away, a siren caterwauled, like a thousand cats.

"Incoming," shouted Huan.

"Incoming," bellowed DuLac.

Marie handed the baby's chart to Reese. An intern from Atlanta. Still queasy about blood.

DuLac came to stand beside her. Two sentries waiting for the glass doors to slide open. Behind them were Huan and El.

The ambulance was careening, swerving through New Orleans's narrow, tourist-choked streets. Marie could hear the *whoop, whoop* sound as it crossed intersections.

The ambulance slowed, then stopped. Doors—front and back—banged open.

DuLac moved forward. Automatic doors slid open. Humidity and hot air slid into the ER like melted butter.

"Flatline," yelled a lanky paramedic, the driver.

His stooped, hair-slicked partner leaped out the van, spitting staccato: "Pulse gone, pressure nonexistent, no brain activity. This one's dead. Too late for salvation."

The gurney clattered onto the street.

"Did you do all that was necessary?" asked DuLac.

"Flatline," said the lanky one, now somber like a priest. "Weird as all hell."

"Been dead for hours," said his partner. "Unbelievable."

"Like you fools," murmured El. "Tearing up the streets, driving like bats out of hell. Endangering the living."

"Yours, Marie?"

"Sure, DuLac."

Marie helped push the gurney forward, through the doors, into Station 4, beneath the bright, unforgiving lights.

"Flatline," the paramedic repeated.

She hated the word: "flatline." So disrespectful, as though life was merely a pulse, a beam on an EKG machine. Besides, the machine could be wrong. That's what she'd learned from the Sleeping Beauties case. The women appeared dead, but were merely in a kind of waking stasis. Zombies did exist. There was a scientific explanation: the paralyzing gills of a puffer fish.

Her hands touched the sheet, draping over the gurney's edge. Inexplicably, she felt fear. As if, once she pulled back the thin cotton, she would destroy some essential boundary between the known and the unknown.

"Dead." The two paramedics had followed her, curious, like vultures.

The sheet lifted and fell gracefully.

She sucked in air. She'd never seen anything like it.

The paramedics were wriggling, almost dancing with glee.

"Get out of here."

"Told you. Told you. Weird as shit."

She leaned forward, checking for a pulse, reflexes. The lungs were flat. Deflated, like a balloon. Pupils fixed.

"Get out of here. I need room to work."

"You heard her." A tall, slim man ducked inside the curtain.

"Parks," he said, sliding a badge from his inside suit pocket.

He was young, good looking.

"Looks like a shriveled leprechaun," said Parks.

The body was small—under five feet. Maybe fifty, sixty. "Alive, he couldn't have been more than eighty-five, ninety pounds," said Marie. "No obvious cause of death. Pale. Consistent with blood loss."

"They said you were the right doctor for a weird death."

"Who?"

"Detectives at the scene."

Marie didn't answer. A nursery rhyme floated through her mind: *This old man, he played one, he played knick-knack on my drum.* She sang it to Marie-Claire. *"Knick-knack, paddy-wack, give the dog a bone."* Kind Dog would wag his tail. *"This old man came rolling home."*

A small crowd of technicians, nurses gathered at the green, ringed curtains.

Marie pressed the man's flesh—abdomen, thighs, arms. "There's not much resilience. Dehydration. I don't think there's an ounce of blood left."

The body wasn't much more than a skeleton, brown flesh stretched over bone. Lying on the gurney—bones stiff, skin deflated—the body seemed a cruel joke. A papier-mâché or wood-cut of a body. A made thing, not a dead man. This was the ill Agwé had tried to warn her about.

"Go on, get out of here." Parks pushed back the gawking nurses and technicians, pulling the ringed curtains shut. He stood next to Marie.

"You should let him go," said Parks.

"What?"

"Let him go."

She'd been holding the man's hand. Blunt fingers, scars on his hand, the tip of his index finger lost. Typical injuries for dock workers.

"Where was he found?" asked Marie.

"Wharf. Just as you see him here. No ID. No valuables."

"Why didn't you take him to the coroner's office?"

"I was told I'd do better to bring him here. To you."

"I'm supposed to help?"

"I've been told you are uniquely qualified." His expression was curious. No sarcasm. Or hint of disdain. "Roach—our coroner—is on his way."

"Let's get him down to the morgue." She settled the sheet over the corpse. "Help me?"

"Sure." Parks pushed, she pulled the gurney. Turning a sharp corner, rolling past the nurses' station, the sheet shifted, exposing the dead man's face and torso.

"Did you see that?"

"Bloodsucker."

"Anne Rice must've cast this one."

"Lestat. That's her vampire. Lestat did it."

The nurses squealed.

Parks covered the leathery skull.

El shouted, "Back to work. Be respectful."

Marie felt ancient. Most of the nurses were only a few years younger than she was. She understood their desire to make macabre jokes.

One of the nurses, a brunette with thick-lashed eyes, crossed herself for protection: "Father. Son. Holy Ghost." Marie wondered if she was fearful of her, the dead man, or both?

The morgue was in the basement. Refrigeration units took up half the floor; the other half, held autopsy rooms and labs.

They rolled the blood-drained man to a woman sitting at a metal, traditional school desk, reading a paperback, James Lee Burke's *In the Electric Mist of the Confederate Dead,* and popping gum.

"He needs refrigeration."

"Actually, he doesn't. It's best to look at him fresh. Least, at first." He grinned, making him seem even younger. "Forensics—a hobby."

"You're—?"

"Parks. Detective Daniel Parks. I thought I was making an impression."

"No one ever calls you Dan."

"Am I that obvious? Never liked diminutives." He tapped his chest. "Detective Parks, just as you're Doc—" He glanced at the tag on her right-breast pocket.

"Laveau," she said.

"Yeah. They told me about you. Used to be Levant. Came from Chicago. Discovered you were a Laveau. Voodoo ancestors. Must've been strange."

The technician, wide eyed, popped her gum.

"We'll find an empty theater," said Marie. This time she pushed the gurney, Parks pulled.

Parks was everything Reneaux hadn't been. Clean cut, light brown hair; blue eyes, and suited in a gray cotton business suit, white shirt, polished black shoes. No jewelry anywhere, not even a wedding ring.

She missed Reneaux's faded leather jacket, his hair in a ponytail, the cross stud in his left ear. She missed his velvet black skin.

"This one's clear." Parks pushed the door.

"Wait up."

"That's Roach," said Parks.

"Why do you call him Roach?"

"Don't ask," said Roach, struggling to catch his breath. "Let's look at this baby." He pulled back the sheet and whistled.

Parks flipped open a spiral notepad. He and Reneaux, maybe all cops, had that in common. Lines filled with ink and lead markings.

Roach circled the body.

Marie shivered. The theater was cold. Concrete floor with drainage depressions for blood, bodily fluids. Steel examining table. A portable tray with gleaming tools to cut, dissect, crack chest cavities, drill skulls, spread abdominal walls. There was a metal sink on the right. A scale. The human heart weighed twelve ounces. Brain matter, fourteen. Liver, three pounds. She'd learned this in anatomy. But she'd never liked cadavers—"stiffs." She preferred living tissue; plastic, colored layers of body diagrams; cast models with pretend skin peeled back, cut open; or a computer simulation.

"Let's have a better look at him," said Roach, snapping on latex gloves.

Rigor mortis had settled in like an unwelcome cousin. Arms were shrinking inward; legs, contracting, curling into a fetal position. The body seemed more like a marionette, strings cut, collapsed into an improbable, impossible position. Everything about the fixed joints, the bloodless limbs, seemed inhuman.

"Time of death?"

"Hand me that thermometer, Doc." Roach sliced through flesh, into the liver. And inserted the thermometer. "Time of death. Maybe sometime before midnight—last night. It's hard to tell. Not normal to take a reading from a bloodless liver. Body is unnaturally cold. Bodies rot in New Orleans's heat. Stomach-content analysis might tell us more."

Marie swallowed. She'd been at the jazz club. Was this man dying when Agwé appeared?

"I still don't understand why you brought the body here," she said. "You've got your own facilities."

"My sentiments exactly," said Roach, bent over, almost sniffing the dead man's body, circling him, inspecting skin and bones.

"Call it a hunch," said Parks. "What're you doing, Roach?"

"Checking the neck."

"Dracula's not to blame."

"Relax. Just checking."

A fly was trapped in the morgue. It buzzed, landing on the dead man's hair.

"Have you ever seen anything like this, Dr. Laveau?" Roach's eyes blinked behind his round glasses.

"No. The body has eight pints of blood. To become bloodless is scientifically impossible without some gaping wound, a throat slashed, or artery cut."

"No cuts here. No blood on his clothes."

"Exactly. Free from trauma except for blood loss."

"Fascinating."

The fly buzzed off.

"So we agree," said Parks, standing beside Marie. "This is a re-markable case."

She could smell Parks's aftershave. Too sweet for such a disci-plined, no-nonsense man. She focused on the body.

Roach chuckled, gleeful. "My real name is William Deheny. One of New Orleans's Irish. You do voodoo stuff?"

"Leave it, Roach."

"Priests do hocus-pocus, too. All that incense. Holy water. Come on—wine into blood?"

"Roach," warned Parks.

"Sure, right. He looks like he's ready to be mummified. In all my born days, never seen such a thing. You?"

"No." Marie decided she liked Roach, round, and irreverent. Parks, staring intently, made her feel like a freak show.

Roach took a knife and sliced open the abdomen. The rib spreader showed tissue-paper lungs, dried sinews, collapsed arteries and veins.

Marie murmured: "Bad-luck man. Never got a break. No shoes, only calloused feet. These black marks mean his toes were infected. His pants and jacket are too small, secondhand. Whatever he did, he didn't do well. All his life, he couldn't do anything well. Not even when he tried." She'd seen this man's type often enough. A migrant trying to get by.

"He threatened someone," said Parks.

"Maybe," said Marie, not eager to let the statement rest.

"What did he do that didn't deserve a beating, a knife to the groin, or a bullet at the base of his skull?" asked Roach. "How could he threaten an enemy so much, they'd drain every drop of his blood?"

Marie exhaled. What was she missing? She squeezed her fingers into gloves, then ran her hands over the body. His skin felt like paper, ready to crumble. She caressed his right hand. Missing finger. Scarred. She turned his palm over. "Look. His wrist—"

"Puncture marks."

"Yes. Blood drained here."

"Impossible."

"No, I'm right."

The man's spirit sat up, nodding.

Marie stumbled backward.

"You okay, Doc?"

She looked at Parks, startled. His voice sounded like Reneaux's.

The dead man's spirit was perched, like an elf, on his own chest.

Inhale, exhale. She blinked. "He's still there."

"Who?"

"The dead man."

"'Course he is," said Roach. "I've cut the shit out of him."

"No, I mean, his ghost."

"Where?" Roach dropped his knife.

"You've got to be kidding," said Parks.

"In the body cavity. The chest." *The dead man opened his mouth and howled.*

Marie covered her ears. "Stop. Stop."

"What's wrong with you?" asked Parks.

"Make it stop."

Roach sliced the air, over the chest.

Silence.

"Is he gone?" asked Roach. "Did I kill him?"

"You can't kill a dead man," said Parks.

Marie clutched the dead man's wrist. The wounds were circular, small, reddish brown. "Blood could be siphoned here. Kill a man. This is what Agwé was warning me about."

Roach made the sign of the cross.

"You mean you had a warning about a possible murder? Why didn't you call the police?"

"And say what? Premonition?"

"You said it was a man named Agwé."

"I said, 'Agwé,' Detective Parks. Not a man. A spirit god. Rules the oceans and seas."

"Jesus. Mary. Joseph," said Roach.

"You're joking."

"You came to me, Detective."

"Yeah, that's right, Doc. Detectives told me about you."

"But you didn't believe them? Didn't believe there was a crazy conjure woman with second sight, hexing, doing *ju-ju*." She waved her hand. "No. Don't answer."

"I believe," said Roach, nervously looking around. "He . . . the ghost . . . still here?"

Roach was typical of white New Orleanians', irreligious until spooked.

Marie stroked the dead man's cheek. "No, he's gone."

Parks checked his notes. "'Never got a break,' you said. How do you know?"

"I can sense things."

"Like you can *see* things? Things others can't see?"

"Now I hear the sarcasm, Detective. I thought you were more open-minded."

"It's 'cause he's a northerner."

"Shut up, Roach."

"It's true. Northerners don't believe in anything."

"I don't believe in ghosts. Religious hocus-pocus. Voodoo."

"I believe," said Roach, stubbornly. "She saw a ghost."

"She says she saw a ghost. Isn't that right?"

Marie was studying the dead man's eyes. They were glassy. Not only blood, but all moisture had been drained from his body.

How could a man with no major arteries cut be drained of blood? More important: Why would he be?

Marie rechecked his limbs, behind his knees. His ankles. Parks and Roach were right behind her. She could feel their breaths. Smell the sweat on Roach, the aftershave on Parks.

The little man was looking at her, too. Woebegone, as if she could resurrect him. Reanimate life.

Marie felt as if time were collapsing, two worlds—living and dead—were merging. The spiritual intruding on her medical world.

She looked at the dead man's ghost. A small, hard-driving, workingman. A face that looked forever mournful. A wharf rat. A man who would take bribes, try and influence what cargos got dumped first, hide cargo—human or otherwise—that needed to be forgotten.

"Definitely a violent death," she said hoarsely.

"How do you know?" asked Parks.

"Otherwise his spirit would be gone."

"You saying he's back?" Roach pulled a flask from his trouser pocket, forgetting to take off his exam gloves.

Parks whispered in her ear. "Show me."

She turned her head; their faces, close. His blues eyes staring into her brown.

"Diagonally across. The other side of the body. Touch."

Parks extended his hand. "I don't feel anything."

"Wait."

"Isn't it supposed to be cold?"

"Wait."

"I feel—I feel—"

"What?" shouted Roach.

Parks withdrew his hand. "Nothing."

"Liar." She'd watched his face. Seen the slight widening of his eyes. The twitch in his jaw.

"Let's close up the body."

"Sure," said Roach. "Is he watching?"

"Yes." *The ghost was holding his dead self's hand.* She thought it best not to tell Roach that the ghost was right across from him.

"I was a fool," said Parks. "Complete idiot to have the paramedics bring the body here. Anyone could see he was dead. No question. Should've gone to the city morgue."

"Then we wouldn't know about the ghost," said Roach.

"We still don't know anything. All we've got is Doc's word. I don't think it would hold up in a court of law. Right, Doc? They'd revoke your license."

"You brought him to me."

"A mistake, Doc. Police officers' practical joke. I bit. Hook, line, and sinker. There's nothing here, Doc. Just a body. A murder victim. No ghosts, Doc. There aren't ghosts. Just in fairy tales." Parks's face was flushed.

"Hamlet," murmured Roach.

"Ghosts don't exist. Hear me, Doc? Murder. Clear and simple. You won't believe what I've seen. A million ways to die. There aren't any ghosts. If I'd felt something, I would've told you. Logic and evidence. Just like a doc."

Both Marie and Roach stared at Parks.

Roach shrugged. "'He doth protest too much.'"

"Doc. Logic and evidence." Parks was calmer now. "Nothing else, Doc." His hair had swept forward onto his brow.

"Did you know Detective Reneaux?" she asked.

"Good cop," said Roach.

"Not to speak of," said Parks. "I'm new to the force. Heard about him. How he died. Multiple gunshots."

Marie swallowed. "Yes. He suffered." She tore off her gloves.

"He called me 'Doc' because he knew I hated it. His voice had the same southern lilt yours just had."

"A kid from Jersey doesn't speak southern."

"Right." She stretched her fingers to caress, tuck back his hair, then withdrew. Fair skin. Blue eyes. Parks wasn't her black, Egypt lover man. "I'm sorry," she said.

"Don't be," said Parks.

"I hear things. Voices."

"Trick of memory. You miss him."

"Parks can make a girl forget," said Roach. "He's the department Don Juan. I'd be, if I didn't have a spare tire."

"Shut up, Roach."

"You shut up. I'm senior coroner."

"I'm case detective."

"You sound like children."

Roach laughed.

Parks grimaced, then his face went blank—once again he was the cool, collected officer. "Sorry if we bothered you. Won't happen again."

"It will."

"You predicting murder? Something you're not telling me? Maybe you're an accomplice? Maybe somebody else is already murdered?"

"I help people," she nearly shouted. "Heal. Never hurt." She was trembling with rage.

The ghost's arms were wrapped about his chest, his body rocking.

"Definitely a violent death." Marie started walking.

"Aw, shit," said Parks. "Make me a believer. Explain this death to me."

Marie kept walking. She left the morgue, faking calm at seeing ghosts, at hearing Reneaux's voice coming out of a white man's mouth.

She needed for Roach to cut, dice, slice in the city's morgue. Needed for Parks to solve his own damn crime.

She passed the gum-popping girl. Punched the elevator. The doors opened, then closed. *The ghost was in the elevator.*

She pushed the emergency stop button. Turned.

Miracles had their limits. Just like medicine. There were schisms in logic. Unexplainable reasons for why one person survived while another died. Same treatment, different outcome. Same with spiritual gifts.

"I don't know what to do."

The ghost stretched out his hands, daring her to clasp them. His spirit wasn't shrunken, deformed, just scrawny, his head tilted, his eyes questioning, pleading for help. As if to say: *Who else but you?*

She punched the button; the elevator lurched, rising upward.

✕✷✸◇✖◉✸▥

Blood stirred memories. What it was, it hadn't always been. It had been—where? Nowhere. It hadn't been.

Now it was. In the water. In the air.

It had been called. By sound. It remembered sound. The call of drums.

JT's blood had filled it. Fed it.

It knew as it was draining blood—warm, bitter, and sweet—the man was dying while it was becoming more alive.

THREE

Six AM. Shift over.

Marie unbuttoned her coat, slid off her stethoscope, grabbed her backpack, and padlocked her locker. She yelled 'bye to El and DuLac, hello to the incoming crew of nurses and residents. Within seconds, everyone would know the gossip. Believe the drained man was hexed.

Sully, the security guard, waved her over. His body overflowed the metal chair; his legs, turned out like a ballerina's.

Sully was the sentinel between two worlds—outside versus inside, the sick and the sicker. A few years ago, she'd given a morphine high to his friend, dying of dozens of stab wounds. Sully thanked her by calling her "Almost Doctor." His name for second-year residents. Even though she was first year. It had been then that she'd first been marked as apart—engendering jealousy, misperceptions, and downright hatefulness.

"Rough night?"

She looked at the elfin ghost, shifting its legs, its weightlessness.

"Yes."

"You'll make it.

"As a *voodooienne* or a doctor?"

"I don't know nothin' about the first." Sully shifted his eyes downward, but not before she'd seen a flicker of fear.

"Sure."

"Here." He pulled a brown paper sack from under his folding chair. "Bones." His blue-black lips spread into a smile.

"Kind Dog would like a Sunday walk."

"I'll be over. You think he'd like to go to Riverwalk?" Sully was asking in all seriousness.

Marie patted his puffy hand.

"With you, Kind Dog would be happy to go anywhere."

Sully smiled, as if she'd told him Dog was a woman, flattered by his attention.

Gently, without knowing why, she stroked his cheek. Black silk. "How come you never go home?"

"I can sit here as well as there. Here, I'm useful."

"'Night, Sully."

The glass doors slid open. Sun smacked her eyes. Marie staggered, shading her face.

The ghost stumbled out from behind a trash bin.

She stopped. Head cocked, alert, studying the dead man with his tight crop of gray hair. "Were you hiding?"

Why would a ghost need to hide?

Musing, she started walking again. What was it Marie Laveau's journal had said? "*The unquiet dead—those without peace, those who'd died violently, those who needed to do penance, seek forgive-ness . . . those who'd been uncharitable, corrupt, who couldn't accept their dying . . . those who needed to send one last message—these souls moved restlessly between worlds."* Afterlife versus real life. Day-light, their souls were supposed to rest. Like mythic vampires. Yet unquiet souls felt no relief.

Marie passed a pharmacy and a drunk peeing on a lamppost.

"I should sing a song for you."

The little man kept trailing her.

"I sing off-key, so it won't be very good."

He opened his mouth and a thin wail floated out.

"You can't sing either."

Marie crossed the street. She walked quickly, moving from Charity, the medical district, past buildings belonging to Tulane, then a downtrodden business district on the French Quarter's edge. Stepping onto the ancient cobblestones of Rue Chartres, she broke into a run. Tourists staggered out of bars; a couple petted and kissed. Musicians, bleary eyed, carted instruments to a white van.

The ghost wasn't beside her; instead, she saw snatches, glimpses of him inside shop windows, in the alleys between buildings, sitting on a loading dock. She even saw him, his arms wrapped around a tree. Once, swinging from a stoplight, blinking yellow. He was strangely companionable.

Marie kept running through the Quarter, sweat lacing her skin.

Church bells tolled.

Street sweepers brushed away blood, dirt, rum-soaked paper cups. The aftermath of the nightly party. The sun was burning off the day's mist. And Marie felt elation, running in the shadows of buildings, the handiwork of ghosts long past. Delicate iron filigree. White lattice trim, pink shutters. Hidden courtyards where old women lounged, where young women met lovers. Fountains decorated with birds, cupids, griffins, and gargoyles, or the Virgin Mary. New Orleans, rising out of the swamp, steeped in the corrupt race-mixing, religion-blending, slave-and-caste system of the 1700s.

The ancient mixed with the modern. Past, present, or future, depending upon how you viewed it, existed simultaneously. The only city like it in America.

She dodged a silver-painted tin man who'd played statue for tourists all night, now dragging himself home. A tarot card diviner was setting up her stool and table; a chess shark was counting money fleeced from tourists. Transvestites and wobbly-kneed prostitutes headed for Mass then, afterward, the Café du Monde for café au lait, beignets, and gossip.

Puzzle it out, she told herself. Puzzle it out. If she could see the elfin man, maybe, one day, she'd see Reneaux. Or her mother's spirit. Both murder victims. Unquiet spirits.

Voodoo taught that with great ill, came great good. With hate, love. Despair, hope. There was always hope. Affirmation.

She began to sing: "This old man, he played one. He played knick-knack, paddy-wack on my drum. With a knick-knack, paddy-wack, give the dog a bone. This old man came rolling home."

She sang, not caring that hungover, red-eyed tourists stared.

New Orleans residents never minded music in any form—gospel shouts, Cajun stomps, blues clapping, Preservation Hall jazz, a washbucket shuffle, it didn't matter.

Marie slowed her run and began skipping like a child.

By the time she sang, "... he played seven. He played knick-knack, paddy-wack in heaven. With a knick-knack, paddy-wack, give the dog a bone...," Marie had rolled herself home. To her apartment where she tried to maintain a semblance of normalcy for Marie-Claire.

Before turning her key, she looked down the narrow stairwell. She couldn't see anyone. Spirits weren't allowed inside. She turned the key, then stopped, looking down the stairwell again.

Crooked shadows ran deep across the steps. At the bottom of the stairs, a narrow tunnel led to an enclosed, too-private court-yard where anything could happen. Where no one could see. No one could hear.

Cross Antiques, on the first floor, hadn't opened. Upstairs, it was just her, the baby, and Kind Dog; and Louise asleep on the couch.

She drew herself tall. Someone was there. Probably a drunk.

The ghost—paddy-wack man—emerged from the shadows. He touched his fingers to his brow and bowed.

She was touched. Moved by his gentility. Had he ever been a patient in the ER? Maybe she'd cauterized his missing finger, wrapped his hand carefully in linen?

Looking spent, frail enough for a sea breeze to blow away, he sat, his back to her, on the bottom step.

She knew he'd wait while she slept.

Just a little rest. Breakfast for Marie-Claire. Day care. A prayer to Agwé. Damballah. Then, solve the crime. Or at least try.

She stepped into her apartment and felt relief. Home. No better place.

"Louise, I'm here."

Louise yawned. Ridges from the couch marked her face. "You don't need me tonight? What is it, Monday?"

"Yes. It's my night off."

"Good. That child needs her mother."

Marie winced. Of all people, she'd expected Louise to understand. She'd raised her children. Worked every day. Sometimes two jobs. Marie needed to support her child, too.

Besides, Marie enjoyed her work. It was important for Marie-Claire to know that.

Kind Dog licked her hand.

"See you, Louise." Marie slipped off her shoes, took Louise's place on the couch. Kind Dog lay on her feet. She was exhausted. Maybe she'd get a few hours sleep before Marie-Claire hollered for breakfast.

✕

She heard chimes. Fighting her way up from deep sleep, she thought she was dreaming. Chimes again. Then a pounding, rattling, at the door.

Kind Dog, barking, leaped off the coach.

"Doc? Dr. Laveau?"

Marie-Claire started crying.

"It's me. Detective Parks. You all right?" He banged on the door frame. "Answer. Else I'm coming in."

"You're scaring the baby," she shouted, opening the door.

"I'm sorry."

Dog was growling. Let him growl.

"I thought you didn't need me."

"There's been another murder. Blood drained."

"Hush, Dog." She stepped back, letting Parks in. "Let me get the baby."

Dog swept past her, sniffing Detective Parks like a hound.

She held a wide-eyed Marie-Claire on her hip. "You like dogs?"

"Cats."

"Well, Dog likes you."

It was true. Dog was sitting beside Parks, his body even with Parks's knee, his tongue licking Parks's hand. Parks patted the furry head.

Marie-Claire puckered her face and let out a wail.

"Is she hungry?"

"I think so." She feathered Marie-Claire's face with kisses, until her cry became giggles.

She walked back toward the kitchen. Parks followed her. Marie-Claire, peeking over Marie's shoulder, watched him. Kind Dog trailed, last.

Marie poured instant oatmeal into a bowl, added milk, then put it in the microwave.

"What's her name?"

"Marie-Claire."

"Pretty baby."

"Not a baby," Marie-Claire chimed.

"She speaks."

"Especially when she warms up to you. Do you have children?"

"Not married."

"Neither am I." He didn't flinch, lift an eyebrow in disapproval, or tighten his mouth. She had to give him credit. "You want my help?"

"Yes, please. I was out of line before."

"You're lying again, Detective. It's my life, and even, sometimes, I don't believe all the weird stuff."

"Okay. I admit it. I'm desperate. A good cop doesn't close doors."

"Here." Marie handed him Marie-Claire. She took out the oatmeal, sprinkled cinnamon on it, and added cold milk. She poured orange juice into a 'Little Kitty' cup. Kind Dog chewed his bone.

"Put her in the high chair. She's messy when she eats."

"Hi," said Marie-Claire. "Hi."

"Hi," answered Parks, awkwardly sliding her in the high chair.

"Eat your oatmeal."

"O'meal." Marie-Claire banged her spoon.

Parks straightened his tie.

"You're not around children much."

"No. Or dogs." He looked down at Kind Dog.

Dog raised his head.

Marie-Claire squealed, "Dog. Kind Dog." She let oatmeal slip from her spoon to the floor. Kind Dog lapped it up.

Marie slid into a chair. "Tell me the details."

Detective Parks flipped open his notepad. Frowned at his scrawl. "This one's a musician. His name's Rudy. Rudy 'Sweet Lips' Johnston.

"Found backstage. Dozens of people must've passed him. Time of death still unknown. Pending autopsy. My guess is that it was between two and four AM. Special recording set, *Live at Preservation Hall.*

"After the break, Rudy went missing. Some thought he'd gone to the bathroom. Others, that he was sneaking a drink. The sound

mixer found him. In the shadows. Pressed against the back wall."
Parks looked up.

Marie concentrated on Marie-Claire. The tug and release of her
lips. The oatmeal smudge above her mouth.

"Rudy was like the body at the hospital."

"You mean paddy-wack man? That's what I call him."

Parks flipped another page. "His name was JT. Jean Toulouse
DuVaille. Haitian. Didn't report for work this morning. Got a tip."

"Both men drained of blood? No major wounds? Punctures on
the wrist?"

"Like a snake's."

Marie frowned. Then she stilled, her head cocked. Marie-Claire
turned, looking past the doorway into the living room. Kind Dog
hustled up, raced to the front door, barking.

Marie grabbed the salt, heading for the front door. Kind Dog
growled.

"He's here," said Marie, opening the door.

"Who?"

"Rudy. Go. Go away," she shouted at the ghost on the landing.
She poured salt on the threshold, hollering: "JT. He has to stay with
you. JT."

"Can I help?" Parks positioned himself in front of the high
chair.

"Stay with Marie-Claire. Dog!" Marie ordered. "Marie-Claire."

Kind Dog raced back to the kitchen. Parks gathered Marie-
Claire in his arms, patting her back, bouncing her as she cried.

Marie stared at the ghost at the bottom of the stairs. Darker
than JT, he had the heavy chest of a horn player.

Rudy, hands crossed over his heart, looked at her yearningly.

"I'll help. I promise. Stay in the courtyard. You'll be revenged."

She slammed the door. Slumped against it. Damn. She looked into the kitchen. Dog was quiet. Standing, ears, eyes alert. Tail tall. Parks held Marie-Claire. A tight, protective embrace.

"Graveyard dust works better," she murmured, walking toward them.

"Police work isn't about vengeance," said Parks softly.

"Neither is voodoo. But these spirits—JT and Rudy—are." She held out her hands for Marie-Claire. "Day care. Shall we go see Miz Lola?"

"Lola. Lola."

"That's right, baby." She smiled. "Parks. Dog's leash is in the closet. I'll get Marie-Claire dressed."

Dog knew "leash"; he pawed the closet door.

"I don't understand."

"You might be a good detective. But you need common sense."

"Potty," said Marie-Claire, emphatic.

"Take Dog to do his business. When you come back, we'll take Marie-Claire to day care."

"Then Preservation Hall?"

"Right," she drawled, teasing. "Smart cop." Then she called over her shoulder, "Don't let JT and Rudy touch you."

"How am I supposed to know they're there?"

"Dog," she shouted over her shoulder. "He'll bark." Then cooed, "Who's my baby? My oh, so pretty baby?"

"Me," piped, Marie-Claire.

FOUR

PRESERVATION HALL, FRENCH QUARTER

MONDAY MORNING

Preservation Hall was spare inside. Hard to believe any music magic was made here. Dark floor, dark chairs. A stage only a foot high, unimposing. Yet this was where some of the greatest jazz legends played, where audiences were charmed, seduced by New Orleans's unique sounds.

Dim inside, the hall had its own time—atmospheric, like a cave reverberating with memories of songs played a day ago, a year ago, decade and decades ago.

Musicians, comfortable with calloused fingers, lips, and unfiltered cigarettes, were staggering about the hall, some nodding off, some in a stupor of straight gin—clear like water so patrons wouldn't notice—some antsy, tap-tapping feet, hands, like they needed a fix. Maybe they did. Cops, gathering evidence, stumbling over each other, were a deterrent. The musicians nodded at Detective Parks. Their lids were half-lowered, covering their bloodshot, dilated eyes.

A man stepped forward. A front-office man, in cheap polyester, concerned, but frightened, too. "We need to open tonight. Y'all need to get on with it. Let the musicians go. They need sleep. We have a show."

"Sure," said Parks, then promptly ignored him. "Roach," he hollered.

"Back here."

Parks and Marie moved stage left, stepping over electric cords, around amplifiers, into an alcove.

"Isn't much to go on," said Roach. "Just a backstage cavern. We dusted a wide area. Floor, walls, props."

Tarp covered the body. A big man. Much bigger than JT.

Marie stood over the body, reluctant to look down. On her left, Parks's blue eyes were fixed on her, on her right, Roach.

Roach cleared his throat. "Course, there's the official exam. Autopsy to come. Seems same manner of death." Brow furrowed. "But the manner of death is impossible. Punctures or not. Even his dick is spent, sucked dry."

"That's enough, Roach."

Roach blinked behind spectacles. "In my day, the young weren't so prudish."

"You are a roach," said Parks, disgusted.

Marie touched the wall. Frayed, chipped paint. Smoke stains. When she squinted, she thought she saw letters. Some kind of calligraphy? No, an image. Agwé's sign? Also, another mark, drying, a still-damp brown-red. Shaped like two Vs. Valleys. Open-ended triangles.

She dropped her hand.

"They call me Roach 'cause I once collected a corpse covered in them."

"Nobody else would touch it."

"It's my job," Roach said, scowling. "William. Bill. My momma called me Bill." His voice slipped into a New Orleans drawl.

She turned her back on Parks. "I understand, Bill. Sometimes folks don't appreciate professionalism. There're squeamish doctors, just like cops." The red-mop man smiled, gold glinting in the back of his mouth. "I'll see if transport is here."

"You do that," said Parks. "Are you okay, Doc? Dr. Laveau?"

"Sure." She stooped, lifting up the tarp.

She sucked in air. Autopsy, surgery, even cancer deaths were nothing compared to this. An absolute drain of body fluids. Taut, leathery flesh covering bone. All the bones—clear, heightened, in bold relief. Inhale, exhale. Don't get emotional, she told herself. Still some muscle and fat. Just limp, flaccid, without blood flow.

Parks squatted beside her. She imagined they looked like little kids staring at a dead, malnourished cat in a sandbox.

Except this was a man. Skin poured over bones. No sense of organs, everything depressed, caved in, bloodless. Nails, yellow. Eyes, wide open, bulging with a glazed look of surprise. His wrist had three punctures, right along the vein.

"Trumpet."

"What?"

"He played the trumpet," said Parks.

Marie squinted at Rudy's ring. Something etched on the gold. Were the markings linked to the wall? A dialogue in some ancient tongue?

"If anyone deserved dying, he did."

Parks stood. "Who might you be?"

"Dede. Stage manager. I've been here forever."

Marie stretched the tarp over the dead man's head. Parks, surprisingly gentle, put his hand under her elbow. Helped her rise.

"Thanks," she said.

"Real gentleman," scowled Dede.

"Show some manners," said Parks.

"Why?" asked Marie. "I mean, why did he deserve it?"

Dede crossed his fat hands over his chest. Scrunched his lips.

"Say something. Else I can take you down to the station for questioning."

Dede looked at Parks as if *he* were a roach. He licked his lips, sly, hesitating, like a dying man. "Everything about him was corrupt." His voice was soft, more melancholic than damning. "He'd sell his sister . . . lie to his mother . . . steal from his brother. Called no man friend. Ornery. A good musician, but no soul. Not supposed to be that way. Feelings supposed to make great music. Everything in him was hate."

Marie shifted from foot to foot. Dede was staring at her. She thought of the ancient mariner. Except Dede wasn't confessing his sins. He was confessing someone else's; strangely, he was warning her.

"You going to take him?"

"Ready to load," said Roach, returning.

"He deserves a shout-out," said Dede. "He's still one of us."

"Shout-out? What's that?"

"A moment of praise. Witness. Recognition that he was one of the group," said Marie.

Dede nodded. He looked around the room, slapped his hands against his thigh. One beat, two.

"My man," replied a sandy man, hair slicked back, drumming

sticks on the table, a syncopated rat-a-tat-tat. Marie recognized him. He was the drummer possessed at the club.

Someone else added a slapping. A steady rhythm against his chest. Then another. Marie looked at the fluttering hands. Another. Thighs. Chests. Tables. A gray-haired man slammed his flattened palm on wood. Dede began stomping his feet. Then all of them were slapping, stomping. Not cat's gut strung tight over drums, but a haunting, improvised sound. Loud. Louder. Leather soles pounding. Dede, steadily watching her.

She swallowed, clapped her hands. Syncopating, counterpointing the men's beats.

Musicians—black, white, high yellow, cinnamon brown, and all the colors in between. Some with gold in their mouths; some with no teeth, few teeth; some young, others old. They all had weary "been there, done that" looks and smiles that recognized the secrets in men's and women's souls.

More soul stirring, less slick than the Preservation Band sound.

Ceremonial. The sound growing louder, the beat more intense. Their bodies as drums, harkening back to an ancient time. A time when communication was just rhythm, when hands against flesh mirrored beating hearts. Like an African juba. A community using rhythm for spiritual release.

All the men were looking at her. They were in need, needed something from her.

She raised her hands high. The drumming quickened. As if the roof could lift. High. Higher.

"Spirit find peace," she hollered. "We've honored, witnessed your life." The musicians were nodding. "Rudy, be gone."

The men abruptly stopped their drumming.

Dede smiled crookedly.

The men and the room seemed to have lost air, exhaled energy. It was now a near-empty, dirty bar filled with tired, disillusioned men.

"I don't get it," said Parks. "What just happened?"

"I need to be outside."

"Don't go far," said Parks.

"Or you'll arrest me?"

"No. I'm worried about you. Be careful."

She exited through the back door, into a courtyard. It felt odd having a man be concerned for her. Not since Reneaux—Detective Reneaux—had someone looked at her as Parks had. Like he cared.

She looked about the courtyard, searching for Rudy.

Rudy's ghost was leaning against the south wall, licking his lips. JT, shoulders slumped, looked as mournful as a freshly neutered cat.

"What connects you?" Marie asked.

"Talking to yourself?"

"You following me?"

Parks shrugged.

"No. To them," said Marie, pointing.

"Whatever you say, Doc." Parks lit a cigarette.

"Bad for you."

"This case is bad for me."

"For a doctor, cases are the ones we try to keep alive."

"Mine are homicides. Without a doubt, dead."

Parks blew smoke right through the ghosts. He looked at Marie, his shoulder leaning against concrete. "I didn't hear a shout-out. Except you—saying 'be gone.' Did it work?"

"No. I said what they wanted to hear."

"Trickery?"

"No. The shout-out was in the music. The rhythm. Each of the gods has its special rhythm."

"Whose rhythm were they playing?"

"Agwé's. The sea god."

"What's that supposed to mean?"

"That's what I'm trying to find out."

"You think they know something? Something they're not telling?"

"No. I think the rhythm was instinctive. Spirits do shape things. Like the markings on the wall."

"There's writing on the wall?" Parks stood upright.

He had the longest lashes she'd ever seen on a man. "Inside," she murmured. "Markings. Above the body."

"A message? Some clue other than impossibly dead bodies?" His voice was soft.

Marie knew he was angry.

Parks pressed his cigarette against the wall, sparks flying. He went back inside.

Marie stayed outside. The ghosts were gone. She—who'd seen all manner of dying—had never seen two men drained of blood. She leaned against the brick wall, her fingers digging in the crevices, the cracks. Scraping at mortar over a hundred years old.

Parks was again in the doorway. She could see him straining to hold himself back, not to get in her face. He lit a cigarette, then stared at the matchstick flame, watching it burn down to his fingertips, before blowing it out.

"What does it mean?"

"Agwé's sign, I think. But it's not finished. Just the shape of a bow, a line for a mast. And something else—uncompleted. Perhaps two Vs."

"Why didn't you tell me earlier?"

Marie just looked at him. "I think there are going to be more deaths."

Face taut, he gripped her shoulders. He seemed to be looking inside her—probing her anxiety, her fears, her heart's secrets.

She felt the strength in him, the strength behind his usual careless posture, his pretty-boy looks. Here was the man who liked tracking murderers. Who could stare at all manner of abuse—homicide by knife, strangulation, beating . . . and now what? vampirism?—and not be undone. She couldn't help wondering whether he'd been born or made that way. Nature versus nurture.

"Never thought I'd be tracking a voodoo killer," said Parks.

"It isn't voodoo."

"Markings indicate a ritualistic killing. Your involvement—your ghosts make it seem voodoo enough for me."

"Then you're a fool."

He stepped back, dragged on his cigarette. "You don't like cops."

"Nothing to do with the profession."

"So it's me you don't like. If you respected me, you would've told me about the drawing sooner. You wouldn't have withheld it, thinking I'm stupid."

"I don't think you're stupid. Slow, perhaps. Needing to be reminded to take a dog to pee."

Parks smiled slightly. "All right. I admit that one." His voice lowered. "But I don't want to admit there'll be more murders. How do you know?"

The courtyard was grungy. Cigarette butts, the tips of rolled weed, a few empty pints of Jack Daniel's. This was where the musicians rested between sets. A small square. At night, she imagined, they could see flickering stars.

"I just know."

"Concrete, tangible evidence. That's what I'm interested in, Doc."

"Sure. Except with Rudy dead, you came to me. When his ghost was at my door, you didn't question. You protected Marie-Claire. I'm grateful for that."

Parks blew smoke at the clouds.

"Bad for you," she sighed.

"This job. This place is bad for me. Ten AM and my clothes are already sticking to me like water."

"Why are you here? New Orleans."

Parks flicked the cigarette onto the cobblestones, watching it burn between crevices.

"A woman," Marie whispered.

Parks froze, expressionless.

Marie felt his suppressed longing, melancholy. Funny how emotions radiated. The more you suppressed them, the more powerful they became.

"Failed love affair," she said, "and you blame New Orleans."

"No. Just her. She knew I was a cop. She wanted to be with her people. What's that? Her people?" He tapped the Marlboro pack against his palm. "Was it my fault New Orleans is the murder capital of the South, hey, maybe the whole damned United States?" He lit another cigarette.

Marie clasped his hand. For a second, he held hers, staring at their fingers, entwined, before letting his hand go limp.

"You love her."

"Stop creeping me out."

"Just a woman's intuition."

"And you? In love?"

His eyes were ocean blue. And, for a second, she imagined she could fall into them. That beyond the blue was brown.

"Parks," shouted Roach.

They stepped apart.

"The body is loaded. We're ready to roll." Roach looked at one, then the other. His eyes blinked behind glass.

"I'm coming," said Parks.

"Take your time. A woman always appreciates that."

Marie bobbed her head. A blush spread across her cheeks.

"Don't mind Roach. Good man. Just crass sometimes."

"No matter. Besides, he's right." She smiled.

Now it was Parks's turn to blush.

"Look," said Parks. "I don't understand what's going on. But I admit it. I need you."

"I, you."

His brow arched.

"Things happen for a reason," she murmured. "The world is full of signs."

"I'm a sign?" He grinned.

"A big one." They both laughed.

"Let me have a patrolman drive you home. I'll get back to you after the autopsy."

"I'd rather walk. Helps me think."

"You sure?"

Marie pressed her fingertips to her eyes. She'd like nothing better than to crawl into bed. But something was awry in the world;

she was smack in the middle of it. That made it dangerous for Marie-Claire, for everyone she loved.

"I'm sure," she said.

She went inside the musty hall. Several musicians were still straddling chairs; some, packing instruments; others, already slipping out the front door. A saxophonist was sleeping on the floor, his coat his pillow, his instrument cradled like a lover.

Parks had slipped beside Roach. Comparing notes. Beat cops yawned.

The hall wasn't much. Yet here, magic was made. Music—a universal human endeavor. Slaves had used it to save their own souls. Preservation Hall, "preservation"—protecting something from loss or danger; salvation; self-preservation; to conserve. In medical terms, "preservation" meant a process to save organic substances from decay; embalmment, fixation, hardening tissue to resemble, as much as possible, living tissue.

Her head hurt. She turned to go, but her mind didn't connect with her body.

She blinked. Her sight narrowed, focusing on the bandstand. *JT stood beside the drums.*

Her respiration increased; sweat beaded on her neck. *As in a ceremony, she was both here and not here, in two worlds. Present/ future. Present/past. Which would it be?*

Time converged. Space receding; streaks of color. Wait, she said to herself. Wait. For the vision.

The world bleached gray, then blanched yellow. Sickly, feverish yellow.

Like a picture show, she saw JT. Saw herself, standing, beside him.

Marie cleared her mind. Let the miracle happen. Be it. In it.

She stepped inside JT's ghostly body.

Loneliness. Heavy as a mountain. A river of tears dammed inside.

On the dock. Keeping lookout. Fearful police will arrive. Water crested. A swell of white foam.

She remembered playing as a child, on the beach. Marching with a stick in her hand, wearing an admiral's hat. Mama—lovely and young, embracing her, feathering her face with kisses. Placing a bag about her neck.

Something burst from the water.

"Mama?" Arms outstretched, trying to embrace the past. "Agwé?"

The water was still like a glass pane, but dirtied from mud, refuse, sewage.

Hands high, lowering, she slapped out a rhythm. Flesh against flesh. Hands to chest. Agwé's rhythm.

Darkness, a floating mist rose from the water. Coming. Closer. Agwé inspires. Redeems.

Impact. Wood digging into flesh. Lungs aching for air.

Horror as her wrist twisted, arched, as the snake drained blood.

"JT, fight. Fight. " But her words inside the spirit had no sound. She felt him letting himself die. Giving in. She died with him.

Welcoming sleep. A sweet exhale. JT believed he had nothing to live for. That Agwé was punishing him, making the world right.

"Doc?"

Marie looked at Parks. He needed a shave; a lock of hair kept falling over his eye; there were brown flecks in his irises. She smelled him: his worry, his sweet aftershave.

"You're crying."

"JT thought he'd dishonored his mother's god. Agwé. Thought he deserved to die."

"Woman's intuition?"

"Voodoo, this time. I was him. In him."

She swayed.

Parks held her upright. "You need rest, Doc."

"No. There isn't time. It's the music. JT and Rudy. Connected by music."

"JT was a dockworker," said Parks.

"But he called Agwé. Like the shout-out, he drummed his body.

"When I first saw him, his spirit," her words tumbled out, "the tune was in my head. Knick-knack, paddy-wack. He played one, he played knick-knack paddy-wack on my drum. I've just seen him. Drumming. He thought Agwé killed him. But it couldn't have been Agwé. It was darkness. A snake."

"The devil, then." Parks brushed back his hair. "I can't believe I'm saying this."

"Snakes aren't evil."

Outside, the ambulance whoop-whooped twice. Rudy's body was being taken away.

"JT thought Agwé was punishing him. Rudy must've thought so, too. That would account for the drawing. He was trying to pacify Agwé."

Raucous singing, from outside, filtered into the hall. *"Oh, when the saints . . . Lord, how I want to be in that number. . . . "*

Marie hated the song. In her mind's eye, she could see the tourists' hips shaking, fingers snapping, taking up the anthem, dancing in the street. Trumpets blared.

"Everybody dead gets a party in New Orleans," cursed Parks. He stomped out his cigarette. "I think we should await evidence. Follow police procedure."

She touched her throat, feeling her carotid artery. Her pulse, ebbing and flowing. "Did JT have a bag around his neck? Or near his body?"

"Nothing."

"As a child, his mother gave him a mojo bag."

Parks raised his brows.

"A corrupted version of *mojuba*," she responded. "'To give praise.' An African charm. Sometimes called gris-gris. Trick bags. Agwé was JT's guardian."

"Sure, Doc."

"Something must've happened to the bag. It would account for why he was such a bad-luck man."

Grimacing, Parks stepped back warily. "I'll escort you home."

"Parks. Listen to me. You've got to believe me. Nothing of this world is going to solve this crime."

"I'm not going to end up like Reneaux."

"What're you talking about?"

"Everybody admired him. Don't get me wrong. But there's talk—you and your voodoo drove him crazy. He let himself slip as a cop. That's why he got killed."

She slapped Parks. Hard. Then slapped him again.

Parks clutched Marie's wrist. The two of them, breathing heavily, their gazes fixed, angry.

A patrolman stepped near. "Need help?"

"Get the hell out," answered Parks. He held Marie's wrist, gaze unwavering. "Concrete. Tangible evidence. Nothing less."

Cymbals clashed; the bass drum sounded. The snare fell over.

"What the hell—"

"JT's trying to provide evidence."

Quick as lightning, JT hid the drumsticks behind a speaker.

"I'm out of my mind. Ghost drummers. Vampires. Witches."

"I'm not a witch."

"Voodoo."

The sandy-haired drummer reset his drums. Hollered, "Elroy, if you fucked with me—" He slammed down an empty leather bag on the snare. "Them's my lucky sticks. Elroy, I'll bust your ass."

"Who's Elroy?" asked Parks as Marie asked, "You've lost them?"

The drummer, skinny like a rope, stared at her. He looked piti-ful, desperate.

"Your sticks are gone," she said.

"I always put them back in my case. Always. Elroy, a clarinetist, is fucking with me."

"Why would he do that?"

The drummer hooted. "I soaked his reeds in gin."

"A joker," said Parks.

"Look in your bag again," said Marie.

"I'm tellin' you. They're not there."

"I think they are. Will be."

The drummer slipped his hand in the bag. "Nothing."

"Wait."

JT pushed the sticks, watching them roll across the band floor.

"I'll be damned," said Parks.

"Wait," said Marie as the drummer bent for the sticks.

JT lifted the sticks, slipping them inside the leather bag lying on the drummer's chair.

The drummer's face twisted, awestruck. "Rudy? Rudy took my sticks? Son of a bitch."

"No. Someone else. Another spirit."

Like a minstrel, JT slapped his chest and thighs.

Parks sat backward in a chair, his head on his crossed arms; Marie patted his back.

"I can't believe I'm asking this," said Parks. "Do you know why a ghost would want your sticks?"

"Drum's everything," the drummer said, shrugging, palms up. "She knows. Ask her."

"Drums call the spirits," said Marie, more certain than ever that this was the drummer who'd been possessed at La Mer.

"Always been that way. Since the beginning. If a ghost had my sticks, he's asking for someone to be called."

"And providing concrete evidence of the unseen."

"Okay, Doc. I get it. I'm along for the ride." Parks paused in lighting another cigarette. "Why yours?"

"Huh?" The drummer slid his sticks, lovingly, from the bag.

"I mean, why yours? Your sticks?"

The drummer twirled on his chair, then beat a crescendo drumroll. Cymbals crashed, punctuating a period. "My people."

Parks rolled his eyes, muttering, "My people."

"Come from a long line of drummers. Back to Africa."

"Where can we reach you?"

"Algiers. Just ask. Everybody can tell you where I be."

"Name?"

"Wire. As in skinny as a wire."

"I would've said rope."

Wire shrugged. "I prefer Cat. Like cat skins."

"I don't understand," said Parks.

"African drums are made with animal hides," answered Marie.

"*Ela kuku dea 'gbe wu la gbagbe*. A dead animal cries louder than a live one."

"Anlo-Ewe? from Ghana?" asked Marie.

"You're the one, Maman Marie." Wire pointed his drumstick. He tossed his sticks high. They twirled, spinning and spinning, until he snatched them and banged twice on the snare. "Interesting times," he crowed. "Dee-vine. Dee-vine."

"What do you say, Detective? Enough evidence? JT took the sticks, then brought them back. Just for you."

"Me?"

"You're the skeptic. And JT wants you to believe. Drumming is the clue. Connecting the murders. Maybe even offering the cure."

"Better believe it," said Wire, placing sunglasses over his eyes, beginning a slow rhythm, hypnotic on his drums. "Miz Marie, you're gonna need me."

"You think so?"

"Know so." Beats fell fast, furious. Wire sang off-key, "Conjure woman, turn your life around. Upside down. Marie Laveau."

"Come on, Parks. We need to get ready."

"For what?"

"A voodoo ceremony."

"You're shitting me."

Marie's smile faded. "I wish I was. Ceremonies are meant to enlighten, heal. This one might be dangerous." She looked at Wire. "You'll come?"

"I wouldn't miss it."

"You know where?"

"Everybody knows where."

Marie nodded. "You okay with this, Parks?" She held her breath, knowing his answer could alter everything.

She knew as surely as she knew mosquitoes drained blood, evil didn't necessarily disappear because of prayer. Both a *voodooienne* and a cop would be needed to solve this crime.

Parks looked at the underside of his wrist. His veins, blue. A scar of a tattoo disappearing under his jacket, his shirt cuff.

Parks looked at her coolly. "Teach me," he said. "This world, the next. Don't matter. Murder is still murder."

In the sea, it had been resting with the bones. Slaves tossed overboard, murdered pirates, drowned seafarers. Been resting among the empty shells of mollusks, snails, among coral reefs and mounds of trash. Once the water had been sparkling green, blue, and white foam, now it was muddied with silt, soil, and waste from New Orleans. It had been his city once.

Part of the city, it still recognized—the Quarter. It didn't recognize the tall buildings, the moving things—trolleys, cars?—was that what they were called? Buses. Strange replacements for a horse between a man's thighs, trotting to the cadence of a whip.

Blood fed it memories. Rudy's blood had been sour.

Music sweet, blood bitter. Like the man. Needle in his arm. Passed out on a floor. Forgetfulness. It dove deeper, draining blood farther away from the heart. A girl. Hair the color of dark cherries. Hands caressing, an embrace. A kiss.

It remembered. Touch. Feel. It slowed its draining. Lulled by a remembrance—of what? Who?

Rudy's secret. Deep in his blood, sinews. Strangling the cherry-haired woman with his bare hands. Seconds seem like hours. She can't get away.

Can't make hands release. Rudy presses, harder . . . harder still. Inside her, thrusting in and out. A welling ecstasy. Her eyes, bug eyed. Her jaw, slack. Her hands trying to pull his hands away. Her hands slip to her sides; her eyes dull. His body explodes. Joy, standing over a pliant body. He draped over her, his tongue licking her, blowing against her breast, as he would a trumpet. Her areola his reed.

It felt Rudy's and the woman's life both draining, dissolving. Two deaths, satisfying its hunger. One, actual; the other, blood memories.

It understood Rudy's emotions. Better than JT's.

It remembered women.

It understood without knowing why, how—it understood killing a woman.

Understood how killing could be better than a kiss.

With Rudy's blood, it smeared, marked the wall.

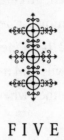

FIVE

Marie stood in the shadows, leaning against a wall, just outside the circle of a streetlamp's glow. She stared at Charity, her second home, rising like a series of turreted monoliths piercing the sky.

In 1736, it was originally called, L'Hospital des Pauvres de la Charité, Hospital for the Poor. Its mission never changed even as sites did, as it grew exponentially, becoming a storied complex with a thousand window eyes. A labyrinth of floors, dark stairwells, and whirring elevators ferrying up the living, sending down the dead.

Marie swatted at a blood-sucking mosquito. With the back of her hand, she wiped sweat from her brow.

DuLac had ordered her to stay home—to rest, prepare for the ceremony. But after Marie-Claire fell asleep, she called Louise to babysit, told Kind Dog to stay alert, and walked out the door in a T-shirt, tattered jeans, and sandals.

She'd never once imagined, given an unexpected night off, the choice of sleep, she'd be yearning for her graveyard shift.

She remembered DuLac from new resident orientation, his eyes bloodshot, barking, "Devils find it easy to move at night. More folks shoot, stab, beat each other when the sun goes down. More than any other time."

As a first-year resident, she'd smothered a laugh. But she'd learned DuLac never lied. Three years later and not a night had passed when she didn't have to change a wet, bloodied lab coat. Fight for a life. Or tell someone that a loved one had died.

She'd learned, too, that while DuLac meant "devils" as in "bad-behaving people," others, especially Catholics, meant "devils" literally, as in demons, Satan.

Marie knew voodoo, in its origins, resisted simplistic definitions of good and evil. The snake in the Garden of Eden offered knowledge. Always a good. Humanity didn't "fall" from grace into sin. Humanity was a never-ending blending of impulses: to heal and to hurt; to help and to harm.

But, in New Orleans, African-based faiths blended with Catholicism, and linguistic, cultural shifts changed *Voudu* into voodoo, with resonant echoes in hoodoo, folk *magick*, and southern rootwork. In the New World, faith, like people, became a "mixed-blood stew." Evil, as a concept, thrived until it turned on the faith itself—pop culture stereotypes convinced both blacks and whites that the slaves' ancient faith was steeped in barbarism with an evil, killing intent.

Part of her struggle was to stir, re-spice, the "stew"—reclaiming, reasserting, voodoo's nurturing, beneficent power. "Your *fa*, your fate," DuLac declared when he recognized her power. Still, it had been two centuries since Marie Laveau died, and unlike Harry Potter tales, there weren't any schools for a Voodoo Queen.

Marie crossed the street. A pinch-faced woman rushed a swaddled baby into the ER. Probably fever. A touch of pneumonia. But you could never be too careful. Among immigrants, it could be TB. Among citizens whose parents forgot or couldn't afford the vaccine, it could be measles. Or chicken pox.

Marie longed to walk into the ER. To follow the woman and her baby.

The ER was Charity's heart. Two ambulances were parked; another was arriving, wailing, red lights flaring. A homeless man played with the electric sliding glass doors, stepping on and off the mat.

She saw sweet Sully speak to the man, then guide him by the hand into the ER, the glass doors sliding shut. Immediately, the glass misted with humidity, making the ER seem out of focus. She knew Sully would give the man some of his dinner, red beans and rice, chicory-spiced coffee from his thermos.

Marie felt an itch, like red ants, trailing down her neck. She turned.

JT and Rudy were standing behind her. Up against the convenience store's graffiti-filled wall. Both looking patient, woeful.

She bit her lip, turned away.

She'd rather be inside Charity's lighted corridors, fighting death, than outside, standing in the thick night air, trying to avoid thinking about conducting a ceremony to quell a monster. Trying to avoid the burden of unnaturally murdered ghosts.

She was tempted to believe unquiet souls might have the capacity for pure evil. Not JT and Rudy, though. She felt sure both had been fallible, imperfect men who may have done evil; but as spirits, they were looking for justice, for peace. Unlike the spirit that had killed them.

"Damn." She needed to be inside Charity, where science did its best to cut life and death into digestible, bite-size pieces.

She wanted to do what she was trained to do. Use modern medicine's tools. Take a history. Blood pressure, temperature, pulse. Order tests. Interpret an X-ray. Stop bleeding. Suture wounds.

Be a doctor and heal.

The ambulance, its wail suddenly quieted, its red light still, pulled into the parking bay.

She couldn't help running to the van, throwing open the doors to a cursing kid, sixteen, seventeen, with a bandaged shoulder, bleeding sluggishly.

"I'll walk. Won't be carried," said the street tough, trying to peacock his courage. Only his restless eyes showed fear. Shock.

Marie nodded at the EMTs—Luella, who'd ridden with the patient; Eddie, the driver. They both recognized her.

"I told you, I'll walk."

Exasperated, Eddie spit on the sidewalk. Luella rolled her eyes.

"How about a wheelchair? Keep you from dripping blood on the sidewalk and floor." Hands on her hips, Marie cocked her head.

The glass doors slid open. Huan, her ponytail bobbing, arrived, breathless. "Hey."

"Hey," Marie answered. "I've got him." She swerved a wheelchair forward.

"I sure would like to get you," snapped the boy. "Fine as chocolate cream. You a doctor?"

"You a patient?" Marie pointed. "Sit."

Wincing, the boy climbed out of the ambulance. He was handsome, lean. His sleeveless shirt, cut at the midriff, showed off his hard abs, a skull and bones tattoo identified his gang. The Buccaneers. By her guess, he'd been lucky. Shot clean through. No major damage, just a lot of blood. His baggy jeans rode low on his hips. Fruit Of The Loom underwear showed, tearing between the cotton and the elastic. His pants looked ready to fall off, just like a toddler's. In a year or two, he'd probably be dead. His youth wasted.

"DuLac isn't going to like this," whispered Huan. "He should be on a stretcher."

"Tell me about it," said Luella.

The young man's face paled. His bandage turned crimson, flowering blood.

Marie wheeled the chair around. The doors parted. "This isn't all DuLac isn't going to like."

DuLac walked toward her, his face grim. "I thought I told you to take the night off."

Staff and patients stared. K-Paul winked. Two nurses twittered behind their hands. El, with her witch's nails, shooed them away. "Get to work."

DuLac pulled Marie by the arm, shouting to Huan, "Take over."

"Hey, give me back my doc."

"I'll give you what for," snarled El, startling the bleeding boy into submission. Huan wheeled him to Curtain Three.

DuLac pushed Marie inside his office, slamming his door. Rigid, he stared at her. She'd never seen him so furious. Absent his Southern charm.

"You have a ceremony to prepare for."

"Tell me something I don't know." Then, defensively, "I was going stir-crazy."

DuLac studied her, his weight pressing into his hands, onto his desk.

Marie willed herself not to flinch or shift her gaze.

"Proper food?"

"Yes."

"Altar candles? Offerings? Incense?"

"Yes, they're all ready."

"Then you should be preparing your mind."

"You tell me, then," Marie demanded, "what should I be doing? How exactly do I prepare for a creature no one's seen? Perhaps can't see. But, amazingly, drains blood? All of it.

"I'm not even sure I can call it to a ceremony. This thing. This creature. Whatever it is. Spirit *loas,* that's what I know. Agwé. Ezili. Ogun. Damballah. If you know better, DuLac, then you do it. You prepare."

DuLac's gaze was hooded, lids half closed, as if he were looking inside himself.

"I'm sorry," murmured Marie.

Three years ago, DuLac drank heavily. Staff covered for him, making sure no one was hurt; but it was only a matter of time before he harmed someone. Lost his license. Been jailed.

Reneaux had confided that DuLac drank because he'd dreamed of being a *houngan.* But the spiritual gifts weren't his to carry.

They were hers.

She whispered, "DuLac—you know I love you. I've done all I could to prepare for tomorrow's ceremony. Reviewed Laveau's journal. Assembled food and costumes. I'm as ready as I'll ever be and I just have to pray that's good enough." She raised her hand, forestalling his words. "I'm grateful for your training. All you've done for me. But I'm me. A twenty-first-century *voodooienne* and a doctor. I need to do what I think is right. Faith healing, science healing, I need to be useful. Charity needs me. I'm going to work. I need to work."

Hands in his pockets, DuLac rocked back on his heels. "*Bien.* You're more woman than I thought. Let's go."

Her mouth dropped open with surprise.

He opened the office door. The bright hall light flooded DuLac's small, dim office. "You coming? Finish what you started? Huan might need a second opinion."

Marie grinned. "Don't think you've got the upper hand. I won the argument."

"Argument? What argument? I see a Voodoo Queen, a woman who's coming into her own. Besides, I knew you'd come here."

"Sure you did."

"You've got your own bloodlust." DuLac turned, seeing Marie's stricken gaze. He shut the door, his back against it. "That came out wrong. You're nothing like the creature."

She dipped her head. But, guiltily, she felt there was some truth in DuLac's word: "bloodlust." She loved stemming its flow, mastering it. In surgery, blood was predictable; in the ER, on any given night, blood flowed everywhere—from any and all orifices, from all types of wounds.

DuLac stepped forward, clasping Marie's face with his palms. "I'm not jealous of you. I used to wallow in self-pity, wanting the gift of prophecy. Sight. No one else in Orleans seemed ready to carry it. Or those who did were pretenders. Corrupt. All I want to do is serve you."

"You mean teach me?"

"After the first year, you outpaced my knowledge. Even as a doctor, your skills are beyond mine."

"No."

"Yes. Let me be proud of you."

Marie felt mournful, sensing their relationship was about to change irrevocably. She didn't want DuLac thinking she was better than he was.

DuLac kissed her brow. "It's the way of fathers and daughters. Children outpacing their parents. Daughters scratching their rough edges on their fathers. No wonder I'm turning gray."

She embraced him, holding tight. Blinking back tears.

"Sass. Too much sass."

She felt giddy, happy. DuLac was still her family. That hadn't changed.

"Get to work. Proper clothes, please."

"Sure, boss." Marie flung open the door. "I've got a lab coat in my locker."

EI had been watching for her. Brow furrowed, mouth tight.

Marie nodded, smiling like a Cheshire cat.

Like lightning, EI shouted, "Hallelujah," then turned, berating a lab technician for moving too slow.

Sweat gathered beneath her shoulder blades, beneath her T-shirt, her lab coat. She worked like a fiend. Nurses couldn't keep up with her. K-Paul tried. Huan just offered help.

EI kept the patients flowing.

Marie loved every minute of it.

They'd sent the gangbanger home, but not before he'd brushed his hand against her breast. She'd slapped his hand. Told him to "Keep safe. Be good."

The boy had grinned. "Sucker bait."

She whispered a prayer.

Four in the morning. Two hours to go.

JT and Rudy sat in the waiting room. Looking like old pals.

Inexplicably, the ER was almost deserted. Sully, his feet on his desk, snored. The homeless were sprawled on chairs. Flu patients were still waiting to be called.

"Hear from Parks?" DuLac handed her mud-thick coffee.

"No."

"That's good." He drank from his mug.

"It isn't over."

"Not good."

"No news means a lull. JT and Rudy still haven't left. They're still needy."

"Still here?"

"Two chairs down from Sully."

DuLac started, squinted at the folding chairs.

"Sight," she exhaled. "Not always a blessing." She pretended not to hear DuLac murmuring, "I'd give up my career."

The ER doors slid wide, letting in a warm blast of early morning air.

"Don't she look pitiful," said EI, coming to stand beside Marie and DuLac. "Barefoot and pregnant."

All three moved toward the girl, in a floral-print dress, with red, flyaway hair.

It was Marie's hand the girl took. "Baby's coming," she said, her voice soft as a cloud. "Been rolling, heaving, all day."

K-Paul offered a wheelchair.

Marie mouthed, "Thanks."

"Exam One is open," said El. "Need help?"

"I've got it," said Marie.

DuLac nodded, walking away, sparing a glance for the empty ER chairs.

Marie pushed the wheelchair through the green curtains, then closed them tightly. "I need to examine you. Let me help you up."

The girl had saucer eyes. Hazel. Something about their dullness made her look dumb. No, that wasn't it. Disinterested. Passive.

"How old are you?"

"Thirteen."

"Have you ever had a GYN exam?"

"What?" For the first time, the girl moaned. Lowing—the deep distress sound of laboring mothers.

Marie touched the girl's belly, feeling a contraction. "How many months?"

"Don't know." She moaned again and Marie stroked her loose hair. It was heavy, thick with grease.

"What's your name?"

"Sue."

"Sue what?"

"Just Sue."

"Let me help you up." Marie extended her arm. "Just lie down and relax. Good." She extended the stirrups. "Put your feet here. That's it. One by one."

Sue's bare feet were cracked and dirty. She carried no purse. She must've walked to Charity. A bayou backwoods girl. During rural volunteering, Marie had seen such girls. They gave birth unaware of professional midwives, doctors. When nothing went wrong, there was sheer beauty—a young girl, birthing, surrounded by wiser women. When the birth was breech or the umbilical cord strangled the baby, the too-young mothers writhed in pain, often dying with their babies.

"I need you to relax," said Marie reassuringly. "See how far you've dilated."

"What's die-lat-ed?"

"It lets me know if the baby's fully engaged in the canal."

Sue frowned.

"Tells me how fast the baby's coming."

"It's coming. I know it." Sue turned her head, staring at the wall, her body limp. Like she'd given up resisting. Knees parted, her belly rippling, she looked like a beached whale. Her pink belly button hyperextended.

"You can sit up now."

Freckles dusted Sue's nose. Stubborn, her lips puckered. "I want it born in Charity."

Marie nodded. "It," Sue had said, not "he" or "she."

"Better than the back bedroom. Tommy says we ought not to pay for what comes natural." The girl clutched her belly, looking every bit her age.

"I'm scared."

"Where's your mother? Is there no woman to help you?"

Strangely, Sue's eyes closed. Like she'd drifted to sleep, sitting upright. Just shut down and left.

Marie swung back the curtain. "EI, call Social Services."

The girl started screaming, "No. Just a doctor. For my baby."

"I'm a doctor."

Sue trembled. Pushing her thin shift over her abdomen, trying to slip off the exam table.

"Stay, please."

"I need to go upstairs to have my baby. Babies are born upstairs, ain't they?" Sue clutched Marie's lab coat. Fading, orange-purple bruises marked her arms. Someone had pinched, shaken, maybe slapped her.

Marie clasped Sue's hands. "Listen to me. You're having Braxton Hicks. False contractions. The baby isn't ready."

"It is. It has to come out." Sue's mouth puckered, like a baby bird's.

"Not yet. The baby isn't ready. You'll have to trust me."

Sue cried big, silent tears, wiping her nose with her sleeve. "There'll be trouble."

"From who? Your mother? Tommy?"

"What about my pains?"

"They're real. Just not effective." When Sue didn't answer, Marie added, "Social Services can help. My friend Antoinette can help."

"That's the trouble. Social Services. I was told not to truck with them."

"By Tommy?"

Suddenly, the girl's eyes were sly. She'd stopped crying. "I feel better now."

"Where're you from? Have you had prenatal care? Seen a doctor?"

"You're a doctor?"

"Yes. Dr. Laveau."

The girl surprised Marie by embracing her. On her tiptoes, she whispered in Marie's ear, "Can you help me get rid of it?"

Then the girl stepped back, her mouth a wide O. "That's a sin. I'm a sinner."

"What've you got, Marie?" Antoinette, in a tailored suit, looking like a banker rather than someone who cared for people at their worst, their most helpless, glanced between the two.

Sue bolted.

"Catch her," shouted Marie.

K-Paul, notating charts, reached for Sue, but his hand caught air.

Sue, eel slippery, dashed outside the automatic sliding glass doors.

Marie called, "Wait."

Outside, Marie looked left, then right. Already the air was hot, damp, smothering breath.

Then she saw Sue, near visitor parking. Preternaturally still. Stopped on the sidewalk's edge.

"How'd you get here?"

Any second, she'd flee, across the street.

Marie knew she had only one chance for success. "I'll deliver the baby, Sue. See you safe."

"Promise? Hope to die?" She trembled, like a doe ready to dart.

"Hope to die."

The streetlamp snapped and buzzed, ready to expire. Sue

looked up, smiling at the moths fluttering against the glass. She shaded her eyes, looking toward the horizon. An orange-filled haze was heralding the sun.

Marie walked slowly, deliberately, toward Sue, holding out a twenty.

The girl snatched it. "Thank y'all." Then, looking neither left nor right, she dashed across the street.

"Sue," Marie yelled. "Sue."

She didn't stop.

"You'll come back? Please?" Her voice was strained, raw. "Please."

Sue turned. Her shift, tight across her abdomen, fell below her knees. A bayou girl's dress.

Sue held up her hand. The white palm, delicate, small, high in the morning air. Her hand fell, clasping her belly. Then she turned, running like a ghost. Racing into a shadowed alley.

Marie went back inside the ER. It was too bright. Her head hurt. "Not now, Antoinette. Not now."

Antoinette responded, "She'll be back."

Marie wasn't sure.

Maybe Parks could help her track a backwoods girl? How many pregnant thirteen-year-olds could there be? Marie grimaced. In New Orleans, plenty. But not many like Sue. Possibly rural Acadian. A runaway? And who was Tommy? Another youth? Lost in the city.

Marie felt worn and wrung out.

"El. DuLac. I'm going home. I'll do better tomorrow. No, today. Tonight."

She looked at the folding chairs. Sully was looking worriedly at her.

JT and Rudy had disappeared.

She walked out of Charity, almost sprinting, her lab coat billowing. Her stethoscope cradled her neck. Past the ambulances. Cars. The shift workers. Past new patients arriving. She ran, tracing Sue's path.

Stopped dead at the alley's mouth.

She suddenly feared Sue and her baby would be drained. Killed.

DuLac was right. She needed to prepare. Stop the monster.

Marie yelled into the alleyway, "Sue. Sue." The sound was guttural.

"Sue." Her voice changed into a scream, roiling, exploding from her gut. Filled with all her anguish, uncertainty. Fear and frustration.

A cat, startled, scooted by. Street-corner boys, on the southeast corner, hailed her, clapping. Two of them started howling, their tenor voices urging each other to a new high.

A taxi cruised by.

New Orleans was stirring awake. An in-between time. Night still claimed the streets but building tops were starting to lighten.

A bus hissed and stopped. Weary casino cashiers, hotel maids, and bellhops trudged home. To some, Marie was just another drunk hollering "Sue." To others, she wasn't crazy enough for them to pay her any mind.

Marie felt staggered by fury.

Her work in the ER mattered. She did and would do good. She might, one day, save the young man she patched up, might, one day, help Sue birth her baby.

She blinked.

JT and Rudy were glimmering before her. Oddly comforting.

Marie listened for clues in the night air:

Sounds intensified: a strain of music from far off; rubber tires slapping against the road; the soft roar of the Mississippi. She thought she even heard the wings of a bird, trolling the water for fish.

She heard, too, the sound of no sound—a pregnant stillness, the creature waiting in the night.

For now, Sue was safe.

Her raised hand had been a promise. Hadn't it?

She'd avenge JT and Rudy. Wouldn't she?

Marie yelled, this time a warrior's cry, filled with rage.

And she hoped everyone, every creature in New Orleans, below and at sea level, heard her. Heard her violence hiding, stirring inside.

☒≋✿◇✖◉✿▓

It heard her. The sound moved through water. Distinct from ordinary sounds. Primitive. Raw.

Just as it sensed memories in blood, it sensed feelings in sound.

This sound. Assertive. A call to battle.

It felt kinship. Remembered battles. Struggles for power, control. It had won until . . . until. . . . It couldn't remember. It remembered pain, dying.

It stirred in the warm water, still gathering itself, rising despite the bones pushing it down, the underwater sea god thwarting it.

It was waiting to be reborn. Resurrected.

Waiting for the other sound that called it ashore . . . waiting for when it would make its own sound and rise from the water's realm to live again. On land.

SIX

LILA'S YARD

WEDNESDAY, LATE EVENING

Marie danced, twirling in her white shift, praying for spirits.

Drums resounded. One hard beat, then two. No drumsticks, only a focused sputtering of palms, cupped and flat, articulations of fingers pounding on cat skins.

Boudom.

Wire's face was drenched in sweat. He played as if his soul depended upon it. The twins, Renee and Raoul, drummed on either side of him. Sometimes she'd see the twins on a street corner: baggy pants, gold chains swinging from their necks. They'd be playing on trash can tops, shouting insults at street dancers, cigarettes dangling, like magic wands, from their mouths. They never acknowledged her, nor she them. Street toughs who had the magic to summon gods. Tonight their power was magnified by Wire's relentless drumming.

But, still, the gods didn't come.

DuLac had been right. She should've spent more time preparing. But doing what? She'd done everything required.

Except she'd worked the ER—a shift that had left her restless. Unable to sleep. She should've conserved her energy.

Marie swayed, stepping and sliding within the circle marked by votive candles grounded in dirt.

She prayed: "Agwé, don't forsake me."

Rituals followed a specific pattern. Offerings at the altar. Beans. Rice. The drummers call to Legba, an old man with a walking stick, to open the spirit gates. Once Legba possessed a parishioner, then other spirits arrived, the drummers playing their rhythms . . . until one spirit above all reigned. Tonight she dedicated to Agwé. God of restless seas. She had his favorite foods: okra and oysters. His saber and admiral's hat.

She'd drawn his symbol on silk.

Nothing happened. No response to the drummer's call.

"Spirits will come," DuLac murmured, his voice encouraging her, blowing softly across her ear. She twirled away from him, contracting her back, letting her arms flail wide. Dulac watched. Like she was a cell under a microscope. Except, she was an organism—a mammal—that spirits could ride. A channel between the living and the dead.

Like hell, she thought. Feeling slightly embarrassed. She was only the medium, yet she couldn't open the gate.

Parks was leaning against the fence, watching, skeptical, as parishioners dressed in white danced. Parks probably thought he was on an abnormal psychology field trip.

Sometimes, she was skeptical, too. Like tonight. After hours of drumming. No signs; no grace. Just heat rising from the small bonfire. Gas torches lighting the backyard's four corners. Christmas lights twinkling in ancient willows.

But when miracles happened, Marie felt like the most powerful woman in the world. Felt more a healer than medicine had ever made her feel.

She felt her followers growing wearier. Disenchanted.

Most of them were elderly, mainly women. Some gap toothed, some rail thin, some, graying; others, with hair as white as cotton. Frail elders who went to Mass on Sunday, confessed venial sins, and said their evening rosary. But they all remembered their youth, their passion . . . the dancing, chanting call to gods. The thrill of spirits entering their bodies. They all remembered seeing or hearing tales of spirit *loas* entering their mother, their mother's mother, their mother's mother before . . . all the way down through the generations. To a distant time when a woman could walk on water. When a woman was the most powerful figure in New Orleans. When a woman could inspire fear, conjure miracles by whispering the words, *"Je suis Marie.* I *am* Marie Laveau."

Marie's body swayed to the timbre of drums. *Boudom.* "Please," she whispered. "Please come."

DuLac gestured grandly at the sky, as if he could call down grace. Parks lit another cigarette.

Lila, a ninety-year-old ex–blues singer, always offered her yard. Marie suspected it was because she was infatuated with DuLac. Eyes, cataract, Lila could hardly see. But she never failed to preen whenever DuLac was near; her near-blind eyes always found him.

Marie felt the drum rhythm change. A syncopated urging in six-eighth time.

Wire was offering up his soul.

Boudom.

Flames flickered from unexpected wind. The silk with Agwé's sign fluttered high, then floated downward, like a waterfall.

Parks was alert. His body leaning forward, like he could sense what she sensed.

Something in the air. The intangible made tangible. Electric.

Marie's heart raced. She surveyed her small band. She knew them twice over: as a doctor and as a priestess.

Madame Yvonne, hands stretched high, waited for spirits to rain upon her. She had hypertension. She was lonely. Her children all lived North.

Petey, known for binge drinking, slept on sidewalks, in alleys, beneath freeway ramps. Wherever he dropped. Tonight, he was stomping his feet, patterning the drums.

Erma, at least eighty, called Auntie by everyone, shuffled gingerly. She had healed fractures—arms, legs, ribs, and face. Auntie had been abused as a young girl plying her sex trade in the Quarter. Some of the damage was done by pimps; some by drug-addled johns. But of all the parishioners, she was the most trusting, believing.

Desiree, sixty-two, visited Charity each month insisting she was in labor. She'd had a hysterectomy when she was twenty-one.

Marie chanted:

> *Legba, remove the barrier for me*
> *So I may pass through.*
> *Legba, remove the barrier*
> *So I may pass through to the spirit world.*

Others joined her. Paul's shout was fierce; he'd worked construction, "paid under the table" all his days. No social security, no pension. He hunted trash for lunch, begged the hospital for vitamins.

Her followers were part of the city's dispossessed. Unloved, unappreciated, forgotten.

Marie moved toward the altar. Magic would happen. DuLac was grinning. Parks watched, expectant.

The drums grew louder, insistent.

Boudom. Followers shouted and moaned. The spirit gate was opening.

Sandlewood, tallow, scented the air. Marie stroked the altar: statues of Saint Peter; the Virgin, smiling benignly; paintings of Legba, the guardian; and Ezili, goddess of beauty and love.

Old bodies seemed young again. Followers moved as if their bodies were water—languid, smooth; others moved as if their bodies were fire—jerking, striking at air.

Arms upraised, Marie felt static in the air. A space opening between worlds.

"Ride," a follower shrieked. The drums cajoled. "Ride," she murmured.

Petey became Legba. He walked bowlegged, with a cane, his back bent. Head cocked, almost darting forward like a bird, Petey puffed on Legba's black pipe.

Followers, in swirls of white, praised him, reaching out to touch his hand.

Then Petey convulsed. Fell to the ground. Limbs twitching.

Desiree's head lolled. Lila clapped, shouting, "Praise be. Praise be." Parishioners chanted: "Legba, Legba."

DuLac laid props and garments on the ground, anticipating the arrival of other gods. Ezili's fan and shawl. Ogun's sword and head-dress.

Parks was transfixed. He moved closer to the swirl of bodies.

Marie slowly turned, studying the worshipper's faces. Ecstatic. Anticipating miracles, spiritual release. But no one was possessed. Haitians called possession *"vevnie de chien," "*ride my horse."

Loas controlled; personality diminished.

Marie kneeled beside Petey. *Cold air surrounded him.* He was trying to tunnel into the dirt. Slobbering, shaking, his eyes rolled high in his head. His pulse was erratic.

She gripped Petey's head, trying to hold it steady, trying to peer into his eyes. For a brief flicker, she saw his irises. *A dark mist clouded his pupils, seeming to bleed like tears.*

Unnerved, she fell back.

The mist elongated, covering Petey's body like a blanket. Salty, crusted with sand.

"What's happening?" shouted Parks.

The drumming stopped. The silence was disorienting, like the aftermath of a hurricane. Worshippers began wailing. Petey gasped, clawing for air. His body flopped like a rag doll.

"DuLac," Marie screamed. "My med kit. DuLac."

DuLac brought the kit. "*Merde.* What is it?"

"He's having a seizure. This darkness—it's hurting him. But the seizure is a secondary symptom."

Parks, on his knees, said, "Use this."

Marie stuck the pen in Petey's mouth. Kept him from swallowing his tongue. Parks held his flailing arms.

"It's freezing," Parks said.

The darkness coiled about Petey's legs, his torso.

"He all right? He all right?" asked Lila.

"Lord, have mercy," said Auntie.

Wire, Renee, and Raoul stood over them. DuLac prepped a needle with a sedative; he pushed the liquid into Petey's veins.

Marie felt the mist, amazingly ephemeral yet substantive. *It uncoiled from Petey and wove up her arms.*

"Marie, watch out," yelled Parks.

DuLac reached for her.

"Keep away," she said, stepping away from DuLac.

The misty darkness brushed through her hair, against her skin. Like ice, it burned. She shuddered.

A voice warned: "Show no fear."

Agwé?

Petey's breathing slowed.

"What's happening?" asked Parks.

The darkness explored her body. Marie kept still, learning about it as it learned about her. She swore she felt textures in the darkness, a shape molding to her skin.

Before, the creature was invisible, but she could tell by her followers' terror, DuLac's curiosity, Parks's horror that the spirit had become visible to them.

The darkness withdrew, coalescing into a tight ball. It hung, suspended in the air, then elongated, seeming to form a mouth, pressing against Petey's wrist.

Blood dripped from Petey's arm.

"No," Marie shouted, gripping Petey's arm, beating the dark air.

Petey's body rattled like a crazed marionette. He was unconscious, the drug dominated, but his wrist was still twisting in the darkness, draining, losing blood.

"Be gone," Marie screamed. "Agwé, help me. Send me your grace."

At the word "Agwé," Wire renewed his drumming. Rene and Raoul supported him, pounding the pattern of waves crashing against the shore, beating against a ship's bow.

Marie quivered; Agwé answered their plea.

Possessed, she grabbed Agwé's sword, feeling as powerful as a tide, swiping, stabbing at the creature. She could see the elements in the darkness, the particles disintegrating with each stab, thrust. But, quickly, the particles reassembled, the damage minimal.

Agwé roared: "What comes from the sea, belongs to me."

The darkness pushed back. A test of wills. Energy that pushed, prodded each other. Like a chain reaction. Building, pulsing, explosive power.

Marie cried out, fell backward.

Agwé flew. So, too, the darkness.

Petey's wrist lay limp.

"It's gone," said DuLac, checking Petey's pulse and heart.

Parks helped her to sit up.

Followers crowded: Auntie, Desiree, Erma. "You all right, Miz Marie? You all right?"

"I'm fine." Marie looked at Wire, somber; at Renee and Raoul, disappointed and scared, like vulnerable teenagers.

Marie touched Petey's chest. His carotid artery. "He's alive."

DuLac wrapped Petey's wrist. "He may need a transfusion. I'll call an ambulance."

Marie rested her head on Parks's shoulder. Fireflies danced, a mosquito tried to draw Petey's blood. She swatted it.

The air was warm, sticky. Wet. The moon was growing full. Petey's body was ice cold.

"Everyone go home," said Parks. "This is a police matter now."

Lila, Yvonne, Paul, and the others began ambling away. Elderly, they'd seen worse. Renee tipped his hat, then, he and his brother were off.

Wire squatted. "I wasn't much use tonight."

Marie squeezed his hand. "No. You did fine. Agwé didn't have the strength to stay."

"All my life I heard about my family's history. Part of me never really believed my father's stories. How our drumming was all powerful."

"Do you believe now?"

"Yes, I do. And, tonight, I feel as though I failed you."

"You didn't."

"I commit myself to your service." Unexpectedly, he knelt, his chin on his chest, all pride washed out of him. His brow, dripping sweat, stained the dirt. "Bless me. I'll make myself worthy."

Parks was looking at her strangely.

Marie laid her hand on Wire's head. "I accept your service."

Wire clutched her hand, kissing the inside of her palm. Abruptly he stood, gathering his drum. Leaving through the backyard gate.

DuLac covered Petey with his jacket.

Two years ago, she'd envisioned a bad end for Petey; she'd lied, telling him he'd die in bed. Whatever his end, she hoped this wasn't it.

She looked at Parks. "New clue," she said softly. "It's becoming stronger. Agwé can't slay it. It's from the sea, but it's something else. Something Agwé has no sway over. I've never known anything like it."

His blue eyes looked into her brown eyes. "Are you okay? That's all I need to know."

Marie cocked her head. "You're a strange man."

She looked at her hand. Blood rising to the surface, she stared at the crazy quilt of veins. Life was mapped by blood, DNA, all the way back to Eve.

"It won't die," she murmured. Her knees buckled, and she slipped into darkness.

"Doc?"

She was in Parks's squad car, her head leaning against the window. She remembered Parks lifting, carrying her. The parishioners huddling like scared mice.

"DuLac?" she asked.

"He called an ambulance for Petey."

"I need to help."

"No." Parks reached across her, snapping her seat belt. "DuLac told me to take care of you. Take you home."

"I need to speak with him."

"Doctor's orders."

"But he doesn't know—" She stopped. What? What could she possibly tell him that would be useful? She slumped back against the seat. "This is the second time you've rescued me. Won't happen again," she said, defensive.

"Didn't expect it would. Figured this was unusual. Like the case."

Parks started the engine. Turned on the *whoosh* of the air conditioner. Flicked his headlights to high as he tried to maneuver out of a too-tight spot.

Parks was a good man. Marie pressed her face against the window. Staring at the row houses: folks, inside, listening to music, soaking their sore feet after a ten-hour shift in the Riverwalk casinos; folks, outside, playing cards, participating vicariously in the voodoo ritual in Lila's backyard. For hours, drums had resounded throughout the neighborhood and no one had seemed to mind. Or, if they did, they kept their mouths shut. Most New Orleanians were believers; and those who weren't believed well enough to leave voodoo alone.

She touched her palm to the window. Wire was standing on the sidewalk, grim, his hand held high. He'd called something all right. And she wondered if he regretted it, felt sorry about it.

Headlights flared diagonally, illuminating parked cars, the road. The car stopped as a whooping ambulance rounded the corner. She and Parks were, for seconds, drenched in red.

The car jerked forward.

"It fought with Agwé," she marveled. "Shut the gate. Opened its own."

"I don't understand a word you're saying."

"I wonder if it's a new kind of spirit? A new *loa*?"

"Seemed plain evil to me. DuLac thought Petey had rib fractures. Internal injuries."

"In voodoo, gods are like people, a mixture of both good and evil."

Parks glanced at her, then focused on the empty road. "You feel anything good?"

She shook her head.

"It's going to rain. Smell it."

Marie rolled down the window, sticking her head into the air. Salt, diesel oil, fish. Body smells—sweat, tears, sex—were heavy in the air. The sky was smoky black, the clouds gray. The moon was crystal white, pregnant. A hurricane was stirring off the Florida Keys, roiling its way eastward, toward the Carribbean Sea and the Gulf. Sailors were battening their sails, hatches. Murmuring curses and prayers.

The car's clock read 2:13 AM.

"Have you ever gotten lost, Detective?"

"All the time. Clues get me lost. Always chaos before I can figure it out. Who did what to whom. And why."

"That's how I feel. Lost. Chaos. Can't figure it out. It'll be a full moon soon. The tides are rising. All around the earth. Amazing—how that happens."

She shifted in her seat, studying Parks's profile. High cheekbones, a nose etched sharp. Thin lips.

"Legba opens the gate. Agwé should've arrived first. Instead, an unnamed thing taunted me."

"Taunted?" He looked sharply at her.

"No, pushed back. Against Agwé. It explored me." She paused, reliving the feel of an inexplicably hard but soft darkness. It couldn't be a *loa;* there was too much substance. Presence.

If she'd shown fear, would it have attacked? Had Agwé warned her? Or had there been another spirit present?

Her breathing slowed, she closed her eyes, trying to see connections in the dark.

"Show no fear." It had felt like a woman's voice. Cautioning that the creature sensed emotions.

Did it feed on fear as well as blood?

"Where are you?"

"What?"

"It's like you go somewhere else. Disappear. From the here. You know what I mean."

She shuddered. "I'm in another world. Inside myself. Thinking. Trying to travel roads I don't understand. Roads my ancestors have traveled."

"I thought you—"

"What?"

"Thought you, voodoo people, controlled things. Hey, I'm not saying I believe." He pumped the brakes, realizing he had been speeding. "I mean, I believe something is happening. If you're not in control, who is?"

"Good question."

She pressed the button on the armrest, watching the window rise. The glass reflected streetlights. She saw her face. Sad. Dirty, hair awry.

The car, a nondescript black Taurus, rolled through the streets of the Garden District. Ancient trees shading the road. Gnarled roots. Mansions with deep porches; windows like jaundiced eyes. Such lovely glory, yet, decaying. Insects burrowing into trees. Soft soil alive with weeds.

Sin City. Decadent. Corruption beyond the neon, the raucous music. Behind elegant mansion doors. Inside tourist bedrooms. Modest cottages. An unforgiving past. Slavery, opium, and fever. Preternatural possibilities.

New Orleans reeked. Caught between the Mississippi River and Lake Ponchartrain. Swamps to the south. It was unsettling living below sea level, it always felt as if destruction was imminent. For decades, the Canal Street pumps had drained streets when it rained. Brackish water mixing with sewer overflow.

Parks said nothing. Just drove.

She wiped tears from her cheeks.

She didn't understand why she felt at such a loss. All her life, she'd been strong. When her mother died, when she was left in foster care, she'd survived.

Had it been her mother who warned her to show no fear? Or someone else? Another ancestor stirring in her blood?

Times like this she felt unprepared. Didn't know enough. Funny, her mother had escaped from New Orleans and her heritage; Marie had felt drawn, like a moth to a flame.

"Here." Parks handed her a handkerchief.

"I didn't expect you to carry a kerchief for a crying girl."

"My mother taught me manners."

"And to be prepared?"

"That was the Eagle Scouts." Parks turned the steering wheel left. "You did a remarkable thing. I don't understand any of it. But I understand you saved Petey's life."

Parks's head dipped and bobbed. He was scanning the streets for crime. Reneaux had driven the same way.

She stuffed the kerchief against her mouth, muffling her wail.

The air conditioner kicked in again, whirring. Even at night, New Orleans was often too hot. Steam rising from the pavement; from the bumping of bodies, personalities trying to thrive in a decadent, desultory world.

Rain started to fall, soft as petals. Marie promised herself that this was the last time she'd ever cry.

�%✕♢⊗◉✕𝍷

Not enough blood. The man's blood had been thin. Filled with regrets, petty crimes. Old blood for an old man.

It enjoyed the victim's fear—the horror when it approached, when the blood began draining.

She didn't fear. Curious.

What secrets stirred in her blood? What memories?

Her blood would be thick, rich with emotions.

It needed not just blood, but the memories the blood sustained. Memories coupled with feelings helped it remember. Feel.

What it was now, it hadn't been. It had been more real.

What was real?

It gathered itself, high above the candles, the bonfire smoldering. It listened for a call. Hungering.

For the girl without fear.

SEVEN

MARIE'S APARTMENT

THURSDAY NOON

Marie sat, her feet propped on the balcony rail. Kind Dog lay at her feet, panting. He was hot, would've preferred being inside, but he wasn't going to leave her.

She patted his head. "Good boy," she said. "We'll go in soon."

Inside her apartment, she felt as if she couldn't get enough air. Outside, the sun shining, watching the street life, she could pretend it was an ordinary day and she hadn't any failures. Maybe because she'd been raised in Chicago, she found the sun soothed what ailed her. Even when she complained about the heat and humidity, she felt grateful it wasn't snow. Wasn't ice.

"Hey, Doc. Doc!"

She lowered her feet, peering over the rail. "Parks?"

Dog stood, waving his tail, his nose pushed between the wrought-iron rails.

"Can I come up?"

"Only if you've got good news."

Parks's shoulders drooped. He lifted high a paper bag.

Dog barked. Sharp. Then barked again.

"Guess I'm overruled," said Marie.

"Door unlatched?"

"No. I'll get it for you." She rose, looking at Dog, his brown eyes soulful. "You should open the door. You invited him in."

She stepped inside the house. Dog padded behind her. She pulled two beers from the refrigerator.

Parks entered, looking unbelievably cool in jacket and tie. Dog, his tail waving mightily, pawed at the bag.

"He's smart." Parks pulled out a bone. Raw, fresh with meat and marrow, from the butcher. "An associate runs a shop."

"A good associate?"

"No. A bad one. A snitch. Good for me. But bad for criminals. He didn't have a tip. So I asked for bones instead."

Dog barked. Tired of waiting patiently.

"Can I?"

"Sure. Dog will bite you if you don't."

Parks placed a bone in Dog's mouth. He went to the fridge. "Save the rest for later."

Marie offered him a beer.

Parks declined. "I'm on duty."

"Suit yourself," she said, walking through her bedroom to the balcony. "Grab a kitchen chair."

Parks lifted jeans off the floor. Folded them, laid them on the bed. Squatting, he studied books strewn on the floor.

His tattoo showed—just a little, blue with a red outline. Marie wondered how far it extended. She could see, too, that his hair was a bit too long for a cop, curling on his neck, over his dress shirt. His hair was a subtle rebellion.

"You're not a neat freak?"

"No." Parks stood, smoothing the front of his suit.

"Sure you're not. Come on, watch me drink." She swallowed the cool foam.

In New Orleans, beer could be as potent as a shot of vodka. There weren't any alcohol limits.

"You're not planning to work tonight?" asked Parks.

"What else should I do?"

"Another ceremony?"

"Doesn't work that way. It's not like turning a lightbulb on and off."

"I didn't think it was."

"I need to regroup."

Parks sat on the chair. Dog gnawed his bone.

"Working at the hospital. Checking on Petey is as good as anything."

Parks nodded at the bottle.

"One drink won't kill me," she said irritably.

"Hey, why are you mad at me?"

"You're here." She swallowed more beer. "Why are you here? Don't tell me it's because of dog bones."

"I thought you might remember something."

"Useful?" She pitched forward, her elbows on her knees. "Tell me. What did you think? Old men and women dancing like there'd be no tomorrow? Me, flailing in the dirt? You think I'm a fake?"

"I told you. You did a good thing." Parks dug into his jacket for his cigarettes.

"Can I have one?"

"No, it's not good for you."

"I'm cranky."

"You're still not getting a smoke. I don't corrupt others."

"Yeah, I bet." She tilted the bottle. "Guess I'll stick with beer."

Parks looked away, blowing smoke rings. "Marie-Claire at day care?"

"No, El has the day off. She's watching her. She's the ER head nurse. I met her and DuLac my first day here. In New Orleans. My surrogate family."

"My first day here I met Roach. And a body that a killer had hacked to pieces."

"You complaining?"

"No. Just stating a fact. The boyfriend did it." Tilting the chair on two legs, his feet on the rail, hands behind his head, Parks's tattoo was more visible. Lines as intricate as a spider's webs.

"Is that why you wear long-sleeved shirts? A jacket? So no one will see your tattoo? I didn't know Eagle Scouts did tattoos."

Parks lowered his arms. He turned. His knee touched Marie's. "I think I believe."

"You think? Or are you just changing the subject?"

"Both." His gaze was hard. "Got any more clues, Doc? Anything you remember?"

There were flecks in his eyes. Dark patterns, shifting in the blue. *Hazel irises deepening to brown. Sable.*

"Doc, I'm just trying to do my job."

"Were you once a bad boy like Reneaux? A teenage rebel? Is that a prerequisite for detectives?"

"I told you, I'm not Reneaux. Don't mess with my mind."

"Funny. Sometimes I think Reneaux is messing with you. Me."

"You see his ghost, too?"

"No. I wish I did." She gripped the railing, staring at nothingness.

Dog sat up, whimpering.

"He knows you're sad," said Parks.

"I'm beginning to believe I won't ever see Reneaux. Unquiet souls roam. Between this world and the next. But Reneaux was shot on duty. I think he's made his peace with it. He did his job."

Unlike me, she thought.

"Look. You saved a life last night. Pretty special, if you ask me. Though I don't know what else I supposed would happen. You'd vanquish the creature? Use your hocus-pocus?" He pulled out his notebook. "I told you before—evidence. I gather clues."

"So. You're hedging your bets?"

Parks grinned. "I'm sticking with you until we solve these crimes."

She grinned back. The sun felt good. She raised her bottle. Then, without sipping, set it down. "DuLac says Petey is hanging on."

"I know. I called."

She looked at him wonderingly.

Slouching, Parks loosened his tie. "I do like a New Orleans sky. Reminds me of days on the shore."

Companionably, they sat, watching billowy streaks fanning across the sky. Thin clouds illuminating blue and gold.

"A rainbow," she said.

It was dim, midhigh in the sky. Shift your gaze, slightly, and it disappeared; stare, just right, and the colors revealed themselves. Streaks of red, yellow, blue.

"Damballah's sign."

"Who's he?"

"Father to all the gods."

"Even Agwé?"

"Yes. Like a Zeus. Some say the Greeks based their pantheon on African gods."

Marie laughed at Parks's expression.

"I wasn't taught that in school."

"A great deal isn't taught in school. I'm proof of that. Evidence."

She tapped his breast pocket. "Answer your phone."

"It isn't ringing."

"It will."

The cell phone chimed.

"Parks." His hand covering the mouthpiece, he whispered, "I believe." Then, "Yeah, I'm still here." His smile faded, his jaw locked; his face, stone.

Marie picked up her bottle. Whistled for Kind Dog.

Parks followed her into the apartment. Watched her put a leash on a happy Dog.

"I'm ready to go," she said, "once I take Dog out. Not unless he can come with us? He might be useful."

"You know? Or just guessing?"

"I know you shouldn't wear suits."

"Doc." He scowled.

"Yes, I know. No time for levity. Yin and yang. Shadow and light. Sometimes," she said, "there's a rebalancing."

"You call somebody dead a 'rebalancing'?"

"No. The thing doing the killing."

"So what's the point?"

"You, a detective, asking that?"

"The killers keep coming."

"One at a time, you tilt the scales back to good."

"Spiritual world. Physical world, the same?"

"Always."

"Maybe I need a new job. New state. New country."

"Let's do this, Parks."

Parks squared his shoulders. "Come on, Dog. Help, and you'll get another bone. Maybe some gravy."

"It's bad," said Roach, opening the door as soon as Parks stopped the car. Kind Dog bounded out the car.

"What's this?" asked Roach, scratching Dog's ear.

"I deputized him. How come you're not inside?"

Roach looked away, crossed himself. "I needed a break."

"You, Roach?" asked Parks, skeptical.

"Let it rest, Parks. He needed a break," said Marie.

Roach nodded gratefully. "One of my great-aunts used to be a nun here."

"The Ursulines," said Marie. "Founded in Italy, spread to Ireland in the eighteenth century, then America with the immigration of the Irish. Ahead of their time. Famous for educating women."

Kind Dog dashed forward, sat on the steps.

"Used to be a place of good," said Roach.

The building was dilapidated. Two stories with ironwork and crosses on the doors and windows. A plaster Virgin was in the overgrown yard; her palms open, upraised. Her white gown chipped, the blue paint of her veil faded.

"It's still owned by the church," said Roach. "A kind of halfway house for priests. Those exported from Boston, New Mexico, Chicago. Get my drift?"

"Pedophiles," whistled Parks. He looked up and down the street. "Where's the police tape? I see the forensic's van, not much crew."

"Special request from the diocese."

"Figures. Low profile," replied Parks, sarcastic.

"Hey, watch the faith."

"Yes," said Marie. "Watch the faith."

Parks rolled his eyes.

All three followed Kind Dog.

The basement windows were dirty, covered with spider webs. Pamphlets on the door announced AA meetings. Free legal advice. Yoga and meditation. Dance classes.

"It's also some kind of community center," said Roach.

"You've got to be kidding," said Parks, stopping. "I hope kids aren't involved."

Priests loitered in the hall. Some dressed in black pants, white shirts, crosses hanging from their throats; others were in uniform, wearing nineteenth-century tunics, the black skirts damp, sticking to their legs.

"Fathers," she murmured.

None of them looked her in the eye. One priest, thinner than Wire, almost skeletal, patted Kind Dog. His blue-veined hands unnerved her; even Dog dipped his head and skittered away.

She could smell Evil. A distilled essence. An evil, inhuman and unlike any spirit she'd known. Even Satan had once been God's favorite.

She walked the first-floor hallway. Men's musk and sweat. Humidity accelerating decay. Creating mold spores in the walls, toxic and pungent.

She swallowed. *Death blended with an odd, burnt taste. A sickly smell assailed her.*

It was hard to breathe. She understood how Roach, an experienced coroner, was avoiding the scene not because the murder was so grim but because it involved religion. Someone who shouldn't have behaved sinfully had.

Marie sympathized with the priests. Trying to meet inhuman expectations: celibacy, suppressed emotions in a veil of piety. Even Mother Teresa had felt darkness. Christ, too, had questioned the need to die on the cross.

Marie knew she could never shoulder a priest's burden.

Voodoo was more accepting of basic humanity. Far less guilt. Just striving to heal, to do good. To be better.

Still, hurting a child was unforgivable.

Marie looked back at the wraiths of men, milling in the hallway, outside their cloistered doors. The Ursulines' nunnery had become purgatory.

"Did any of you see anything? Hear anything?" asked Parks.

The priests drifted away. Some, furtively, shut their doors.

"I'm told we can interview them at the diocese. Not here. Too public," said Roach.

"One of them could be the murderer," Parks protested.

"I don't think so," said Roach. "You'll never get me to believe priests can be vampires."

"After Marie's ceremony, I'm leaning toward believing anything is possible."

"Should we go in?" asked Marie, halfway down the hall. "It's here. In this room. I can smell it. Dog, too."

"You picked right," said Roach.

Parks pulled his gun.

"It's secure," said Roach.

"Like to be sure." Parks slipped in front of Marie. "Ready to do your job, Roach?" Parks asked.

Roach blushed red. "All of us got our tipping point, Parks. You'll get yours."

"Stop it. Both of you."

"Sorry, Doc." Parks opened the door.

The room smelled like a multiple-trauma scene. Dried blood. Festering wounds. Urine, loose bowels.

Windows sealed from the inside. Christ, crucified, hung on every wall. Flies buzzed, covering trays of rotted and rotting food.

Parks gagged, coughing the smell out of his lungs. "Roach, you sure this is the same M.O. None of the other victims had this smell."

"Yeah. Same M.O. with a difference."

Kind Dog howled.

"Hush, Dog," said Marie

"Seems," said Roach, "Father Xavier never left his room. Been here five weeks. Priests brought food to the door. Maybe he was trying to starve himself. Or else keep himself barely alive."

The dresser had a mirror. An unusual vanity for a priest. Marie stared at her reflection. She wondered what horrors, what false piety the mirror had seen.

"Where is he?" asked Parks.

"There," said Marie, seeing the body before she actually saw it.

He'd fallen, squeezed between the wall and the twin, single-mattress bed.

She could see him, trying to get away, scuttling like a crab into the tight space. He'd been drained just the same. Pinpricks marked his wrist. Both arms thrown over his head.

Frenzied, Dog started chasing his tail.

"Dog, go outside." Marie braced herself.

Blood drained; flesh deflated. Sores, fresh and scabbed, covered the priest's body. The grotesqueness was multiplied by lack of moisture. He looked like Kafka's dead and shriveled bug.

"What's that?" asked Parks. "Something's under the bed. Above his head."

Roach crawled over the bed, lifting a whip from the floor.

"A flagellant," said Marie.

"A what?" asked Parks.

"Medieval period. Whipping one's self as penance. Each strike, wounding, tearing of flesh was symbolic of God's wrath."

"Give me a break," said Parks.

"Our murderer cornered him. He must've sensed it, whatever it was, coming."

"Yeah, and he cowered," said Roach, studying the blood streaks on the floor. The spattering on the dresser, the bed, and the walls. "He must've been on his knees. Beating himself. Then he scuttled away from the attack. Wonder if he thought God's wrath had visited him? Vampirism beats flagellation."

"Maybe," said Marie.

"Who's to say it wasn't God?" said Parks. "Seems reasonable to me. Though I can't imagine what connects a pedophile with JT and Rudy."

Marie felt nauseous. As a doctor and *voodooienne,* people harming themselves affronted and angered her.

"I don't need to see any more," she said. "At least not here. Perhaps after the autopsy."

Marie clasped Roach's pudgy hand. "Sorry you have to do this."

"It's the Irish in me. Shouldn't have to view a murdered priest or one who abused children. Still. I feel sorry for him. No one to give absolution. A priest should have absolution."

"After what he did?" sneered Parks.

Marie glared at Parks, then squeezed Roach's hand. "You're right. Everyone deserves forgiveness."

Roach's eyes blinked rapidly behind his glasses.

Marie stared at Parks.

Parks shrugged, as if to say, "What?" Then, shifting his weight into his hip, murmured, "Roach, I'm sorry. Buy you a drink later?"

"Yeah." Roach wiped his eyes. "Go on, get out of here." Shirt untucked, his belly folding over his belt, Roach looked bewildered, staring at the priest's body.

"Hey," said Parks. "Let me send another coroner."

"No, no. I've got it." He stooped: one hand on the bed to steady himself, the other lifting the priest's flaccid hand, marked with pinpricks, like bites from a snake.

Outside, Marie inhaled, letting the fresh air clear her lungs. Eyes closed, she tilted her face skyward.

Parks lit a cigarette. "Weirdness. Can't wait until I leave this town. Imagine, Roach upset like that."

Eyes still shut, Marie could hear a rope slapping against concrete. Children jumping double Dutch, chanting rhymes.

"Did you see his ghost? Or is that only at night? Think you'll see him? Our pedophile priest?"

"I don't know," she murmured. "And he's not my priest."

"Point taken." Parks blew smoke rings. "I say he's in hell."

"I don't believe in hell," said Marie. She whistled and Dog bounded toward her. "Dog and I are going to walk home. I need time to think."

"Connect the dots?"

"Yes."

"I'll try and do that here. Look for clues. Fingerprints."

"Won't find any. Other than the victim's."

"Yeah, well, procedure. I'll buy Roach a drink. Two drinks. Talk to the priests at the diocese. Doc? Meet up tonight?"

Before she could answer, Parks, brow furrowed, slapped his notebook against his hand. "Got to be some connection. Wharf rat. Jazz man. Priest."

Marie wandered across the unkempt lawn. Dog, head low, trailed behind her.

"Hey," shouted Parks. "Give Dog the bones. The whole damn bag."

Dog didn't bother to lift his head. Marie didn't turn, just held up her hand, feeling the warm breeze on her fingers. The air was tinted with the smell of magnolias and fish.

From far off, she heard music, a poignant duet between piano and sax. Maybe some blues or jazz men who'd decided, no, *needed,* after a night of playing music for tourists, to play their soul's desire. Fingers skimming ivory. Lips kissing metal while lungs blew air. They'd play until they were spent, sleep a few hours, then play all night, until dawn, buoyant tunes for drunk, happy-time patrons.

"Doc. Doc."

Parks's voice was melodic. A deep timbre, rising to a call, slicing the air. "Doc—"

She and Dog kept walking. It was impossible not to hear music in New Orleans.

Music connected JT and Rudy.

Why not the priest?

⁂ ☷ ❖ ◇ ⊗ ◎ ❖ ▦

The blood had been thick with sin. Richly aromatic. The wounded flesh, seductive. This blood, more than the other two, was sustaining. It felt itself gathering texture and strength. It had been. A walker on two legs.

A creature of needs, desire.

Still. Blood filled. Fulfilled. Carried memories.

Touching flesh. Smooth, yielding. Then, not yielding. Holding tight. Tighter. Bowing the child's back. Tears, wails. Resistance, thrilling.

Thrilling, too, the self-abnegation. Pleas for forgiveness. Lying prostrate before the child. Children who never failed to say, "I forgive you."

Such innocence demanded blood.

Another type of ecstasy as skin cracked, sliced. Blood mingled with pain, flowing, flowering into blooms.

How sweet the taste. How sweet the blood.

EIGHT

Marie's cell chimed, melodic and startling. Playing a few bars of the Neville Brothers's "Yellow Moon":

> *Yellow moon, yellow moon,*
> *Why you keep peeping in my window?*
> *Do you know something I don't know?*

She didn't know anything. The more the case dragged on, the less she knew.

She was outside the Café du Monde. Kind Dog begged while young women and children petted him, letting him lick powdered sugar from their hands.

Normally Marie enjoyed watching Dog charm a crowd. But the dead priest was still sharp in her mind.

She stared at the Mississippi, trying to sense Agwé. Trying to

remember precedents for murder. There weren't any. Not in au-
thentic voodoo.

The song stopped. She exhaled. Let the message go to voice
mail. If Charity needed her, her pager would buzz.

"*Yellow moon, yellow moon, why you keep peeping . . .*"

She flipped open the cell phone.

"Marie. *Merde,* Marie. Answer the phone!" DuLac shouted.

"Here."

"Are you all right?"

"I'm fine. Stop shouting."

"You should answer your phone. Parks called. Said you had an
unpleasant case."

"Silly man. All our cases are unpleasant."

"Silly or not. He thought you might need some support."

Marie stared at the horizon. Gray clouds. The sun seemed suspended by strings. Offshore, a storm was feeding. " Even though I
walk through the valley of the shadow of death . . . '"

"Marie?"

"Twenty-third Psalm. 'The Lord is my shepherd.'"

"You're a shepherd, too."

"I know. Damballah's priestess. My flock is small."

"You're renewing it. Besides, slaves didn't mind mixing African
drums with Christian hymns. No different today. Except folks keep
quiet about it. Hide it."

"You're right. Baptist, AME Methodist, Roman Catholic—when
they've given up hope, they come to me."

"Don't be bitter. I'm going to call a friend. Professor Alafin, a special-
ist in indigenous and indigenous-inspired religions. African. Haitian
Voudon. Rastafarian. There's no precedent for a blood-draining spirit."

DuLac was breathing heavily. She imagined him sitting at his desk, his head in his hand.

"I can't help but believe we're at the beginning, DuLac. Not the end."

"This is *fa*. Your destiny."

"Why does it have to be so hard? So brutal?"

"What? What did you say?"

"Nothing." She was sure he'd heard her.

"Parks said 'Bushmills.' He bought Roach a Bushmills. Said you'd understand."

Marie laughed. Bushmills. A good Irish whiskey.

"I'll see you tonight?"

"Yes. I want to check on Petey. He's still holding on?"

"*Oui.* You're sure you're all right?"

"Sure. Kind Dog is with me. We're going to visit Father Donnelly."

"Stay Safe."

"*Au'voir* Later." She clicked her cell shut.

"Have you come to confess?" Father Donnelly looked up from the pew, a rosary wrapped around his hand.

"Maybe next year. Though, if you want, I can confess to some wicked fantasies."

"You're a mother now."

"That's why I have fantasies."

Father Donnelly laughed. Not yet forty, his hair salt and pepper, he patted for Marie to sit beside him.

Born in Baton Rouge, Father Donnelly knew New Orleans's

history better than anyone, knew about the nineteenth-century's intersections of race, religion, class. Voodoo ceremonies in Congo Square. Quadroon balls. French aristocrats tricking innocent girls into false marriages; priests who collected alms to buy opium.

"I thought you'd visit."

"Mind if we go outside?"

"You used to think my church was beautiful."

"It still is," said Marie, studying the soaring stained glass. The woodcut stations of the cross; the gold candelabras on the altar. The Catholic Church's pageantry always stirred her. "Dog's outside."

"Let's go then." Father Donnelly genuflected before the altar, before the Christ nailed to the crucifix. "I've missed Dog."

Kind Dog's entire body shook with joy.

"He remembers you."

Father Donnelly snapped a tree branch. "Here, boy." He threw. Dog woofed and ran after it.

"Simple pleasures. God's creatures bring great pleasure."

"You should get a dog."

"The Church won't allow it. Smacks of vanity. Besides, I have you and Kind Dog to visit me." Playfully, he brushed Dog's head. "Is it true about Father—"

"You know?"

"Clergy gossip is swift. Is it true?" he asked, watching her expression closely. "Bloodless?"

"Yes, it's true."

He crossed himself.

"What is it with you Irish?"

Father laughed. "Are my freckles getting red?"

"No, but your eyes are smiling."

"Can't help my Irish eyes."

Feeling suddenly tired, Marie sat on the church steps. Pigeons fluttered, pecked at the grass. She threw the stick again for Dog.

Father Donnelly sat, his voice mimicking Lugosi's: "'Vampires. They want to suck your blood.'"

"Not funny, Father."

"Dysfunctional humor. I'm sorry," he said. "Did you know Transylvania's always been Catholic? My Irish ancestors believed in elves, fairy folk. Benign beings compared with the devil's blood-sucker."

"So you think it's Satan?"

"Certainly no African god you worship."

"Thanks for that."

"Pre-missionaries, I'm not one to believe the African continent was dark."

"You're one of the few. But whoever said, 'Dark is evil'?"

"Sorry again. I misspoke."

"I'm giving you a hard time. But it's true—ever since Cain was branded black for murdering his brother, Christians see color as an excuse for prejudice."

"Personally, I believe Christ was dark. Finding Lucy's bones means we all are. Or once were."

"Careful. Your parishioners might hear you."

"It's not them I'm worried about. The Church hierarchy is growing more conservative. The archbishop is always upset with me for something."

They sat companionably on the steps. Dog lay down when no one threw his stick.

"Who do you think killed Father—?"

"I don't know. I've never seen anything like it. But I'm not sure it's Satan."

"Father Xavier was a tortured soul."

"The other victims—"

"Others?"

"Two."

Father crossed himself again. "I'll say prayers. Tell me about the others."

"A Haitian refugee. An African-American jazz man."

"As different from a New England priest as you could possibly be."

Marie raised her brows. "New England?"

"Nantucket."

"Maybe that explains the water."

"Meaning?"

"Agwé, the sea god. One death happened near water. The other— a saxophonist died trying to draw Agwé's sign." She hesitated.

"Go on."

"And I've felt Agwé's presence. Heard his rhythms."

"Have you called him?"

"Careful, Father. You might get excommunicated."

"Don't patronize me, Marie. I'm a Delta boy. Southern to my core."

"I called Agwé." She hugged herself, remembering the cold. "He wasn't strong enough to stop the creature from attacking Petey, one of my followers. Nothing about my ceremony went right."

She shuddered, remembering the cold touch.

"Father Xavier abused nearly a dozen boys. Normally, I don't believe in retribution. Deuteronomy 19:21: 'Life shall go for life, eye for eye, tooth for tooth.' The Old Testament God sent slaying angels—many times . . ."

"You're not saying this is a manifestation of God? You can't be serious. What about Christ's suffering? His mercy? Don't tell me I'm more of a believer than you are."

Father stood. Dog, too.

"I'll light a candle for you."

"You're offended."

"Why did you come to me, Marie?" Father Donnelly's face was red, his expression despairing. "You wanted to know my thoughts? Maybe it's a demon. Satan's calumny knows no bounds. Maybe it's God? 'An eye for an eye.' Maybe that's what this world needs. The sword. Wrath. The fearful guise of God."

"You're trembling."

"I have work to do."

"Wait." She clutched his hands. Soft, almost feminine. His eyes, usually compassionate, were hard.

"Tell me. What's wrong?"

"We were in seminary together. Even then there were whispers."

"You feel complicit. Guilty."

Marie wanted to go home, take a bath, hug Marie-Claire. Instead, she kept hold of Father Donnelly's hands. "Did you ever see him touch a child? Have evidence that he touched a child?"

"No."

"Then you would've condemned prematurely."

"You're only trying to make me feel better."

"Those who buried the evidence deserve condemnation. Did you do that? Bury evidence? Not report a crime?"

"No."

"Did you move him from parish to parish? During decades of abuse? Post him in New Orleans to rot?"

"No."

"Good." Her stomach roiled. She slapped her hand against her thigh, calling Dog to heel.

"I didn't help you at all, did I?"

"I'm not sure anything in this world can."

"You're a better priestess than I am a priest."

"Nonsense."

Both she and Father Donnelly were aware that she hadn't mentioned confession. Confessional sanctity protected even the most abhorrent crimes.

"Here," he said, handing Marie his well-worn rosary. "It may help. Always works in vampire movies."

"Don't be having a crisis of faith."

"Is that what this is?" he answered cryptically, turning toward the church's hard oak door.

"Father. Tony. It isn't your God. Nor one of mine. Agwé says it comes from the sea."

"You're a good woman, Marie. I need to pray." Eyes bleak, he slipped inside the church.

"Dog," Marie called.

He pawed a willow tree.

"Dog!"

His brown eyes stared at her. Bright and splendid. Marie felt Dog's intelligence. She moved closer. "What do you see? A squirrel? A bird?"

Shading her eyes, Marie stepped inside the tree's lacelike curtain. Dozens upon dozens of fanning branches hung, quivering like falling stars.

JT and Rudy were perched on a limb. So intangible, a slight gust of wind could scatter them, like dust in the air.

She was relieved she didn't see the murdered priest. "Good. Father Xavier isn't part of my flock." Her palm pressed the rough bark. "What do you say, JT? A false lead? Rudy, how did you know to call upon Agwé? What word were you trying to write?"

Passersby looked at her strangely. A crazy woman talking to a tree.

A portly man stopped and looked up, into the sunlight-streaked branches. He shook his head. Meandered on.

A child, suspenders clipped to his shorts, pointed. "I see. I see them." His mother hushed and tugged him, crossing to the other side of the street.

A peddler pushed a cart of New Age crystals: wind chimes, hearts on a string. Unicorns. He shook his knotted dreads, like Father Xavier's cat-o'-nine-tails.

Sun burst through the crystals. Rainbows snaked up the tree.

Like a mirage, JT and Rudy vanished.

The peddler moved on.

Marie looked east, west, north, and south. Families strolling the Quarter. Con artists playing shell games. Tourists, wide eyed, bushy tailed, eager for sin. The church bells tolled.

Marie thought she was losing her mind. Even reality didn't seem real.

NINE

In three days, there'd be a full moon, affecting tides, creating greater waves of lunatics in an already crazy town. A thwarted lover would beat his beloved to death; an unemployed worker would find solace in a killing spree; a lonely, mild-mannered teacher would commit suicide. She could see it all before it had happened; part intuition, part sight.

The storm was coming. Like rising air pressure, the ER over the next few days would become even more crowded. More drunks, druggies, gunshot wounds, stabbings, and accidents—all adding to the uninsured seeking care.

Marie slipped on her lab coat. Ready to work. Another shift. Here, inside Charity's flat, white-colored walls. But she knew this job. This was comfort. All afternoon with Dog at her feet, she'd been studying Laveau's nineteenth-century journal. She couldn't find any clues. Couldn't discard Father Donnelly's pain. Or JT and Rudy's haunting.

Tomorrow, she'd meet DuLac's friend, the anthropologist. Maybe he could help. For now, she'd do what she knew best. Be a doctor and heal.

Her cell rang: "Yellow moon, yellow moon . . ." On her break, she'd download something innocuous, stupid. "Raindrops Keep Falling on My Head," "MacArthur Park," "Rhinestone Cowboy."

"Doc?"

"Here."

"JT, Rudy, Father Xavier. All dead; same cause. Blood loss."

"Tell me something I don't know."

"Rudy marked Agwé's sign with his ring. Some kind of signet. Maybe a Mason? We're looking into it. The other mark—the letter, letters, whatever it is—was in blood."

"Rudy's?"

"Yeah."

"Was there—"

"—blood on Rudy's fingertips? No. None."

Her knees nearly buckled. "It's communicating." She wanted to run far away. "I've got to go, Parks. Work."

"You'll need a ride home, Doc? What do you say?"

She ducked inside an empty exam room. Panting, trying to catch her breath. Her worlds were colliding again.

"Doc? You still there?"

She powered off her cell. She didn't want to speak with Parks.

On her break, she'd go upstairs and visit Petey. Maybe he'd re-member something essential.

But here, now—she needed to be a doctor. In New Orleans. Her home. A city, like Vegas, where housewives, businessmen, convenience-store clerks, librarians, doctors planned on visiting to shed inhibitions. Of course, some didn't; they were shocked voyeurs. Planned on that, too. Like a tourist planning to spend too much money, eat too much, drink too much, they planned on squealing, being shocked by sex in the streets, transvestites walking in three-inch heels, and dachshunds dressed as clowns.

Vegas, its mob roots suppressed, had become an R-rated DisneyWorld.

New Orleans still shimmered with its XXX-rated pride. Slavery's sorrow, the wounds and pain of war, yellow jack epidemics, and hurricane disasters, all had roots plumbing miles deep beneath New Orleans's gaiety.

Now there was a new evil in town.

Come hell or high water, she'd draw the line.

She smoothed her hair, coat, drawing back the curtain to Exam One. "Mr. Layton. Did you lose your false teeth again?"

"Sure did." He grinned like a recalcitrant child.

Rudy and JT stood at the head of the bed.

Marie almost waved, then cocked her head, considering. Why weren't Rudy and JT at yesterday's ceremony?

She smiled for Mr. Layton. "We'll see if Antoinette, the hospital's social worker, can help. Maybe a spare set of teeth."

"That'll be right nice."

She pressed the stethoscope to his chest, back, listening for possible pneumonia. His airways were clear; his eyes and ears, fine; but his throat and lips, dry, his skin, taut.

She spoke to the young nurse, Delores. "Give Mr. Layton three cc's of saline." *The ghosts nodded their heads.* "It'll hydrate you.

You'll live to one hundred. Just remember to drink. Water, not tea. Or rum. You'll be fine."

"Thank you, Doctor."

She patted his wrinkled hand. Marie wished the city would subsidize air-conditioning for its elderly poor. In the ER, all she could do was hydrate and send them home.

She walked toward the patient board. What was next? A sports fracture. Impacted bowels. A vomiting drunk. "From Wisconsin," an ER nurse hissed, disdainfully. Tourists from the Midwest were the craziest.

She should call Parks. Were ghosts concrete evidence enough? Was their absence a clue?

"Hey, we need help here." A threesome—two men dressed in tight black pants, the woman in a halter and floral skirt—entered the ER. The elder man, white haired, but still lean and fit, his arms around his companions, limped. "Fell down stairs," he said. "Awful."

"Wait your turn," hollered El.

"Do you know who this is? Greatest samba teacher ever."

"He should learn how to walk then."

Nurse Delores giggled.

"Best in New Orleans," said the high-yellow woman, her hair falling in cascades. "A treasure."

"I don't care who he is," said El.

The woman, red lips pouting, answered, "Don't you care about Mardi Gras? We will be the best," she said, shimmying her shoulders and breasts.

El waved her away, like a fly. "Sit."

The girl extended her hand to her curly-haired partner, black as midnight, and he smiled, catching and cradling her hand to his chest. He stroked her waist and pulled her tightly against him, almost as if they were about to tango.

"Play," he said, never once looking away from her eyes.

"*Sí, sí,*" said the teacher. "Make love. Dance with your soul." He pressed the button on his cheap cassette. Marimbas, drums, guitars, swirled. Echoing, cresting like a tidal wave in the ER. The two were dancing, hips shaking, hands fluttering like butterflies. The woman's breasts jiggled; the men in the waiting room couldn't shake their eyes. The two were seductive. The fluorescent glare seemed to dim; the white walls seemed tinted with passion. The ER was a dance hall—a pretaste of a Mardi Gras parade—among the sick. Feverish waiting room patients clapped; a man requiring stitches started to sway. Another man, a huge bump on his head, set down his ice and began finger snapping.

"Turn that off," shouted El. The two kept dancing in and around chairs, giggling like truant schoolchildren. The patients were conspirators, blocking El as the dancers moved among the small tables and chairs. Even the nurses grinned, swiveling their hips.

Unbridled joy in the ER. Even DuLac tapped his feet, nodding, staring appreciatively at the woman dancer.

El swatted at the couple. The samba teacher, holding his stomach, doubled over laughing. "Security," screamed El. But Sully was clapping, eager to catch the glimpse of thigh beneath the girl's skirt.

Marie looked to see if Rudy and JT were enjoying the music. It had to be better than haunting her. Better than the sick and the dying. Better than seeing their bodies splayed in the morgue. Lord, she was truly crazy—worrying about the feelings of the dead.

She scanned the room. She didn't see them.

Patients, standing on chairs, shaking hips, shouting, "Samba," defeated El. She retreated to her station, lips pursed, and tried to focus on paperwork. Huan, who'd never danced in her life, was tripping over K-Paul's feet, startled by his hips shaking beneath his physician's coat.

The music was infectious. Sully, overweight yet light on his feet, twirled. Incredibly graceful and sweet.

Marie looked for her ghosts. *She saw a shimmer, light shifting like water, in the far-right corner, near the coffee machine.* Ghosts, spirits, didn't displace air.

She felt unsettled.

Strangely, everyone else in the ER was happy. Even El hummed, snapping her fingers.

Her back to his front, the woman shook her hips from side to side, up and down. Marie was acutely aware of the sexual panto-mime. Men had lust in their eyes; and the women, sick and old, were fluttering their hands like fans. Marie felt a stirring in her crotch.

A technician rocked, eyes glazed, his hands on his thighs. A couple—one with a stomach ailment, the other needing a diabetic check—danced as if they were long-lost lovers.

Time out of mind. The give and take of motion; sweating, bodies exuding pheromones, the chemical aphrodisiac. She shook her butt a bit, trying to remember that she was thirty, not eighty.

K-Paul murmured in her ear, "Maybe we should just heal with music. Not one of those folks acts sick." He spun her around, dipped, and swayed. His lips swooped down, kissing her. "I'm willing if you are," he drawled, then, danced away.

She thought, Why the hell not?

The man with deep knife wounds across his arm didn't mind the uproar. Eyes closed, he was cupping his crotch. A crying baby now gurgled. Amazing. Each and every one transformed.

"Let's close the ER and go home," said El. "They can dance all night for all I care."

Marie couldn't help chuckling. Sully bowed and asked a woman who looked anorexic to dance. Fat and slim, they looked charming.

K-Paul was boogying with his Cajun soul. Marie undressed him in her mind. She ducked her head, blushing, looking across the counter to see if DuLac had seen her prowling. He was tap-tapping his hands, appreciating the dancers' sensuality.

K-Paul grabbed her arm again. "Dance."

K-Paul's good-natured smile, his gentle hands, felt just right. She wanted to pretend everything was fine. Enjoy a sweet moment in a man's arms.

Holding tight to K-Paul, her body following its own rhythm, she looked again at the corner.

Rudy and JT were squeezing themselves small, banding together like brothers.

"You all right?"

Marie stopped dancing.

Rudy and JT were afraid. What could scare the dead?

Music. Her heart raced.

She exhaled, watched her breath condense. Everyone else was sweating; she was cold. *She heard a plaintive wail, echoing from a distance, from underwater. An anguished cry beneath bright samba beats.*

Across the room, DuLac cocked a brow. He'd always had a sixth sense about her—it had only grown stronger as they shared ceremonies and work. He stood at attention, watching her as she carefully watched the room.

K-Paul kept repeating, "What's wrong? What's wrong?"

She tried to stare at the invisible—the space between air, between worlds. Imagining herself here, now, in a ceremony. Through the whirl of color, bodies, and sound, she tried to discover who or what was keening.

The ER's smell had become rancid, like kelp decomposing on the shore.

The dancer, red lips stretched in horror, her black hair falling like a curtain, was arched backward over a chair, her arms extended, flailing; some force was flattening, pressing her hard, until the chair collapsed.

The dancers and the ER patients jerked away; some toppled over chairs; others clung to one another, wailing; still others staggered for the exit.

The girl screamed, "Get it off me. Get it off."

Once a carnival, the ER now resembled a fun house mirror. Everything the eye saw didn't seem real. It wasn't real—watching a woman pinioned to the floor by a mist. Wasn't real seeing the primeval fear in her, the distaste, the voyeurism in the others. The stares. The girl dancer crying, Sully moaning, "Lord, have mercy," patients making the sign of the cross.

Marie grabbed the girl's wrist. Her pulse quickening; her lungs spastic, hyperventilating. *The mist pressing hard against her flesh.*

"Get phenobarbital. Now," she shouted at K-Paul.

The girl's other hand rose, as if someone held it in midair. Blood appeared on her wrist.

Marie extended her hand, feeling cold, the tangible mist, the suction pulling blood through the girl's veins.

When her fingers covered the bite marks, the bleeding stopped. When she removed her fingers, the bleeding renewed, doubling in ferocity. Disappearing into air.

"Mother of God, Lord have mercy." There were shouts of stigmata. Most fled, stumbling over the folding chairs. Tough El fell to her knees.

"A tourniquet," Marie commanded softly. "Get me three cc's of BeneFix. Huan, get bandages. A neck brace."

"What the hell?" said K-Paul.

"We've got to stop the bleeding. She'll be drained. A coagulate may help. It won't do worse. We'll relax her, try to contain her body. Ride it out."

"Should we strap her to a gurney?" asked K-Paul.

"No. The more rigid the body, the more damage might be done."

Music, reverberating crazily, mocked.

"Turn off that music," Marie shouted.

El stomped on it; the cassette door popped open, the brown tape spilling, coiling out.

Huan dropped beside her. Marie injected the drugs. Almost immediately, the girl's body went limp. Her bloodied arm fell. Huan gently grabbed the wrist, applying antiseptic, bandaging it with gauze.

Marie checked the girl's pulse, her eyes, reflexes. She was deep asleep.

The spirit was gone.

Parks swept in, pulling his gun. "What's going on?"

"Almost another victim," said Marie. "K-Paul, find her a bed for observation."

"Sure thing."

El yelled, "Order, folks. This is a hospital."

K-Paul and Huan lifted the beautiful dancer. Her dress fluttering gracefully, her ruffled hem ripped.

Marie sighed, sitting cross-legged on the floor.

"I came just in time," said Parks.

Marie smiled. "Sure you did, Detective."

Like a tidal wave, there was a vacuum, then energy roaring— entering Marie, forcing her back. She cried out; her head hit the floor. *She was in the eye of the wave, a swirling maelstrom of emotions, voices.*

Parks was shouting; Huan, sobbing.

She moaned. *The spirit clutched her throat. Her head arched; she saw pockmarks on the ceiling. Pieces of the ceiling broke and fell.*

Nothing touched her. Yet, something touched her. Almost as if a face was right above hers. All she saw was a threatening sky, storm clouds gathering, and a pale moon hovering over roiling water.

Parks was on his knees, shouting; she couldn't hear. *Cold. Her organs becoming ice.* Hypothermia, no visible cause. The scientist in her couldn't help but be curious. Forensics would be stumped. Cold. Blood loss.

"Doc, can you hear me? Doc?"

She tried to say, "Don't touch."

Huan was holding Parks's hand, chattering in Vietnamese and repeating after each phrase, "No, no. No."

Good. Huan understood. Perverse, the spirit might move from her to Parks.

Don't touch, the spirit mocked, moving aggressively against her.

She felt a searing pain. Her wrist had been punctured. *She was no longer in the ER, in New Orleans, in this world. She saw Rudy and JT, crystal clear. They were mourning for her.*

Blood drained from her wrist.

She felt the priest. He'd enjoyed his suffering. Mea culpa. As his blood drained, he'd screamed for help.

No one heard him because of the drums.

Dancing. There'd been dancing in the basement. In her mind, she saw the leaflet. Afro-Cuban dancing. A strange absurdity.

Like feeling the roar of blood, rushing toward the wounds on her wrist.

So this is what it felt like to die. She was on the floor . . . her heart beating faster . . . then slower . . . she could feel with each pulse, blood leaving her body. *With it, snatches of her history, memories. Blood memories.*

Sitting in church with her mother, both holding their rosaries. Sammy, a sixth-grader, screaming, "Poor, nigger black." Her mother, dead, on the floor. Eyes wide open.

Reneaux, tenderly loving her. Sleeping in his embrace.

The spirit sucked, draining, tough and hard, like a child would a breast. Flashes of the present: Parks mouthing words; Huan's tear-stained cheeks; K-Paul refilling a syringe. She wanted to be unconscious. She ached. The invisible weight pressed deeper into sinews, muscles, and veins. Devouring, controlling her body, draining her blood like an IV line in reverse.

It wouldn't take long to die. She'd join JT and Rudy as ghosts.

K-Paul tried to inject her.

The darkness lashed out. The syringe skittered across the floor. K-Paul cursed.

The creature learned; it wouldn't be fooled twice.

Furious, DuLac yelled: "You fight, Marie, you hear me? Fight. Who you be? *Comment t'appelle-tu?* You tell me. Tell me your name," DuLac demanded. "Tell me."

"Marie." The word was a whisper.

"*Oui, Marie.*"

"Marie." *She felt the spirit withdrawing, retreating.*

"*Je suis* Marie," she said, her voice gaining strength.

"Marie," said DuLac.

"Marie," she repeated. *Her mind felt a further retreat. Her blood stopped draining. The air warmed.* She spoke louder. "*Je suis* Marie. I am Marie. Marie Laveau."

The spirit flew.

"It's gone."

"Doc." Parks embraced her, lifting her in his arms.

"Let me bandage you," said Huan. "Spirits don't scare me."

Marie squeezed her hand.

"They scare me," said Parks.

"Curtain Two," said El. "I'm going to clean up this mess. Huan, you got her?"

Beneath the efficient veneer, Marie could see El's fright. Shaken to the core, she looked old, uncertain. K-Paul slipped his arm about her.

Parks lifted her up on the gurney; DuLac, the consummate doctor, began his exam. Parks held her hand and Marie felt comforted.

"It knew me."

"Are you sure?" asked DuLac.

"Yes." She looked at both men, watching her. "It didn't like my name. Me," she rasped. "Didn't like me."

＊≋✧◇✕◉◎✕ᵉᵉᵉᵉ

Marie. The name had frightened it. Stirred memories.

    It knew her face. But couldn't gather up the particles of thoughts. Just felt desire, then hurt. Wanted to hurt her. Some grudge needed tending.

    Marie. It knew her. Had known her. It had a past.

    Touch. Hurt. Touch. Hurt.

    Touch.

    A mother had touched her. Reneaux—had touched her. Held her. Who was Reneaux?

    Who was Marie?

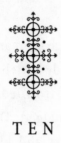

T E N

The office was ramshackle. Dimly lit, filled with books, glass paper-weights, statues of assorted cultural gods. Isis. Buddha. Vishnu. Skulls—human and chimp—religious medallions, and jars filled with dead specimens—tree frogs, beetles—littered the file cabinets and desk. Cornhusk dolls, rosaries, bottles filled with multicolored oils cluttered the floor, the bookshelves.

Professor Alafin wore a tweed vest in the hot, windowless room. A chain watch dangled from his pocket. He wore a clip-on bow tie and tortoiseshell-rimmed glasses. Gray dreads scraped his collar.

"You're an interesting crew," said Alafin, shaking DuLac's hand.

"Think so?" asked Marie.

"Sure. My friend DuLac, who's never worried, looks worried. Perhaps a bit scared? No insult intended, old friend."

"None taken."

"A lovely young woman." Alafin stepped closer. "Pale. Unsettled. Are you well?"

"I'm fine," she said. Though she'd argued with both DuLac and Parks to let her come. Her body hurt; her head throbbed.

"Are you sure?" Alafin frowned, his brows touching between his eyes. "Wrist bandaged. Dressed to downplay your loveliness in a black T-shirt and blue jeans. And you," said Alafin, intent on Parks, "haven't got the sense not to look like a cop. Or is it a G-man?"

"G-man," said Parks. "I haven't heard that term in a while."

"I'm dated."

"Alafin lives in the present only when he has to," said DuLac.

"And DuLac visits me only when he has a puzzle. Sit."

Parks peered at captive beetles, moths, and butterflies pinned to a mat beneath glass. "What is it you do?"

"A bit of everything. Social anthropology, philosophy, religion—mystics and canonical—cultural history. Folklore. Ethnomusicology."

"Eclectic," said DuLac.

Alafin chuckled. "More like the perennial associate professor. At least according to my department chair. He says my research lacks focus. Significance. Whereas I believe any human inquiry has meaning. And all inquiries loop back to the essential question: Why are we alive?"

"To do good," answered Parks.

"A naive answer."

Parks bristled. "I'm a cop. Not a philosopher."

"I didn't mean to insult you. My own cynicism. Twenty-five years studying, searching, and I wonder whether it's that simple—'to do good.' If your answer is correct, then much of my life has been wasted, hasn't it? My chair thinks my research is a waste."

Marie found Alafin slightly distasteful. Doing good was her foundation.

Alafin sat behind his desk, his hands cupped under his chin, his elbows on his desk. He was a dark man; bright, black, inquiring eyes; medium size. His hands showed his age; years of digging, unearthing mysteries, secrets, and ancient societies had taken their toll. His hands curled like claws, wrinkled and discolored from clay, mud, the earth's minerals. He watched Marie, intent, curious. As if he'd guessed her disapproval.

"You know who I am," Marie murmured.

"I knew you when DuLac suspected you were you."

She looked at DuLac.

"Don't be upset with DuLac. Confirmation. He wanted confirmation."

"You don't even know me."

"I know how you came into being. How history, ancestors, have crafted you. A descendant of Laveau, who descended from a powerful African priestess. See, I have it all here. Five generations." He opened a lineage map, a tree of her female ancestors.

Marie bristled. Part of her wanted to study the tree. To ask questions. Ultimately, it was upsetting that he knew more about her than she him. That DuLac had discussed her with him.

"Don't be upset, *chérie,*" said DuLac. "I needed help. With my understanding."

Parks interjected, "We need help with a crime."

"Something to do with the bandaged wrists?"

"A spirit's been draining blood," said DuLac. "Not a spirit called during voodoo ritual."

"But called by music," said Parks. "Isn't that right, Doc? Except Father Xavier's murder doesn't fit the pattern."

"It does," she said. "Check. There'd been a dance class the night he was murdered. Drums in the basement. The room beneath his."

"How do you know this?" complained Parks. "Damnit, Doc—"

"It tried to drain you?" interrupted Alafin.

"I survived." Her left hand covered her bandage.

"Let me see. Please."

She felt Alafin's desperation. Mouth slightly parted, his hands clenched together as if to rein himself in, he could barely contain himself from grabbing, from ripping away gauze.

Marie unrolled her bandage. Layer after layer.

Her flesh was red, as if scalded by steam. Three punctures. Parallel to her bruised veins.

"What did it feel like?"

Marie didn't answer. DuLac was studying her. He wanted to know how she knew about the drums. The music in the basement.

Alafin touched her hole-shaped wounds. "*Wazimamoto.*"

He searched his shelves of books. His blue polyester clothes were too big; a ripped pant cuff scraped dirt from the floor. He needed a shave and a haircut. "Here." Alafin grabbed a book, on the far left, from the next to the highest shelf. "Vampires."

"You've got to be kidding," said Parks.

"Quiet," chastised DuLac.

"Not researched much," said Alafin. "Really an unexplored area. One I haven't given much attention. No one has." He flipped through pages, his fingers resting on one particular page. He read silently, the researcher in him forgetting anyone else was in the room.

"What do you know, Alafin?" asked DuLac. "We're among friends."

Alafin lifted his head, focusing on Parks, DuLac, then Marie. He clutched the book tightly against his chest. "I've spent my whole life studying the mystical. Searching for miracles—I've seen things. In Haiti, Brazil, Nigeria, Belize.

"Seen zombies, as you have, Marie. Seen shamans shape-shift. Yes," he said to a sneering Parks. "Seen a man become a cat then a man again. Seen seers predict volcanic eruptions, a woman's labor. All religions, cultures, have their miraculous tales. Christ's image appearing in cloth. The reincarnation of the Dalai Lama. Aboriginal firewalkers. But I've never had the miraculous walk into my office."

"I'm just a woman," said Marie.

"Shame. There's no hope for you then."

Marie stared at Alafin. "Show me," she said. "Show me what you've seen. What you see."

Alafin laid the book on the desk. Black leather, red-trimmed edges on the pages. Leather straps for closure.

DuLac, Parks, and Marie gathered round the book and desk. Alafin adjusted the lamp; the book gleamed.

"Colonial period," said Alafin. "Written when Africa seemed a banquet for Europeans to consume, like a greedy plague."

Marie stroked the cover. She hesitated, knowing that once opened, her life would be forever changed.

Unlike Christianity, with its command not to be tempted by the snake, voodoo proclaimed all knowledge good. Like a snake eating its own tail, renewing itself by shedding its skin, knowledge was infinite, necessary to being human. There was no "two-edged sword." In voodoo, Prometheus would have been celebrated, never chained.

Gently, Marie opened the frayed pages, originally a kind of beige, with red, a reddish-brown, leaking from the edges into the page's interior.

"That's blood," said Parks.

DuLac rubbed the paper between his thumb and fingers. "This page, it isn't flesh, but something close."

"Cowhide," said Alafin. "Seared with elaborate woodblock prints. These, too, dipped in blood. Pages upon pages. All hand-crafted. Art embodying the caution. Embodying life and death."

"Amazing," exhaled Marie.

"One of the few books in the world documenting African vampires. It was written by a 1920s missionary. A priest and a village shaman. A unique partnership. Written to warn. Bear witness to humanity's sins begetting sins."

Picture upon picture: African villages, straw-thatched huts, women tilling the soil, carrying infants on their back, children playing by the roadside. Men conversed in small groups, their heads and eyes averted. In the far-left corner, two officers looked down at a splayed body, blood draining from its wrist.

Another: a seemingly unending chain of Africans, each whispering in another's ear. Officers were dragging a man into jail.

Another: moon high and full, a deserted plain. Amid the stalks and high grasses, there were a dozen bodies, emaciated, drained, their wrists blood speckled. A pride of lions ignored them. A soldier with a bayonet, gleaming black boots, counted out coins to a barefoot villager.

"But there's nothing about race here," muttered Parks.

"Are you sure, Detective?"

"The officers are all white, the villagers black. Colonialism. All about race. Class. Part of the psychology. Whites were *wazimamotos*. Colonizers. See, the officers are implicated in the killings. Explicitly, here, they're dragging a man to jail. Everyone knows he won't return. He'll be killed. They'll say: '*wazimamoto*.'"

"It's a metaphor," said Marie.

"Yes. But it's also suspected to be real. Evil takes physical form in the world. The *loas* teach us that. The gods, themselves, can be reflections of hate, jealousy, envy. See this—a small group of black men, wearing badges—men who were probably given power similar to a deputy. They've become spies on their own community. Traitors. Africans, literally and mentally, colonized.

"*Wazimamotos* could be either a white spirit punishing blacks or a colonized, assimilated black—"

"You mean an Uncle Tom?"

"Yes. A black feeding on its own. Similar to African kings who sold their enemies into slavery. That was evil. But a *wazimamoto* can also be someone who commits evil because he identifies with his oppressors, he wants to *be* the colonizer, the master. These black men here are wielding machetes, dismembering this black man— and, by extension, metaphorically dismembering, destroying, their noncolonized selves."

"But a free Africa is still engaging in slavery, brutality."

"I'm not saying, Detective, that evil behavior doesn't exist. It's rampant in all cultures. Throughout history. The Incas' sacrifices. The Romans' feeding of Christians to lions. You need only to read today's paper to know that across the globe, evil thrives. I'm speaking about motivation. Sometimes evil is a product of self-hatred. Learned behavior. When individuals identify with the oppressor. Intraracial, not interracial, prejudice. People feeding off the blood of their own people. Oppressing within their social group to cull favor with the colonizer, the enslaver.

"In these instances, the motivation stems from the legacy of the first evil—a people systematically demeaning, brutalizing, another people."

Marie slammed the book shut. As a physician, she'd seen some of evil's physical results. But she wasn't required to think of the source. For her medical work, it didn't matter; as a *voodooienne,* it did.

The three men watched her.

"Tea?" asked Alafin.

"*Oui,*" said DuLac.

"Scotch," said Parks.

"I have that, too." Without asking, Alafin poured a drink for Marie.

She sipped. The heat in her mouth felt good. "It possessed me. No, that's not right. It was inside me. But it didn't overtake me. I was conscious."

"So it's not a god, not a true spirit *loa.* But other," said DuLac.

"A human creation," said Alafin. "*Wazimamoto.*"

"How can that be? It's a monster," said Parks. "Besides, we don't live in a colonized world."

"Are you sure?" asked Alafin.

"New Orleans is the epitome of colonization," said DuLac. "Multiple colonizations taken to their logical conclusion."

"We're all Americans."

"Some living better than others," said DuLac. "Why is it that the more pigment you have, the more oppressed you seem to be," said DuLac. "Not just in New Orleans. But especially in New Orleans."

"Aw, come on, DuLac," said Parks. "New Orleans has a black mayor. Black police chief."

"It also has a legacy," said Alafin, "from the eighteenth and nineteenth centuries. Colonial distinctions detailing the worth of a black—house slave, field slave, a Creole, free colored, mulatto, quadroon, octoroon."

"Who still controls the wealth?" said DuLac. "It's not by accident the majority of Charity's patients are black, brown, and yellow people."

"Look. Can we get back to evidence?"

"In part, I think you're both right," said Marie. "Racism still influences New Orleans. How could it not? A historical port city, home to slavers. Colonizers who owned people as easily as ships, cargo. But the Civil Rights era has happened. African Americans have defiantly staked their claim and right to be."

"*Oui*," said DuLac. "We've always been a proud people."

"Yet racism, colonialism, still brutalizes. Perverts," said Marie. "Like a disease spreading, its power would lie at the source. At the historical nexus when its power was unfettered, rampant. If *wazimamotos* exist, they would exist not as twenty-first-century vampires, but as a remnant from the nineteenth, eighteenth—"

"Yes," said Alafin. "That would make sense. The point of cultural contact. When the conflict in society, within the self, would be at its worst."

"That means—" said DuLac, understanding.

"Our vampire is a ghost. A creature from the past."

"Aw, come on. Speculation is well and good, but I can't convict on theories. Hell, I can't arrest what I can't see. It's like trying to lock up Rudy and JT. The ghosts Doc says she sees."

Marie raised her brow.

"Okay, okay. You see them."

"And?"

"I think I've felt them. That's as far as I'll go, Doc. Shit." Parks downed the scotch. "Okay. I felt them. Ghosts. Invisible dead."

"Don't light a cigarette in here," said Alafin.

"Probably send the place up in flames," DuLac said wryly.

"Have another drink, Parks." Marie poured the shot.

"Shit. Shit. Shit." Parks gulped the alcohol.

Marie leaned forward, reopening the book. A white missionary taught a group of native children.

Parks read over Marie's shoulder. "Reeducation." His scotch-tainted breath was sweet. "Why the multiple languages?" he asked. "They all say the same thing? 'Reeducation'?"

Alafin nodded. "English, French, Portuguese, Afrikaner/Dutch—all of them at one time colonized Africa."

"Just as French, Spanish, Americans did—"

"Enough already," said Parks. "Why the draining of blood, Professor? Murder is murder. Why not just slit the throat? Crack a skull?"

"Here," Alafin turned to the last page. "This is the African dialect. Ibo. A kind of epigraph. It says, in effect, that bloodsuckers are emblematic of western culture. Dracula, *nosferatu* were brought to Africa. Not the other way around."

"And this," asked Marie, her fingers tracing letters that had been written on the back binding. A rough scrawl, in blood.

"What does this say?"

"The unsayable. It's name. *Wazimamoto*. This is the only place in the book where the word is written out. The last page. Africans believed saying the name would call it."

"So they used a code," said DuLac.

"Parks," said Marie. "These are like the markings in Preservation Hall. Rudy, I mean the creature had been trying to name itself."

"What are you saying?" asked DuLac.

"There was blood above Rudy's body," said Parks. "But no blood left on or in his body."

"Amazing." Alafin nearly crowed with excitement. "There are origin myths. Tales about how such creatures are born. Knowing one's name, being able to say it, is powerful."

Marie stroked the pages tenderly. Starting from the beginning, she flipped the pages. Arrested.

"What do you see?" asked Parks.

"From the beginning you see fragments of the name. An angled line at first. Then another. Then the angles meeting."

"It's on every page with a death."

"Yes. After each draining."

The next to last page, the angles met, twice: VV. A young woman lying in the grass. Her neck arched back. Hair fanning across her breast. Her simple shift hitched high on her thighs. Her left arm thrown over her head, palm open to the sky, fingers gently bent. Puncture wounds. Deep, red.

"The first letter there. Completed," said Alafin. "Buried in the corner."

Parks's fingers traced the VV.

Marie turned to the last page. "It named itself. Tantamount to coming into being. Like a child learning to spell, to say its name."

"Relying on blood, on killing," said Alafin, "to create the first letter. Does it know what it is—or does the killing account for its knowing, its awareness of self? Maybe it isn't even aware of its self."

Marie thought of the markings on the wall in Preservation Hall. Agwé's sign. Rudy had tried to scratch his salvation. Like the book, the first letter of *wazimamoto* had been scratched in blood. The evidence team had confirmed it.

"Rudy's blood," said Parks.

"What?" asked DuLac.

"This letter," said Marie, tracing, "was drawn with a victim's blood."

"Incredible," said Alafin. "Scribing its self into being."

"Yes and no." She spoke slowly, thinking, trying to articulate connections. "If it's a ghost—then *wazimamoto* is what it *is*—its *genus*, vampire—but not its name. It would've had a life once— before becoming a vampire. A different name."

"Why didn't it write it?" asked Parks.

"Maybe it didn't know it," said DuLac. "Its name. This isn't a normal ghost. JT and Rudy are present day, presumably with present-day memories. This ghost—this *wazimamoto*, has been where? For over a century. Do ghosts have memories?"

"Uncharted territory," said Marie.

"So little we know. Much we don't," said Alafin.

Marie's palms covered the name—*wazimamoto. The page felt alive.*

"Written in blood. Draining blood. Again, why blood?" asked Parks. "Serial killers do it to demonstrate control. But a ghost?"

"All cultures revere blood," answered Alafin. "To lose blood is an offense that violates more than life, it violates human dignity. Implying the capturing of one's essence, the bloodlines. And who is to say the soul doesn't reside in the blood? Theologians talk about the heart—the engine of our blood—as our soul's resting place, our desires animated from the heart's blood."

"Anne Rice couldn't have written it better," said Parks, mumbling.

"Facts, not fiction," insisted DuLac. "Are you such a poor policeman that you abandon facts? What your eyes see? You saw what that thing did to the dancer. To Marie."

Parks studied his hands, clenching, then unclenching them. "Part of me still doesn't want to admit to what I saw. I don't understand anything you've all been saying. It's gibberish."

"Chaos," said Marie, nudging him toward acceptance. Understanding.

"I'm comfortable with chaos. But this is a mystery. Mystical."

"That's why you have me, Parks. The three of us," she said, her look embracing Alafin and DuLac.

"I feel I'm back at square one. Resisting. I'm being honest." He looked frankly at Marie. "Everything in me says I can't go down this path. I'm on it, been journeying. But part of me wants to turn around, keep trekking. Like I never met you. Any of you." He tapped his chest. "Look. If I can't smoke, give me another drink. I can't believe this," Parks said wiping his sweating brow, "drinking on the job."

DuLac poured. "Why'd you become a cop?"

"I hate seeing people victimized. No one should be hurt. Ever."

"You hate what it did to me?" asked Marie.

"Yes."

"Hold on to that, Parks," said DuLac.

"It isn't done with me," said Marie.

"Or with others," said Alafin.

"What do we know?" asked Marie. "Follow the evidence. Music calls it—as it calls the spirits. But, unlike a spirit, it can't possess. It inhabits, controls the body but not the self. This vampire—this *wa-zimamoto*—"

"This response to colonialism," said DuLac. "Racism—"

"We're living in the twenty-first century," said Parks.

"Exactly," said Marie. "The invisible dead. A ghost from some other time."

"It straddles both worlds," said Alafin.

"Multiple worlds," said Marie. "Past. Present. African. American. Old World. New World. Mythic. Real. Living. Dead."

"Why does it kill?"

"The policeman's question."

"Motive, Doc. Like your motivation for evil. Crimes don't happen without it."

"Don't they?" asked DuLac.

"Never," Parks said, adamant. "Even when it seems there isn't motivation—a crazy man losing control—still, the cause is there, just buried. Maybe he was abused. Took mind-bending drugs. Thought his victim was an alien. Even when motives are unknown. Or seemingly not there. They're there. Motives move people. Cause them to act."

"But this isn't a person," said DuLac.

"Parks still has a point," said Marie. "It kills. Why? Why bother, after centuries, to kill? What's gained by the method of killing?"

"Food?" said DuLac. "A need for sustenance?"

"Control," said Alafin. "Claiming power."

"A taste for cruelty," said Parks

"Vlad the Impaler," said Alafin.

"Stoker's Dracula," responded Parks. "Cruel, hungry."

He went to the window and pulled the cord, opening the blinds. "I've got to hit the streets. Sun's going down. Isn't that when vampires thrive? Besides, the French Quarter is jumping, half lit with booze. If music calls this thing—this *wazimamoto*—I can't think of any place better than Bourbon Street."

"I'll come with you."

"I don't think that's wise, Marie," said DuLac.

"Marie-Claire is with Louise. You'll go to her, DuLac? Take care of her until I'm home?"

"You needn't ask."

DuLac embraced her. "Take care. Parks, if you let any harm come to Marie, I'll hurt you myself."

Parks opened the office door; light rushed in from the hall.

"Professor." Marie wanted to ask one final question. "What does Agwé have to do with this?"

"He may be trying to control the creature."

"He's done a good job so far," quipped Parks.

"Or else," said Marie, "that's where it was born. Became re-animated. Inside Agwé. The Mississippi. Flowing out to the Gulf—"

"—out to sea," said Alafin.

"All the way to Africa," said DuLac.

"An ocean littered with bones," said Marie. "Souls."

"You remember that, Marie," said DuLac fiercely. "A lost soul. Not a god. And it feared you. Your name."

"You're not just a woman," said Alafin.

"I know. *Je suis* Marie Laveau." Then Marie smiled, brilliant and expansive. "Thank you, Professor."

Alafin bowed.

"DuLac. I promise to take good care." Marie paused. "Of Detective Parks."

DuLac chortled. "Touché."

"Let's go, Detective," said Marie.

"Women. Worse than vampires," said Parks.

"Don't get me started on detectives," said Marie. The two of them bickered down the hall.

✕ ≋ ✧ ◇ ⊗ ◉ ✕ ⸬

It had been human. Once.

He'd been?

He couldn't remember his name before or after enslavement. He just remembered promises of freedom. But freedom never came. So he killed for it.

Afterward, a woman had helped him.

A woman had betrayed him.

He'd once been a man. Standing, walking, on two legs.

She'd spoken his name. Lovingly. Hatefully.

ELEVEN

BOURBON STREET

FRIDAY EVENING

The French Quarter was jumping. The sky was layered, orange, gray, and black. Neon lights of blue, red, and pink reflected off the pavement, the windows. Some tourists waved carnival glow sticks—green, yellow, blue.

Parks and Marie strolled Bourbon Street. Alert, on edge, both of them searching for ghosts.

Music floated out of bars, restaurants, hotel lounges. Zydeco. The Neville Brothers. Rock. Basin Street Blues. Cajun folk. Wash-bucket shuffle. Tourists in House of Blues T-shirts or tropical-patterned shirts crowded the streets, some their arms slung around each other; others, their hands twisted around drinks; still others, open palmed, touching, stroking the ancient buildings as if they were make-believe, the Disneyland version of the French Quarter. But everything was real—cobblestones placed by slaves; wrought-iron balconies crafted by free coloreds; and cafés constructed in the

1700s to capture the coins of Spanish seamen, American soldiers, and French nobleman.

"What am I looking for?" asked Parks. "Can't see ghosts. Waiji-mojos?"

"*Wazimamotos,* Parks. You can see victims. And potentially save them. If we can get to victims sooner, they might survive." Marie poked her head inside Lafite's Bar.

"Who's Lafite?" asked Parks, his finger tapping on the brass plaque.

"Jean Lafite. The gentleman pirate. Brutal, yet known for his chivalry. Loved women. Especially quadroons." Marie scanned the bar. Middle Americans drank beer and hurricanes; no locals here. Just clean-cut patrons indulging in revelry. Pretending they were pirates or privateers.

It was easy to romanticize the past, but life had been brutal, short. Scurvy. Poor dental care. Inadequate public health. She wondered how many murders, slave trips, pirate rampages had been planned at Lafite's. How many more died of bacteria, fever, syphilis?

"You see something?"

"No. Just thinking about the past. How all of us will become ghosts."

"You've always been this spooky?"

"Let's keep walking," Marie said, shaking her head, focusing on the present.

She and Parks were unlikely beat cops. She walked, senses heightened, looking for signs, disturbances in air, light, smell, or sound—anything that would suggest an aberration. *Wazimamoto*—not a typical ghost, not a spirit *loa*. Something other. And it wanted to hurt her.

A lost soul. New Orleans was filled with them.

Marie peered high, searching, scanning the balconies, shadows.

Parks strode confidently, cocky. His policeman's clarity—direct, forthright manner—was intimidating. Maybe it was just the power of carrying a gun? The bouncers eyed him. Even drunks avoided him. A barker for a peep show stopped hailing, "Nude everywhere," until Parks had passed the marquee with a poster of a blonde, her breasts and crotch decorated with purple feathers.

Parks grimaced. "After this case I'm quitting. Moving to the Jersey shore."

"Lovely?"

"You bet. Should've been a surfer."

Marie laughed.

"I was good."

"Do they even have waves in Jersey?"

"More than here."

"JT's waving."

"Where?" Parks spun, his hand on his jacket, covering his gun.

"Up on the balcony."

JT clutched the antique rail. His expression—more an aura than facial muscles—seemed pensive, almost hopeless.

She wondered if JT knew her odds were poor.

"Not Rudy?" asked Parks.

"He may have moved on."

"They can do that? Move on? Like heaven? Hell?"

"I don't know. All. Either. Neither. 'Every good-bye ain't gone'— it's a folk saying. Everything that existed still exists. Not clear where. Maybe everywhere."

Marie stopped. Tourists swarmed, flowing around her and Parks as if they were an island. She sniffed the damp air. "Everybody dead is still here."

"Tell me," asked Parks, stopping her, touching her arm. "How come you're not crazy?"

"You religious?"

"Lapsed Protestant."

"Would it sound funny to you if I said faith? I believe I have my gifts for a reason."

"Like tracking a bloodsucker?"

"Sure. Why not?"

They smiled in perfect understanding.

Parks's hair fell forward, framing his angular face, his cheekbones. He was a good foot taller than she.

She looked past Parks, scanning the row of iron balconies, the shingled rooftops. "JT's gone."

"So?"

"Our first clue. The *wazimamoto* is near. Just before the hospital attacks, JT and Rudy disappeared."

"And the music?" said Parks. "The second clue? Follow the music."

Marie nodded.

Parks snapped open his holster.

Marie hadn't the heart to tell him his gun was useless.

Follow the music.

At first, all she heard was a cacophony: pulsing, riotous nightlife spilling out of clubs; music overlapping, creating noise. But New Orleans had its own unique sound, too—rhythms built on drums, brass, and bass guitars rather than pianos, violins, and reeds. A raw, urging sound that rose above people's chatter, hollers, and shouts. A melody of jazz—eclectic, improvising, riffing on chords of "God Bless the Child."

They walked east. The Quarter gave way to less commercial, less well-lit streets. Locals ruled intimate clubs catering to the maids, the bellhops of overpriced hotels, the cruise-line workers, the domestic workers, and the town gamblers who played bid whist rather than poker.

"Misty's," said Parks, stopping. A sax wailed, plaintive and yearning. "*Mama may have. Papa may have . . .*"

MISTY'S was written in cursive pink neon. A white Mardi Gras masque flanked the letter M.

The drums clamored, driving the sax higher and higher. Another sound: a scream?

Parks pulled his gun.

Screams.

The music stopped: drums toppling, clanging. The electric guitar whining. The saxophone stopping midcry.

Patrons rushed out of Misty's as Parks, Marie behind him, shoved, trying to rush in.

A small crowd gathered about the door marked LADI S—the *e* missing, the door painted a flat black.

"Police," said Parks. "Move."

A woman, petite, with high heels, her panty hose gathered about her ankles, her thighs bare, sat on the toilet seat, her head dropped forward, lolling on her chest as if she'd simply gone to sleep.

Parks lifted her head, clenching his jaw at the woman's wild, bug-eyed look. Her mouth was wide with a silent scream.

Patrons gasped; some screamed; some made the sign of the cross; others covered their eyes, turning their heads away.

"I found her, I found her," moaned a dyed redhead. "She had to pee, that's all. What's happened to her? What's happened?"

Parks pressed his cell phone's buttons. "Roach. Parks here. Bring the entire crew. Misty's, east of the Quarter. Yeah," said Parks, his voice soft. "Another one."

"She was gone so long. I went to check on her." Mascara smeared down her cheeks. "Thought she'd passed out from those hurricanes. She can't drink worth shit. What's happened to her? She looks a hundred years."

Marie inched closer, studying the wrist. Puncture marks. Neat. Vertical. Right above the artery. A Tiffany heart bracelet had blood on a few links. Otherwise, the suction had been clean.

"Her name?"

"Sarah. Sarah Bruchette. Lord, I've got to call her folks." The red-haired friend started to cry.

"Would you like me to call her parents?" asked Marie. "I'm a doctor."

"Would you?" The girl rummaged in her friend's purse, pulling out a cell phone. "Here. Look up 'Mama.' She called her three, four times a day." The girl swayed and Marie could see she couldn't be more than eighteen. Both girls underage, pretending to be sophisti-cates.

"Go sit down," said Parks, extending a hand. "We'll get a state-ment from you later."

The girl clutched his hand gratefully, then moaned plaintively. Unsteady, her hand covering her mouth, she staggered out the door.

"Everyone out. Cops on the way," Parks shouted at the excited, leering faces—people trying to cram into the bathroom to catch a glimpse of the dead girl.

"You." Parks pointed at a sallow-faced man. "You the owner?"

"Naw. I just work for Misty. She ain't here. I'm Earl." His head jutted forward, transfixed by the girl's bloodless body. "What kind of man would do this?"

"Who said it was a man?" Parks regretted his words as soon as he'd said them. He reached for his Marlboros. He could hear the gossip now. Ghosts. Vampires. Bloodsuckers.

Marie eyed him sympathetically. Outside, ambulance and patrol car sirens wailed, then died. The cavalry had arrived.

"Keep your patrons inside the club," said Parks. "We'll want to question them."

"Misty's gonna be sorry she missed this. She won't be sorry about the money though."

"Murder is good business," said Parks bitterly.

"Damn straight. New Orleanians love scandal. Misty will get her gold."

"And you'll get yours, skimming right off the top."

Earl grinned slyly. "You said 'another one.' There's more?"

"Mind your own business," said Parks.

"And you," Earl said, nodding at Marie, "be the icing on the top. The Voodoo Queen. Somebody's doing bad voodoo, hoodoo, *ju-ju*."

Earl crowed, his voice like a carney barker's, shouting, "Drinks on the house, folks."

Parks grimaced, watching the man waddle and strut. The sax started wailing again. The drums pounding.

"I'll go outside," said Marie. "Call the family."

"Thanks." Parks squatted before the body. "I don't like it."

Marie paused, watching Parks puzzle it out. Skin and bones. Everything that had been lush about the young girl was gone.

"Three men. Now one women. Dead. You think it's random? Or planned?"

Marie didn't answer.

She walked through the bar, her feet crushing peanut shells, as Roach, the officers, and the forensics team were walking in.

"She's all right," said Roach as an officer tried to stop her from leaving.

Marie mouthed, "Thanks."

Police tape and barricades blocked Misty's entrance. People were pushing, shoving, dying to get in. A harried officer yelled, waving his baton.

Marie avoided the crowd by turning left, then left again, into the alley. She walked past the stage door, past the trash bin, the empty liquor and beer crates, a series of loading plat-forms. During the day, there were resale and wholesale shops selling antiques, clothes, paintings, and photography. A kind of flea-market atmosphere interspersed with coffeehouses and bars. At night, street sounds filtered into the alley; mainly, there was the whirr of large-unit air conditioners, cycling on and off.

She stopped under a streetlamp, its bulb flickering, losing its electric charge. A small circle of shadows appeared then disap-peared. But as she looked left then right, the alley looked like one long dark tunnel. A thick blackness that had as much weight as the shapes—abandoned cars, trash bins, an old sofa, a washing machine, barred windows, and metal doors.

The cell phone lit up blue. She hit Contacts. GEORGE. KIKI. AMBER. TONIE. MAMA. She couldn't press the button.

She felt a quivering in the air.

"JT?" Her voice pierced the darkness. She thought she'd felt his presence. Or, maybe, some homeless person, slipping from his hide-a-way?

She looked at the cell screen: MAMA. She pressed the button. She couldn't imagine losing a child. Losing Marie-Claire.

Hair on her neck tingled. She knew about reactions to fear, to stress. It was her imagination.

Was someone approaching, stalking? Her?

Third, fourth ring. Mama wasn't home. Marie lifted her head. "JT?"

No answer.

JT wasn't near.

She felt a chilling cold. She dropped the phone just as a voice answered, groggily, "Hello? Hello?"

There. Behind the industrial trash bins.

Marie faced it. *A black more solid than darkness.*

Two feet away. The air about it, inside her, was frigid, Painful. Making it difficult to breathe.

An outline of a human form.

"Who were you? What do you want?"

No answer. *It flared with a new intensity; she could almost . . . almost see a face.*

"Who are you?"

The cell buzzed. Disconnected.

The wazimamoto seemed gigantic. But Marie guessed it was part of its power, some intangible essence, overwhelming space. She blinked. As a man, it couldn't have been more than six feet. Sturdy, not massive.

A singsong chime startled the night. Mama was returning her call.

Marie stooped to pick up the phone, then spun around, feeling someone caress her hair. "Stop." She shivered.

Standing, at arm's length, was a man, but not a man. *A shadow.* A grotesque version of Peter Pan's runaway shadow.

A substantive darkness—desperate for life.

Though Marie couldn't make out eyes, she knew it was examining her.

Think. In science, energy attracted matter. But what kind of matter shaped itself to resemble a human?

Her heart raced. Skin tingling, hives reddening on her throat. All the clichés, but still a physical reality. The primitive brain—fight or flight. Terror fueled by adrenaline. Her breath shallow. She couldn't scream. Or run.

A scientist's curiosity calmed her.

It was allowing her to watch it. It had more weight, more presence than when she'd seen it in the hospital. And while she felt cold, she also sensed its heat, its life's energy filling the darkness. A kinetic energy.

Move, she told herself. Move.

It stepped closer, awkward, foot heavy.

Shout, scream for Parks; but it was impossible. Her body felt weighted. Fascination overcame fear. And hadn't she been warned to "show no fear"?

Hands—there were *no* hands—*stroked her breasts through her shirt.* Her shirt bunched, moved. Her body responded, nipples hardening. Her breath caught in her throat.

The touch was gentle. Like someone pulling silk across her breasts. Her body betrayed her. The cold felt right, felt good to her heat.

She heard a whisper, but there wasn't any sound. Just vibrations, assaulting her mind. She understood the sense of it—the words that were not words—*"Mine. You're mine."*

Marie stretched out her hands. *She could feel shape, density. See, in the dark, a shadowy face.*

It was stroking her—sweetly, exploring waist, abdomen, thighs. Touching her crotch, making her feel naked. Exposed.

Part of her was drowning in sensation. Another part of her could see the image wasn't complete. *Features were indistinct; connections between eye bones, the nose bridge, and cheekbones were hazy.*

Suddenly, she was sick. Nauseous. The creature arousing her felt more of a violation than when it drained blood.

"Kill me. I dare you." *She slapped, flailed, feeling resistance before her hand broke free, swiping night air.*

"Get the hell away."

Her body was slammed against the wall. *Her throat was being squeezed. Pressure against her esophagus. She clawed at the outline of hands surrounding her throat; but the energy felt like a vice. As strong as steel.*

Oxygen deprivation. She'd become light-headed as cells starved, eventually losing consciousness. Her lungs and heart, shutting down.

She tried to speak but couldn't; inside her head, she chanted, "I am Marie. Marie. Marie. Marie."

Cold touched her ear. "Mine. My Marie."

"Halt," said Parks. "On the ground. Hands on your head. Halt."

Her feet lifted off the ground. She was being held by the throat— face-to-face with what wasn't a face. Only indentations of darkness suggesting eye sockets, forehead, and mouth.

She was losing consciousness. The word "How?" fixed in her mind.

She ceased struggling, her body limp.

Cold brushed, pressed against her lips. She swore she was being kissed.

"Doc," Parks screamed, firing a warning shot. Then another.

It turned. Parks fired four rounds into its head. *The creature vanished, disintegrating like smoke. Breaking into particles.*

Marie stumbled, falling forward.

Parks caught her, clutching her to his chest. Her cheekbone resting on his chest, her ear listening to his heart. Parks was holding on to her for dear life; she, holding him. He was protecting her, she told herself. A frightened girl held close, safe against a man's chest.

She cursed. She was a woman grown. More deeply, she felt ashamed. She'd let herself be seduced—mentally *allowed* herself to be seduced. Damnit to hell.

She pushed Parks away. "Enough."

"What are you talking about?"

Shoulders heaving, she crossed her arms over her chest. She wiped her mouth; her hand was slick.

A substance, gelatinous, covered her mouth and throat. She tasted brine.

"Evidence," she whispered. Unlike ghosts, the *wazimamoto* had been concrete.

Parks staggered backward, then turned, running. "Roach. Roach. We've got evidence here."

As a doctor, Marie was intrigued. She had something to study, to test. She could form a hypothesis—about the *wazimamoto's* nature. Being. She might find a rational explanation.

The woman, Marie, felt sullied. Marked. She wanted to scrub her skin raw.

Marie, the *voodooienne*, knew there was a hidden blood narrative. A story written in red.

Bloodlines.

Deep inside herself, she'd responded to the creature's words: *"Mine. My Marie."*

Her blood had stirred, answering, *"Yes."* Her blood had its own tale. Secrets.

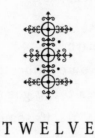

TWELVE

The substance was tinged green. Viscous, it seemed innocuous in the test tube.

Using a metal file, Marie lifted a sample and smeared it on the slide, sliding it beneath the microscope lens. Magnification 1,000 times 1. It was a one-cell organism, the simplest kind of bacteria. It didn't look like salmonella or E. coli. She'd have to run tests to type it.

"What've you got?" Parks strode across the room.

"See for yourself."

He tilted his head, positioning his left eye. "What am I looking at?"

"It's a bacteria. I don't know how or why the creature exuded it."

"Alive?" asked Parks.

"Yes."

"That means we can kill it."

"Maybe."

"What do you mean 'maybe'?"

"Just that. Maybe. There are further tests. Analyses. How it interacts with other chemicals. I've got a hunch it's saline." She tested it with a thin strip. "Yes, its some kind of sea brine. That would explain why Agwé tried to warn me. Why I smelled sea life, tasted salt." She touched her lips, shuddered at the memory of the kiss.

"You're exhausted. Let me take you home," said Parks.

"I don't want to endanger Marie-Claire. This creature, the *wazi-mamoto*, is coming for me."

"DuLac is with her?"

"Yes. He'll protect her with his life."

"Will he need to?"

"Get out of here, Parks. I have work to do." She stared again into the microscope. "Deadly. Beautiful." She couldn't help shivering, dreading the implications of a living substance.

"There's something you're not telling me."

"Look, Parks, if you want to help, help me make more slides. We'll test for chemical reactions."

"Okay. You don't want to talk." Parks slid out of his jacket. "Got a lab coat?" Parks pulled a coat off a hook on the door. "Menotti. He's not using it."

"She. 'Menotti' is a she."

"You think someone might mistake me for a doctor? I took Chem one. And two. Hand me some slides."

"I heard it," Marie said softly, staring at the test tube.

"What?"

"It speaks. Its voice is nothing more than vibrations. But I felt . . . heard its words in my head."

"Why didn't you tell me before?"

"I didn't want to believe it."

"How can I protect you if I don't know what's going on?"

"I never asked you to protect me."

"It comes with the job. 'To serve and protect.'"

"I'm responsible for myself. I thought that was clear. Don't smoke in here."

Frustrated, Parks blew out the flame. "Look, Doc. No one should be a victim."

"I'm not a victim. I'm an adversary."

"One who can't go home."

"Won't. There's a difference."

"Dr. Laveau. This man bothering you?" Carlos entered the lab. He was short, five-one. But his shoulders were broad from swimming, lifting weights. Multi-colored tattoos covered every inch of his arms.

"I'm a cop," said Parks.

Carlos shrugged, baleful. "What do I care? You need help, Dr. Laveau?"

"Science, Carlos. I need help with some tests."

"Sure." Carlos pushed past Parks, his shoulder hitting Parks's arm.

"Funny, a gangbanger in the chem lab."

"A dumb cop in the lab," sneered Carlos. "What've you got, Doctor?"

Marie pointed at the slide.

Carlos looked into the microscope.

"See if you can culture it. If you can, try all the antibiotics you can think of to kill it."

"I can do that."

"It'll take a while for the cultures to grow," said Marie, yawning.

"You should sleep," said Parks.

"I hope it grows fast, before it kills again."

"This? This stuff, Doctor?" Carlos looked again at the cells. "Naw. It's the simplest organism."

"You think so? Let me have the slide." Marie pierced her finger with a scalpel.

"What're you doing?" asked Parks.

She pinched her skin, letting drops of blood fall on the slide.

She anchored the slide under the lens again. The reaction was swift. Cells devoured the blood, gaining nutrients and size, then dividing into more cells. "Look."

Carlos looked into the microscope. "What did you say this was?"

"She didn't say," said Parks.

"I'm not sure what it is. But if I'm right, the cells will need to feed again, and again. As if they're continually starving."

"It feeds?" asked Carlos, kissing his medal depicting the Virgin. "Evil. Devil's work."

"Not a rational opinion," said Parks. "Aren't single-cell organisms amoral?"

Carlos scowled, his broad face serious. "But spirits aren't amoral. Isn't this part of whatever is killing?"

"Carlos is right," said Marie. She pointed toward the south wall. "They're here," she said. "JT, Rudy, Sarah."

"The victims?" said Parks. "I don't see anything."

"Ghosts bearing witness," answered Marie.

"I believe you," said Carlos.

The three spirits were linked, hand to hand, against the far wall. Rudy and JT, protective, flanked Sarah.

"I have to stop it." Marie peered again into the microscope. "It has focus. Instinct. Searching for blood to survive."

"What?" asked Carlos.

"Our *wazimamoto*."

"Our murderer," said Parks.

"Tonight it had form," said Marie, breathless. "Not detailed, but shape. Parks, you even thought it was a man."

"I did."

"This have anything to do with the bloodsucking murder?" asked Carlos.

"See? No secrets," said Marie. "The vampire has followed me to work. It's becoming more solid as it feeds."

"You think the more it feeds, the more stable it becomes?"

"Yes. Somehow this substance allows the spirit to gain form."

"Wait," said Carlos. He opened a small refrigerator.

"Plasma," murmured Marie.

Carlos smeared the slide. He trapped it beneath the lens. "Nothing," he said, disappointed. Then, he sliced his finger. Blood rose. He smeared it on the slide, locking the slide in place again.

"It's feeding?" asked Parks.

Carlos waved Marie to the lens.

"Yes," she said. "It's dividing into new cells. Growing."

Parks's cell chimed, high pitched, alarming.

"Yeah. I'll be there." Parks snapped the cell shut.

"Another murder?"

"Unfortunately. Two in one night, Doc."

"Soon it'll be a man. Using others' blood to be. A true vampire."

"But how could these cells become a man? The science isn't right," said Parks.

"It's not all science. These cells indicate a source. I'm convinced the creature came from the sea. Agwé's realm."

"Agwé?"

"A sea god, Carlos."

"Like the orishas?" asked Carlos. "Water goddesses of Brazil?"

"Yes. It's a reminder that there's a spiritual component. A mystery unexplained. This—" She lifted the test tube, twisting it beneath the fluorescent lights. "These cells are animated by the spirit."

"A resurrection science can't explain," said Carlos, crossing himself again. "*Mi madre* believed in Christ's resurrection. Mysteries of the Black Madonna. The presence of spirits." He tilted his head toward the south wall, toward the spirits he couldn't see.

"Except this mystery isn't faith based," said Marie. "No African-based faith has a legacy of such a creature. It's mine to exorcise."

"Doc, you coming?"

"Go on," said Carlos. "I'll run the cultures. Try to have some answers before morning."

"I didn't mean to get you involved, Carlos."

"No problem. What's this word '*wazimamoto*'?"

"A professor says it's a colonizer, murdering," said Marie. "Or a spirit so colonized it hates itself, its people. This creature wants vengeance."

"Vengeance," echoed Carlos.

"But I don't know why."

"Vengeance is general," said Parks. "Most crimes are specific. Specific targets."

"I'm the target."

"Doc, are you withholding evidence again? Why are you any different from JT, Rudy? Sarah? This creature just kills."

"Sure, Parks," she said, looking at him, lying. "You're right."

"You up to this, Doc?"

"I'm stronger than you imagine."

"I'm not doubting your strength," said Parks.

"Neither am I," added Carlos.

Marie squeezed Carlos's hand. "Beware the cold. Call DuLac for me. Tell him to beware the cold."

"Rain, too," said Carlos.

"It's raining?" asked Marie.

"For the last hour. Heard on the news the Mississippi is rising. Hurricane season, you know."

"I know," said Marie. Hurricanes, seasonal, like clockwork— waves, hungry, licking at the levees.

"Let's go, Parks." *She nodded at JT, Rudy, Sarah. Like the* wazi-mamoto, *they, too, wanted revenge.*

✳ ≋ ✧ ◇ ⊗ ◎ ◉ ✧ ⁞⁞⁞⁞

What it most remembered was her. Soft, yielding flesh. Smell of honeysuckle and lust.

All of who she was had once belonged to what he had been. Marie.

He remembered—her name. Marie.

He longed to write it in blood. Her name. His blood.

Marie.

He'd write her name. When he did, would she scream? Remember?

"John." His name was John.

THIRTEEN

MADAM MAY'S JOY HOUSE

SATURDAY, EARLY MORNING

Rain pelted the street like hail. Agwé was answering in kind, swatting the Mississippi against the levees. Rage and heave. Water rising.

It was still dark outside, but, in a few hours, the sun would rise. Vampires avoided light, sleeping in coffins. What did a *wazimamoto* do? Daylight must be a factor. All the victims had been killed while the moon shone.

Roach held an umbrella for Marie.

"Nice," said Parks.

"I have some manners," said Roach, offering a hand as Marie stepped out of the police car.

"What's the news?"

"Easy ladies' house. May's complaining. Says she's losing forty K a night. Should switch jobs. Be a pimp. What do you think, Parks? Could I run the Joy House?"

"I think I'd like to see the body."

"I was waiting for you to wrap up. The forensics sweep is done. All the tourists and so-called tourists got a walk. Must've been a bribe. Some politician who didn't want to be questioned. Maybe the mayor? Police chief? City councilman? All I know, all the male patrons got a pass. Only the whores left."

"Better than priests," snarled Parks.

"Enough already." Roach shook his umbrella.

Marie stepped over the threshold. A dim interior to make lust appear romantic. Votive candles on the tables. Pornographic paintings on the wall. Poor copies of the Kama Sutra. Advanced Copulating 300.

Multihued women, dressed in silk, satin, and lace, lounged in chairs. On daybeds. A few smoked cigarettes; one prostitute painted her nails.

A woman swiveled on a bar chair. She looked like a CEO. Elegant in a red Dior suit. A mixture of Asian and black heritages. She looked respectable, gorgeous. Only in New Orleans was "madam" a prized social position.

"I'm losing money," said May. "I'm sorry for what happened. But I'm running a business."

Marie ignored May and walked to the sound system. Billie Holiday was singing "Strange Fruit." Marie pulled the plug. How ironic—a lynching protest song in a house of prostitution. Perfect accompaniment for a *wazimamoto*—another kind of Klan man. Marie couldn't imagine how "Strange Fruit" would encourage sex.

She nodded at the two women, bare breasted, in G-strings, sitting on the stage, next to dancing poles. The trick wannabes. Mostly single moms, struggling to survive. Sex-trade workers had their own pecking order. Dancers were dependent on tips. Prostitutes made the real pay—thousands a month. May took her overhead and marketing cut. But May would never end up in Charity's ER, battered, face cut, with vaginal tears or a damaged uterus.

Parks rubbed the day-old growth on his chin. "You ready?"

She looked into Parks's blue eyes. "New Orleans has always been hard on women."

"For what it's worth, the North's no different."

There was a brief moment of companionable understanding. Both detectives and doctors grew tired of seeing the same violent patterns. Sins and hurts, ever repeating.

"Over here," shouted Roach.

Marie moved past Parks, down the hallway with plywood walls and improvised doors. The original rooms had been sectioned into smaller sex quarters.

"Here she is," said Roach.

Marie stepped inside. The room was barely big enough for a twin bed.

Striped mattress, no sheets. The girl, naked. High heels still on, deep scratches across her breasts, bruises on her shoulders and arms. She'd fought. One arm was thrown high above her head. Her torso lay twisted, her head at an odd angle, as if she'd been trying to look back, reach for an escape. Or maybe she was just trying to avert her eyes from her killer.

Overhead was an exposed red bulb.

There were the telltale pinpricks on the girl's wrist. Her body drained, like a balloon without air.

Marie lifted the wrist. No pulse. She touched the carotid artery:

no pulse. Compulsively, she kept checking, rechecking that the poor girl was dead. And she was a girl—her hair still lush—hair didn't depend upon blood—a crystal in her belly button. In her left ear.

"I still can't get an exact fix on time of death. Body's too cold. Folks claim a john left her over an hour ago. No one saw her come out. Or anyone else enter her room. Nobody saw nothing," said Roach.

"Typical," said Parks.

"I think it's the cold that dries the body," Marie said. "Cold can be as drying as heat."

On the floor, the girl's pink lingerie was ripped, shredded. The spirit had found a new talent. Hands that could tear. Ever becoming.

Marie opened the victim's fake leather purse. She smelled Jo Lo's Glow perfume. Working girls loved the scent. No ID. Just a purse full of condoms. Virginia Slims. Birth-control pills. Valium.

Parks asked Roach, "Madam May tell you the victim's name?"

"Pinky. New to the business. Came up from Abbeyville. Country girl wanting to make it big."

"Not much light," said Parks.

"With this bulb off, it would've been completely dark. She might not have known what was happening," said Roach

Marie looked at the girl's crotch. A bikini wax. She wondered if the rape kit would reveal a substance similar to that in the lab. Or maybe not? Could a *wazimamoto* procreate?

Or, maybe, her thoughts were on the wrong track. Maybe Pinky had been mesmerized, seduced; maybe she'd thought, for a blessed instant, that the *wazimamoto* was a sweetheart she'd left in the bayou. Only at the last moment, Marie hoped, had she realized the threat.

Thunder snapped loudly, reverberating inside the room.

Marie sensed a presence. She refused to turn around.

Parks went to the head of the bed. He looked at Marie, then back again at the girl. "She looks like you," he said softly.

"You're wrong."

Parks merely pointed.

Marie walked to the head of the bed. How could she have missed it? Small eyes, slightly upturned nose. Not beautiful, but a symmetrical face, black shoulder-length hair. Her body lean rather than voluptuous.

It felt like a knife turned in her gut.

Marie looked about the room. Bare walls. Not even a chair. A room for sex. Not comfort. Not luxury. Just sex. She ran her fingers over the pane of a slightly cracked open window, left from the original construction.

"She must've been one of May's best. A room with a view," said Parks. "This must've been a third of the original bedroom."

Marie stood at the window. Feeling cold seeping through the cracked window, knowing for certain that the *wazimamoto* was outside, near. She trembled as cold swept across her neck. "It's gone, yet not."

"You see it?"

Marie didn't answer. Parks was behind her; she saw his reflection in the pane.

It was watching her. Had watched her.

Parks didn't see it. Mistaking the darkness for plain night, Parks jotted notes.

The rain fell, drenching the world. Marie could see where the rain didn't penetrate, where it flowed around the creature rather than through it.

"You all right?" Parks was looking at her, speculative.

It was strangely comforting that the creature was outside. Peering through the window, watching her, it wasn't killing.

"We'll take care of her now," said Roach. "Step aside so we can get the gurney in."

"Be gentle," called Marie.

"We'll take good care of her," said Roach.

The two technicians, young, with dyed, spiked hair, both looked like Goths. They were old hands, though, at transporting bodies.

"I'll finish my autopsy at the station," said Roach. "But I think my report will be the same. Blood gone. No known cause. No ID on the puncture marks. No fingerprints. Footprints. Nothing in the room. I'll verify dehydration also due to extreme cold."

Roach directed the cops to lift the body. They lifted her delicately, like she was glass.

Marie stared at the window. The creature was gone.

"Let's get the hell out," said Roach, his belly leading his body. "Load her in the ambulance. I'm going to get Madam May to comp me a drink. Irish whiskey. Straight up."

They were an odd processional, the Goths carrying the body. Roach behind them, wiping his mouth, thirsty for a drink. Then, she and Parks.

Parks's hand touched the small of her back. As if he were escorting her to dinner or she needed guidance to find her way. She wanted to tell him to leave her alone. To let her be.

Instead, she surprised herself, saying, "Take me to your place, Parks."

She wasn't sure he'd heard her; but his hand moved upward, squeezing her shoulder.

Marie lifted her face to the sky, letting the rain stroke her face.

Parks walked around to the driver's seat. He rolled down the window. "You'll catch your death."

Marie opened the door, slid into the passenger seat. "Sorry. I'm getting your seat wet."

"No problem." He started up the car. The radio crackled: "Ten twenty-four on Rampart. Exercise caution." Parks punched the button for mute.

He leaned across Marie, her head leaning against the window, and clicked on her seat belt. "You sure? My place?

"Okay," he said when she didn't answer, cutting the wheel left, turning into the street. Headlights made the rain look like snow. "My apartment."

Marie stared out the darkly tinted glass. Lights, a morass of people, French Quarter revelers, passed by. Parks honked impatiently at the scores of jaywalkers. He didn't live far, on the outskirts, past the fine hotels, strip joints, bars, casinos, close to the Ninth Ward.

"Exactly twenty-eight blocks from the Quarter. Four from the river." He parked in front of a three-story apartment building. "Not much," he said. "Renovated former Section Eight housing. New Orleans's joke of gentrification."

He got out of the car, dashed around to Marie. He offered

his hand, threw his jacket about her shoulders. "Come on, Doc."

Past the courtyard fountain, an impish, algae-covered fairy spitting water out of its mouth. Past the steel door, into a black-and-white-tiled hallway.

A huge gilt mirror was on the right, above the mailboxes. Two had broken locks.

"Not much, but home. Elevator." He pressed the button. "Third floor. You can rest a bit. No one will find you."

"It will. Just not tonight."

"The *wazimamoto?* Not if I can help it."

She smiled wanly. She wished Kind Dog were here.

"You're not seeing those spooks? JT, Rudy?"

"'Ghosts' or 'spirits' is more respectful."

"Are you kidding me? Respect spooks?"

"Yes. If you're with me."

The elevator door closed. Parks hit 3. He smoothed damp hair away from her eyes. "Okay, okay. Spirits, ghosts."

She nodded. That was the difference—how she'd changed. Old Marie versus new improved Marie.

Growing up, her mother had had her sayings: "A broken-wing bird means death"; "Scratch the wall, somebody die"; "Dead don't lie"—useless sayings that added up to nothing about her family legacy.

In New Orleans, she'd stumbled headlong into family mysteries and murder. DuLac had lifted her up, shown her how pieces of herself connected to an ancient tradition. He'd made her a believer.

"Spirits in this world and the next," DuLac had said. "All things alive."

He was right. She'd seen it with her own eyes.

Parks's apartment was a spare one-bedroom. Small kitchenette, a sofa, coffee table, stereo hookup for his iPod. No TV. A two-bar-stool counter for meals. A door leading to the bedroom. Bathroom.

A neon cross, a sign advertising baptism blinked outside, beyond the window; there was also a billboard advertising River-walk and the Big Easy Casino.

"Here. Glenlivet, part of my Scottish heritage. Drink." He tipped the bottom of the glass toward her mouth.

She swallowed.

"Scotch better than Irish whiskey any day."

"Another," she said, holding out her glass.

"Want some music?" He looked sheepish. "I guess better not. Music calls it."

Marie picked up a photograph from the end table. Blond, blue eyed. A southern sorority girl. All bouffant hair and tight sweaters. Whatever made Parks think she'd settle for a Jersey boy? He'd been the exotic. Not she.

She held out her glass. He poured another shot. She drank, appreciating the heat in her throat.

Deliberately, she began undressing. Slipping off her shoes. Pulling her T-shirt over her head, shimmying her jeans down from her hips. No bra. White cotton panties. Nothing like the prostitute's lingerie. And, unlike most prostitutes, she needed sex. Now.

She walked toward his bedroom. "You coming or not?"

"You're drunk."

"Sex. Pure and simple." She faced Parks, her hands at her sides. "I need the connection. Need to be reminded that I'm a woman." "By a man," she could've added. She couldn't help how her body had responded to the *wazimamoto*; but she could still *choose* to respond to someone. A good man. Like Parks.

Parks was frozen, like a stop-action character. The poker-faced cop, trying not to tip his hand. Nonetheless, there were telltale signs. He swallowed. Saliva quickening. Marie knew his respiration, his pulse, would've quickened. The physicality of desire. Blood volume increased. Inside his khakis, he had an erection.

She wasn't lush. Small brown breasts, chocolate areola. Her stomach, flat; thighs, lean. Many men preferred her body type. More boyish than womanly. But she was all woman. Her thumbs hooked her pantie's elastic. She stepped out of them: slowly, one leg at a time. Tiny black matted curls demanded attention. "This isn't about love, Parks. Just sex."

"You mean therapy?"

"Depends how good you are. Are you any good?"

Parks grinned. "The best."

"Don't turn on the lights."

He gripped her buttocks, pulling her close. Spun her, pressing her back against the wall. Grinding his pelvis into hers. Kissing her deep, until she almost screamed for air. Then he lifted her off her feet. Cradling her like a bride. Gently lowering her to the bed.

He stood. A solid dark shape surrounded by darkness, faint

light streaming through the window from streetlamps and blue neon.

She heard his belt unclick. Heard the gentle scrape of his pants against flesh before falling to the floor. She couldn't see him and somehow she found that more erotic. Her hands reached for him, unbuttoning his shirt, undoing his tie, smiling at his old-fashioned boxers as she helped him strip.

His restraint was gone. He pushed her back onto the pillow, hands fiercely caressing her body, his tongue flicking against hers. His hand stroked her clitoris; he whispered, "That's it. More." She squirmed with desire. She felt him guiding her like a wave, his hand rocking her pelvis. Fingers tickling, then moving, in and out.

She gasped. Contracted her muscles around his penis.

She contracted again, trying to squeeze every bit of pleasure, release her pent-up desire. Then her contractions became involuntary. Every ounce of feeling was centered—there. Her back arched. She was desperate, yearning. Her nails dug into his arms.

"More," she said, and he responded. Pushing deeper, urging her.

Almost there. Almost. There. Nothing but feeling; heat flushing her entire body; her muscles utterly relaxing. Peace.

They were both wet, sticky. He lifted off her, spooning, holding her buttocks and back to his chest, his lips kissing the soft down on her neck.

"Thank you, Reneaux."

He pulled away. "I'm not Reneaux." He sat up, flicked on the lamp, opening his nightstand drawer for cigarettes.

"I'm sorry."

He looked over his shoulder. His face, blank; the good cop again, not giving away feelings. He lit his cigarette.

All she could see was his back. White, with a light dusting of freckles, curved like a C as his elbows rested on his knees and his feet were flat on the floor. He dragged deeply on his cigarette.

Marie buried her face in the pillow, her legs pulled into her abdomen, her hands covering her breasts.

Parks stubbed out the cigarette. "You need rest." He tugged until he covered both their bodies with the comforter.

"The other night," he whispered. "I'm sorry for what I said about Reneaux. Heard he was a good man."

"He was."

"You loved him?"

"Yes. He understood me."

"Fair is fair. You know about my love life. Now I know about yours." He turned, reaching for his cigarettes again.

"He died. Big difference."

"I'm sorry."

Parks was looking at her, his eyes unblinking. Not sympathetic, something else. Like he understood. Empathized.

"I haven't told anyone. Not even DuLac." Her voice rushed on. "I healed Reneaux. They shot him. I healed him. Took away the wound and the pain. My hands held a power beyond medicine."

"Like Keanu Reeves in *Matrix*?"

"Yes." She examined his features; he wasn't laughing or mocking her. "Like faith healers down a back road in the bayou. I don't know how I did it."

"Why isn't he alive?"

"They shot him again. My grace was gone." She pressed her face into the pillow. She didn't want to cry. Parks stroked her back.

His touch unleashed a welling tide. Anger, loss, resentment. Love.

His touch lowered, stroking, touching, kneading her buttocks; he rolled his body atop hers, both hands cupping her breasts.

She heard his breath rushing across her ear; she felt desire stirring.

He turned her. Face-to-face. The handsome Jersey boy—the head cheerleader's prize—had faded; he'd become the strong, aggressive cop, intent. Almost feral. The man of passion who could kill, also love.

He held her hands at her sides, kissed, suckled. His mouth moved lower.

She murmured, "Don't."

"I want to." He spread her legs, touching her soft mound, the brown curly hair. He kissed her, his tongue flicking at her sex.

"Parks," he said, biting the inside of her thigh, then burying his mouth against her until she writhed, climaxed. Then he plunged inside her, biting, sucking her neck, her breasts, her earlobes. Teasing her mouth with his tongue. He moved inside her, urgent, watching the tension build in her face. "What's my name?"

"Parks."

"What's my name?"

"Parks," she screamed, her pelvis arching to meet his, her body shuddering, gasping for air.

Parks rolled to the side.

"You didn't come."

His gold hair was slick on the pillow. Sweat beaded on his breastbone. His breathing was normal, as if he hadn't exerted himself. Hadn't felt desire.

"Let me give." She roamed her hands over his abdomen, his cock damp from her body. "Let me love you."

Parks stared at the ceiling. "How long has it been?"

She thought of all the men she'd picked up. The times she'd gotten laid. Times she'd felt less satisfied, more lonely afterward.

"I'm healthy. I've had a few partners. Is that a problem?"

Parks shifted onto his side. He kissed the hollow just above her collarbone. "I'm sorry. I was making a point about me." He gently bit her ear, his hand sliding down to her thigh. "Let me love you as you deserve to be loved. As Reneaux would've loved you."

"He's not here. He's dead."

"Just let me love you."

She held his hand, stopping him from caressing her sex. "My turn."

"There are no turns."

He kissed her, slowly, gently, uncoupling his hand from hers. Exploring crevices.

She moaned, trying to embrace him.

He held her hands high above her head. She was stretched, soft beneath him. "Let me take care of you." He entered her, whispering in her ear, "I'm Reneaux. If that's what you need, I'm Reneaux."

Marie relaxed in his embrace. It had been a long time since she'd let all her guard down. Let herself fully feel. Real love between a man and a woman. Not just lust. Desire. Love beyond the romantic. Love as in charity. Grace.

She arched her breast to meet his mouth. He sucked, fed gently, his mouth in rhythm with his pelvis, moving deep inside her. Making circles inside her, stroking in and out until she screamed. He shouted. Head thrown back.

He pulled her against his chest, burying his face in her hair. One hand stroking her breast, the other draped over her abdomen. "I'm loving you," he murmured. "I'm loving you."

"Parks."

"You smell good." He was the sweet Jersey boy again. All the sexual tension gone, his body seemed vulnerable. His eyes, kind. "You should get some sleep."

She kissed him. "Thank you," she said.

"I could die now and go to heaven."

She punched him, sat up shouting, pulling the pillow, like a shield, against her stomach. "Don't say that. Don't. Everybody I've ever loved died. I'm not saying I love you. I don't even know you. I just don't like the word—'die.' I need—I want to be around people unafraid to live."

"Like you?" He was the inquisitive cop again.

She winced. "I try."

He took away the pillow. "Do me a favor. Don't say anything else." He pulled her into his embrace again, her head on his chest. "Curl up. Sleep. Dream."

"Parks, I—"

"Don't say anything. Just sleep."

Marie studied the planes of his face. How, in the dark, the light from the streetlamps made his skin glow alabaster. Damp tendrils of hair curled on his brow.

"Were you this good to your girlfriend?"

Pain tiptoed across his face. "I tried to be."

"She was a fool," said Marie, settling her head on the pillow. Beneath the sheets, Parks reached for her hand. They clasped hands together, breath matching breath, drifting.

Sleep.

☒☰☒◇☒◉☒▓

Woman's blood. Aromatic, sweet. Satisfying. Sexual tension deepening their fear.

He remembered slaking his thirst on top of—inside—women's bodies. Holding dominion. Yet he also remembered disliking women—his need of them.

He'd enjoyed tormenting the woman. Flipping her facedown on the bed. Entering her. Her hands tearing at air. Her screams as she heard his words inside her head. "Mine. All mine. Scream. No one will come."

And no one did. Not unlike the salons he remembered. Where for gold, a few francs, even the disliked American dollar, there were places where you could do anything to a woman and no one cared. Needy women took their chances. In this New World—so different from the world of his memory—it seemed much the same. Women were easy prey.

Except for one—the woman called Doc. When she spoke her name, Marie, he had hesitated.

Some other memory haunted, served as a warning. The specifics unclear. He'd remember why. With more blood.

Razor sharp, vengeance swelled. He felt a rage to dismember. Hurt.

Vengeance. For what?

He'd watched her; she'd allowed it. Through the window, he'd felt pleasure watching her recognizing that the victim could easily have been her. Similar build. Dark brown hair.

Knew if he kept feeding, she would come to him. Knew she was as curious about him as he about her.

The mystery would be solved. Soon. He was becoming John.

He'd be powerful. Again.

Rest.

More blood would give him substance. More memories.

FOURTEEN

CHARITY HOSPITAL

SATURDAY EVENING

The lab was humming with activity: pregnancy tests, blood typing, HIV screening, diabetes testing, all the usual, standard procedures for an urban hospital. In the far corner, at the last lab station, Carlos slept, sitting on the metal stool, his head on his arms.

Marie shook him gently. "Any luck?" She handed him a Styrofoam cup filled with coffee.

"Nothing but dead ends." Carlos stretched, his arms coming alive with moving tattoos. Roses, a hummingbird, a snake. The Madonna was ink-stained on his other arm.

"Anyone been curious?"

Carlos looked at his lab mates, on the far side of the room. "Told them you had a special project for me. They left me alone. They've already guessed this has something to do with the murders. They think you're tracking Lestat."

"Lestat's more moral than our killer." Marie grimaced. "So, tell me." She pointed at the test tubes.

"Antibiotics, negative. I did a full spectrum. Blood reanimates the cells every time. Can't even grow a culture. It's inert. Won't grow. Not unless you add blood. I've never seen anything like it. Blood only makes it more invulnerable."

"It can't be killed," said Marie.

"What can't? The *wazimamoto*?"

Marie hugged DuLac. "Marie-Claire? Dog?"

"They're with Louise."

"Did you set protections?" asked Marie.

"Salt. Grave dust. Every spell I could think of. Set both Damballah's and Agwé's signs. Marie-Claire will be fine."

"Promise?" Marie asked.

"Promise." He smiled reassuringly. "You helping, Carlos?"

"Doing my best, Dr. DuLac. But nothing in science works."

"What do you mean?"

Marie lifted a vial, tilting the greenish substance. "This is part of the killer. Seems harmless. Sea bacteria. Who knows how old these organisms are? The sea, more than the earth, carries primordial cells, bacteria. Some estimates suppose there are millions of unexplored simple life-forms. These cells, in the water, are harmless. But, outside the water, they feed on blood, grow, and divide."

"They're part of the *wazimamoto*," responded DuLac.

"Yes. It's becoming. More and more manlike."

"It's an invisible presence," said DuLac.

"Not anymore."

"You've seen it?"

"Last night. As close to me as you are now, DuLac. Features not fleshed out, but it's becoming a man."

"A man? Or just mimicking? An imitation?"

"I'm not sure. This"—she held up the test tube—"is a simple organism. What attacked me had substance, strength."

"It tried to hurt you again."

"Not 'again.' The first time it tried to kill me. Last night, it only wanted to hurt. It's stalking me now—like I'm prey."

"Why?" asked DuLac.

Marie tried to quell her emotions. She answered like a scientist, cool and dispassionate. "I don't know. Somehow it knows me. Or it is getting to know me. Remembering, perhaps. A time when it knew another Marie."

Shaken, DuLac sat. "I've checked all my books. On folk culture, religion. There's nothing about such a creature anywhere."

"I thought I'd reread Marie Laveau's journal. There may be something I missed."

Carlos handed Marie his rosary. "The Madonna will keep you safe."

"I may need a stronger power."

"Holy water?" asked DuLac.

Marie felt giddy. "Worth a try. St. Louis Cathedral?"

"I'll get it," said Carlos. "Light a candle, too. Pray." Carlos grabbed his leather jacket from the door hook. "I'll be back as soon as I can."

DuLac looked through the microscope lens. "I've never seen anything like this."

"DuLac, I think I should try to contact Marie Laveau's spirit. If

wazimamotos are recounted in colonial times, then we're talking, particularly, about the seventeenth to nineteenth centuries."

"The most powerful Marie was from the nineteenth."

"Of all the matrilineal line, she was the most gifted. If there's a spell in the word 'Marie,' it's because of her."

"It might work."

"It knows my name, DuLac. Our name—mine and Laveau's. You told me to say my name."

"I wanted you to remember your power."

"The *wazimamoto* remembers, too."

"Precisely, what is it remembering?"

They sat, side by side, on the lab stools, contemplating the slides, test tubes, and petri dishes. The other technicians kept their heads down, focusing on their work—as if it was nothing extraordinary to have two medical doctors staring, in silence, at glass filled with a viscous green.

There'd been vengeance in the assault last night. Marie knew Laveau had had many enemies, false friends. Who had hated her enough to resurrect?

DuLac clasped her hand; she looked, startled. "What happened last night?"

"Two murders."

"Afterward?"

"It's personal."

DuLac smiled. "Something happened. Good for you."

Marie frowned. Normally, she wasn't shy about sex. But Parks had comforted her in a profound way and she didn't feel like sharing.

"You know we missed our Saturday night at La Mer's. First time in a year."

"We'll go again," she said. "If this case ever ends."

DuLac caressed her hair. "It has an end. Have you and Parks got a beginning?"

"I don't know." She tapped her nail on the test tube.

She swore the substance moved.

When the elevator opened, Sully was waiting for her.

"Hey, Doc, remember tomorrow. Bones. Kind Dog for a walk?"

"Sully, some other time. When this is over."

"Your outside business?"

Marie watched his expression. She saw him remembering gossip and tales. Remembering she did both physical and spiritual healing. Mixed with spirits, creatures resurrected from the dead.

"Dog is protecting Marie-Claire?"

"Yes."

Sully beamed as if the dog was his and had been awarded a medal.

"I'll just bring him bones tomorrow. Ham. You know how he likes to lick the marrow."

"Except no bones—Dog has plenty."

"Where from? I always bring him bones."

"Detective Parks brought bones."

Sully frowned.

"Look, what the hell," said Marie, "we'll have an unbirthday for Dog. Let him gorge himself. He'll be happy to see you."

Sully lit up, jovial and content again. A big man with an even bigger heart.

Over the years, Marie had come to understand Sully. Charity

was his hospital; even when he wasn't working security, Sully came in to volunteer. Visiting children and terminal patients.

Loyalty was his hallmark; he'd been loyal to Kind Dog ever since she and Reneaux had rescued him. She'd never forgive herself if Dog wasn't well looked after—and it'd been Sully who helped pick up the slack.

"I'll be home. Dog deserves a walk."

Unexpectedly, Sully hugged her. She smelled Old Spice. "We'll go to the park. Play ball. Watch the steamships," Sully muttered excitedly, walking back to his post.

Marie couldn't help wishing all her problems were so easily solved. She studied the patient board.

Already another busy, outrageous night. "I'll take Lao," she told the shift nurse.

Abdominal pain. Exam Three. She parted the ringed curtain.

"I'm Dr. Laveau. Can I help you?"

Lao pointed to his stomach.

Thin, compact, wiry. Probably a new immigrant, Marie thought. According to his chart, he was forty-five.

Marie palpated his abdomen. Lao kept studying her face; she felt self-conscious. In the left quadrant, she felt a mass. In medical school, they'd taught her to keep her expression neutral. Not to reveal clues to a possible diagnosis.

"Do you understand English?"

Lao nodded.

"You'll need X-rays, maybe an MRI. I'd like to test your blood levels, too."

They stared at each other and Marie couldn't help feeling they were somehow dueling.

"Not good," said Lao.

Marie's heart filled with sympathy. Once again she was startled by how so many knew when the battle was over. Lao had probably carried the pain for months, working, feeding his family.

She sat on the stool, all pretense of neutrality gone. "Is there someone I should call?"

"I'll call." He lifted his cell phone, opening it to a picture of his wife and two grown sons.

"You can fight."

"I will."

"Why don't I believe you?"

"Not give up. Difference." His brow furrowed. "Accept."

"Mr. Lao, you've known about this."

He nodded. "Six months. Hurting."

"Why didn't you come for treatment?"

"I did. Now."

"But now may be too late."

"From the start it was too late." His face was unlined. "Baosheng Dadi said I would die."

A Chinese folk religion, Marie remembered. A compilation of ancestor veneration, an acceptance of fate and hundreds of gods. Baosheng Dadi was the divine physician.

"I prayed. Made sacrifice. But not to be. Come back in the next life."

"Reincarnation?"

He smiled. "Maybe be doctor like you."

"I'll call an admitting nurse."

"No, I go home."

"Then let me write you a prescription." Lao stood while she wrote, his hands at his sides. She handed him the scrip.

"This is the strongest I can give. You'll need to come back. Be admitted later."

Lao looked at the white square paper.

"You'll come back?"

He looked at her with empathy, compassion. As if she were the one needing help.

"Mr. Lao, no need to accept pain. Let us, let me, help." Certain men stoically welcomed suffering, ignoring what it did to their families. "You'll come back?"

He didn't answer and she knew his answer. He wouldn't come back. Politeness prevented him from saying so.

"Why bother coming to the hospital now? You've left it too late. You won't let me help."

"I'm in America now. This is how America works. This, my sons will understand."

Suddenly, Marie understood. His Americanized sons didn't value folk religion. Folk medicine. They'd probably use aggressive technology. Put their faith in western medicine despite their father's wishes or suffering.

She sighed. "Mr. Lao," she said, solemnly, "tell your sons there was nothing I could do. Tell them I tried everything. Western medicine couldn't help. It's fate."

Lao bowed, deeply, reverently. She bowed, too. They finally understood each other.

Lao left the exam room, the happiest dying man Marie had ever seen.

※

Next patient. Next. One after another: a heart attack victim; a drunk driver who'd broken his spine; a drug overdose, a possible suicide attempt; a police officer shot in the arm. The entire staff was consumed by traumas, prepping patients for surgery, defibrillating to restore heart rhythms—for a hit-and-run victim, it didn't work— and moving patients to critical care or to a ward upstairs. Everyone danced in a fast, desperate ballet to deliver efficient care.

On uncomfortable ER chairs, the poor with cuts, scrapes, colds, and strep waited . . . and waited.

Two AM. She ducked into the physicians' lounge, dashed water on her face, and started a fresh pot of coffee.

"You're not going to believe who's here."

"Who?"

"Barefoot pregnant girl," answered El. "Except this time, she's got shoes. I put her behind Curtain Two. Called Antoinette."

"Thank you." Marie left the lounge, ready for round two.

Baylee, a homeless woman, complained loudly. "How come that pregnant girl go first? She ain't in labor. I didn't see any laboring. My throat is sore. Real bad. I'm dying."

Weekly, like clockwork, Baylee complained of an ailment. After the nurses showered and fed her, she always declared herself miraculously cured.

Marie pulled back the curtain. "Hello."

Sue's face was pinched, her eyelids heavy. One hand clutched the sheets, the other her abdomen.

"You're in labor?"

"Think so. Waited a while before coming. Waited till Tommy went to sleep."

"Let me examine you."

"You think it's Brax-Hicks?"

"You were listening." Marie smiled encouragingly. "Let's see."

She washed her hands, snapped on latex gloves. "Relax. This will be a bit cold." She inserted the speculum.

Sue squirmed and winced; a contraction crested. She moaned.

"Am I die-lay-ted?"

"Six centimeters. Almost there." She snapped off her gloves. "How'd you get here?"

"Cab. I kept the twenty you gave me."

"Good girl. We'll get you upstairs for labor and delivery."

"You can't deliver here?"

"No. But I'll check on you. I promise."

Sue's eyes were moist; she grunted, her hands clutching, twisting the paper sheet.

Young, no suitcase, no bag filled with baby blankets. How would she ever care for a child? . . . She was a child herself.

"Tommy don't want me here. Said it costs too much."

"Don't worry. Charity provides. Everyone here loves babies."

Antoinette arrived with a wheelchair. "I heard you were in labor."

Sue shrank. Helping her to stand and sit, Marie whispered, "Go with her. I'll come later and help with the baby."

"Promise?" asked Sue, nails digging into Marie's arm as another contraction crested.

"You'll be fine." Marie settled her in the chair, flipping down the metal footrests.

"Yellow moon, yellow moon . . . ," her cell rang. She opened it, simultaneously saying, "Thanks, Antoinette."

"Hold on," Marie murmured into the phone. She quickly kissed Sue's cheek and the girl hugged her as if she wouldn't let go. "You'll be fine." She pulled back.

"Go on now. Delivering your baby is safer upstairs." She looked at Antoinette, who turned the chair, spinning it away.

"Hello. Parks? Another death? No? Good. I'm fine. Sure." She wanted to tell him about Sue, about how sad and scared the girl looked. Instead she said, "I've got a patient. I might be a while. Okay. I'll call you."

"Who's that?" El had snuck up on her; when Marie didn't immediately answer, she asked more loudly, "Who's that? Who you talking to?" Her voice carried loudly to the staff.

Marie glared. El chuckled.

"Boyfriend. About time," said El.

Marie rolled her eyes and went to check the board.

It was a beautiful baby. A girl. Seven pounds, two ounces. Eighteen and a half inches long. Downy blond hair. Brown eyes. Ten fingers and toes. Sue had needed a C-section. But she'd been awake, chattering. Cooing over the baby as if it were a doll.

Marie knew Antoinette would help Sue as best she could. But she also knew there'd be an evaluation to determine if Sue could properly raise a child. For now, the new mother was happy. With luck and prayer, Angeline—that's what Sue had named her—wouldn't become a teen mom, too.

Her shift was over. Parks had said he'd be waiting outside Charity to drive her home. As if she couldn't walk. But it pleased her to get home sooner. To Marie-Claire. A cool bath.

Sex would be good, too. If she was honest, that's why she'd said, "Yes, Parks. Drive me home." She should've just said, "Sex." But Parks, nonetheless, understood. Just as she understood his offer to drive was part of foreplay.

Forget about the bath. Just sex. Then coffee, and rereading Laveau's journal.

"'Night, Sully."

"I'll be there at two," he replied, watching her leave.

She smiled, stepped bravely outside, blinking at the rising sun. The moon, descending, reflected the yellow glow.

She didn't see Parks's car.

Had there been another attack? Police business? He would've called her. Wouldn't he?

She scanned the street: cars cruising, patients leaving the hospital, some arriving. The *Picayune* deliveryman was filling the automatic newsstand. The convenience-store clerk was filling the crates outside the store with apples and bananas. An ordinary day.

Feeling wearier with each passing minute, she counted to a hundred. Another hundred.

She dialed Parks's phone; he didn't pick up.

She started walking. Okay, no sex. Just Laveau's journal. Another day digging for possible clues. Another day to figure out how to kill the *wazimamoto*.

Someone pushed her, and she fell, sprawling, her hands bracing her fall. Gravel tore at her skin. Her head jerked. Her hair was being pulled from its roots. She screamed. Grabbed the fist clutching her hair. Tried to gain traction with her feet. A tennis shoe slipped off.

A fist slammed into her jaw. She moaned, trying to keep clear-headed.

Wazimamoto? No, couldn't be. The attacker was solid. No freezing air. Or music. It was daylight. Think. She was on her hands and knees, trying to crawl away. Keep shock at bay.

She was picked up, thrown against a wall. She felt a rib cracking. She slid down the wall, and someone, smelling of alcohol, his face covered with a ski mask, dragged her, by her legs, down an incline, a driveway leading to an underground storage area for medical waste.

She thrashed, screamed. It wasn't fair. A random assault.

She kicked hard with her feet, hitting her attacker's knee. He dropped her legs and she scrambled, stumbling upward, toward daylight.

The man barreled after her. Spinning her, shoving her to the ground. Bloodshot, crazed eyes. Knees on either side of her. Hands pressing her chest flat; pain radiating, she couldn't catch her breath. His hands clasped her neck.

She kicked, her nails clawing at the mask.

The man cursed. Cajun. He was a backwoods man. Smelling of chewing tobacco, diesel oil.

Light-headed, Marie was losing strength. This was just a man. Not even a vengeful spirit. She thought of Marie-Claire. Enraged, she grabbed her attacker's crotch. Digging in her nails. Twisting.

He screamed. Fell back.

She scrambled up, kicking him. Aiming for his kidneys. Turning, running up the gray, dirty tunnel, screaming, "Parks."

And there he was. Materializing, at the tunnel's mouth, like a ghost.

"A man—"

"Not—?"

"No." She gasped, knees buckling, falling. Parks caught her—she whimpered—and gently lowered her to the ground.

"Just a man," she said.

Staring down the shadowed drive, Parks called for backup. "Wait here." He released the safety on his gun.

Gingerly, Marie fingered her rib cage. Some bruises. One rib broken. Possible hairline fractures on two more.

Two shots echoed in the tunnel.

"Parks," she screamed. Bracing her back against the wall, using her thighs as leverage, she pushed herself up. She was a doctor. Someone would need help.

She winced as she moved, sliding her shoeless foot. She heard footsteps. Heavy, deliberate. Like her, she thought the person must be hurt, trying his best not to fall down. "Parks?"

She could see a man's form. Her pulse raced. "Parks?"

"It's me."

"Where are you hurt?"

"In the gut. He hit like a son of a bitch. I'll be fine."

"Does he need help?"

Parks, his cheek swelling, turning purple-blue, avoided her gaze. "Dead."

"How can you—?"

"I'm sure."

Sirens wailed. "Cavalry's coming."

"You look like hell," she said.

"So do you. Come on." He slipped his arm about her waist. "Lean on me."

A flashlight's beam danced over them. "Parks. Parks, I heard it was you. Distress call." Roach was rushing toward them.

"Victim's below," said Parks. Officers, guns drawn, moved downward, into the tunnel.

"Is it—?"

"No, Roach. A regular murder. Regular bloodletting. Bullet holes. One to his leg. The other, his heart."

Roach whistled.

Parks handed him his gun.

"What's this?"

"Give it to the captain. There'll be an investigation."

A voice called, "I've got ID. Roach—you coming?"

"Give me a minute."

An officer stepped forward, nodding. "Detective Parks. Charity sent an ambulance."

"No, take me home."

"You should get checked out, Doc."

"Take me home, please."

Roach studied Marie and Parks. An ambulance whooped.

The patrolman shrugged. "EMTs already here."

Roach took off his jacket. Wrapped it about Marie. "I'll cover for you. Get her out of here, Parks."

Roach turned, his hands high, waving, like a traffic cop, motioning the medics. "Down here. Man down. We might be able to save him."

Parks lifted Marie; she groaned. The compression of bone, hurt.

"Sorry," Parks said. "I'll get you home."

"I don't want anyone from the hospital to see—"

"I know." He lifted Roach's jacket higher, shielding her face.

Hospital crew and bystanders were already gathering behind

police barriers. Marie buried her face against Parks's chest, taking shallow breaths. "Another bottle of whiskey for Roach."

"Better believe it," said Parks.

Marie tightened her arms about his neck.

✖

Kind Dog whined. He sniffed Marie's hand. Jumped up, trying to see her face.

"Down, boy," said Parks as he maneuvered Marie toward the bedroom.

Louise uncurled herself from the couch. "What's this? What's this?"

"Please, Parks," whispered Marie.

He maneuvered her into the bedroom, laying her softly on the bed. Dog leaped up.

Marie patted Dog's head. "Sssh. Sssh. It's all right."

Parks blocked Louise's view, ushering her toward the front door. "Marie's fine. She needs rest. Here," he said, peeling off twenties.

"Too much," complained Louise.

"Marie-Claire?" he asked.

"Sleeping," said Louise, reddening as Parks pushed her out the door, saying, "Thanks much."

"Marie," Louise called.

"Ssh," said Parks. "You'll wake the baby." He closed the front door.

✖

"Down," said Parks.

Dog lifted his head, turned, and jumped off the bed.

"That's a first," said Marie. "Dog always comes to bed when I do."

"Always?"

"I don't bring men home."

"Hey, what about me?"

"More like you brought me home, don't you think? Besides, if you think you're getting laid—"

"Don't tease," he said, grimly. "You're hurt. You look terrible."

"So do you."

"But you're alive." Parks sat on the bed, cradling her open palms.

He bent his head, kissing the scratches, the cuts. Lightly, pressing his mouth to her palm, then her thumb and fingers. "I knew I was going to shoot him."

"You don't mean that."

"Vengeance."

"Parks, no."

He touched his fingers to her lips. "Don't talk. I can't affect the supernatural. But a man hurting you? That's my realm. I wanted him to pay a price. Planned on it."

"What's going to happen?"

"There'll be an investigation."

"Parks, I'm so sorry."

"Not your fault."

"It was self-defense. Tell them it was self-defense."

"I'm not sure. I could've subdued him. I think I could've."

"You shot him twice?"

"In the thigh first. He kept coming."

"An imminent threat. Self-defense."

"I felt furious, righteous, shooting him in the chest. I'm a cop. I'm not supposed to get angry."

"You're human."

His face crumpled in pain. "I'll have to tell the investigators." He pulled away, elbows on his knees, his head facing down. She tried to reach for his hand.

He pulled away.

"It's the heat," he murmured. "Something in the water. Spirits floating about. Aboveground crypts. Every sin tolerated. Drugs. Alcohol. Prostitution. Gaming. Whatever sin you want to commit, you can commit here, in New Orleans. It's always been that way. Just walk through the Quarter and you can feel the weight of the past. Slavery. Brawls. Beatings. Rapes."

"Don't."

"I'm beginning to understand why New Orleans is the murder capital of the world."

She didn't know what to say. Parks, ever cool, had betrayed himself.

"There's cognac in the kitchen. DuLac likes to drink it when he's here."

His hands on each side of the pillow, his face inches from Marie's, Park spoke, his expression tender. "I'm going to start a bath. Get you a triple cognac. Take Dog out to pee. Then come back and bathe you.

"You've got bandages?"

"In the closet."

"Good. I'll bind your ribs."

"You've been through this before?"

"I'm a cop," said Parks simply. "Cracked ribs hurt like hell. Hurts to breathe. You'll heal soon enough."

"Soon enough to fight the *wazimamoto*?"

"Let's hope so." He kissed her, exploring her mouth gently with his tongue.

He pulled back and, despite her pain, she felt aroused. Felt touched by his vulnerability.

"What's done is done," he said, smiling, willing his spirits to lift.

She touched his cheek. "We should take care of this bruise— antiseptic, ice."

Angling his head, he kissed her palm. "After we take care of you."

"You're not falling in love?" She regretted her words as soon as she'd said them.

Parks pulled back.

True, she couldn't live without sex, passion. But it was also true that a decade of foster care had taught her it was risky to love.

Wordless, Parks got up, turned on the bathtub faucet, left the bedroom, and brought back a full glass of cognac, then whistled for Kind Dog.

She heard her apartment door close.

All she had to do was say she was sorry, reach out to him; but she couldn't. Not now. Her feelings and body were too raw.

It'd be easy to give up and let Parks take care of her. But she wasn't that woman. She appreciated kindness, tenderness. Good sex reminded her she was alive. And with a generous lover, she responded in kind. Maybe that's why she was confused about her feelings. Parks had been beyond generous.

Wincing, holding her left side, she sat up. She drank deeply, feeling the cognac burn its way down her throat.

The *wazimamoto* was intent on destroying her. To survive, she needed to understand the world as Laveau had understood it.

Parks was distracting. She, Marie-Claire, and Kind Dog were enough. DuLac and El were enough. They were a family. What more could a woman want?

Gently, she slipped off her blouse; gently, she unbuttoned her jeans. Her chest ached; a hot bath would feel good.

In the medicine cabinet, all she had was Advil. She swallowed three tablets with water from a Scooby-Doo paper cup.

She turned off the bathtub faucet. Steam rose from the water. Condensation clouded the mirror.

The water shone like glass, reflecting the bright white porcelain. Were words, memories, as powerful as water?

She'd had patients who drowned in bathwater. Children, by accident, or murdered. Suicides. Not much water was needed to die.

New Orleans was drowning in water, slowly sinking, losing landmass. In another hundred years, the city would probably vanish.

All that would be left would be water.

Bones, in the water. Pirates, sailors, slaves, native peoples, hurricane victims.

Agwé had birthed a monster. Were there more? Waiting to overtake land?

Water burst from the faucet—hot, rushing. Causing waves, a rising waterline. Grimacing, she turned the tap. Nothing happened. *The water spilled over the tub, covering the bathroom tile.* She threw towels on the floor. Tried turning the tap again. Nothing. Her feet slipped; her side hit the tub. She felt excruciating pain. She clutched the sink's rim. *A face, vague, undefined—but still a face—a man's face, watched her.* She turned, groaning; no spirit was behind her.

The water stopped flowing.

It still covered the floor, her feet . . . and the water turned a subtle green. A trick of the light? *There was life in the water, microbes. Particles coalescing into some aberration of human life.* She wouldn't scream.

Water covered her feet, seeping over the door ledge into her bedroom. Deep, ever so deep, she knew it would be a life-and-death struggle between her and the *wazimamoto*.

She stood. Even Agwé couldn't save her. That was the message. And given enough time, enough blood, the night wouldn't hold it. Him.

FIFTEEN

MARIE'S APARTMENT

SUNDAY AFTERNOON

"You're awake," said Parks, coming over to the bed. "Let me help you sit."

"Where's Marie-Claire?"

"In the kitchen having red beans with El and DuLac." He plumped the pillows behind her back.

She searched the room. "Dog?"

"Sully's walking him. It's three PM."

"It wasn't a dream?"

"No, it all happened."

"I need to get up."

"Don't you dare move from that bed," said DuLac, entering. "Doctor's orders. Heard voices. Brought you some coffee. Pain relief, too."

"I'm fine, DuLac."

"Liar," said Parks.

"I insist, Marie," said DuLac, tapping the syringe to remove any air. "It'll help you rest. Heal faster."

"I'll be fine," said Marie.

"We need you healed," said Parks. "There's been another murder."

DuLac pierced her arm with the needle.

"Where's your bedside manner?" A bubble of blood rose on her arm.

DuLac dabbed her shoulder with gauze. "You should've waited for Parks to drive you."

Worry had aged DuLac. His skin was taut; dark circles underlined his eyes.

"He wasn't there," she said.

"I'd gotten a call," said Parks. "I'm sorry. So sorry."

"Parks, it wasn't your fault. It just happened."

Marie could feel the morphine washing over her, displacing her pain. "We have a new problem. The *wazimamoto* was here."

"Parks told me," answered DuLac. "Was there music?"

"No. Not here. But the city has sounds. When isn't someone playing music in New Orleans?"

DuLac sat on the bed. "Carlos made slides. I've experimented with everything I can think of—every root, herb, gris-gris charms. Calamine. Foxweed. Absinthe. 'Keep away' spells, destruction prayers, even sacrificed a chicken. Nothing worked."

"Did you try silver and garlic?"

DuLac laughed. "I will."

"You never know," said Parks.

"Never know," Marie repeated. She reached unsteadily for her café au lait. Parks picked it up, placing it in her hand.

"Are you suspended, Parks?"

"The attacker had a history of violence. Spousal, child abuse. Conviction for armed robbery."

"You'll be exonerated?"

"Maybe. But it doesn't matter. After this case, I'm out of here."

Marie, her face neutral, blew air into the coffee's foam.

Parks pulled out his notebook. "Seems the attacker—Thomas Leckie—was the father of one of your patients. Sue Leckie."

"Are you sure?"

"Sure. He finished a six-year term in Angola. When he got out, his wife didn't want him. So he took his eldest daughter."

"She had his baby."

"Real sweet dad. Kept her confined so he wouldn't arouse suspicion. Didn't take kindly to you delivering the baby."

"He expected to get away with it."

"If his daughter didn't die in a home birth," added DuLac. "A hospital meant discovery. That's probably why he attacked you, Marie."

"You ruined his sweet deal."

"Bastard," she said, trembling, recalling her attacker's hands, his sweat and sour breath.

DuLac took the coffee cup from her hand. "Sue and the baby are fine. Antoinette said she's happy her father's dead."

"Don't doubt it," said Parks.

She felt lightheaded. Felt as if her spirit and body were separating. Morphine didn't exactly reduce pain, but focused it. Pain was a hot ball fixed behind her eyes while her body seemed to float, levitate, toward the ceiling.

She slowly enunciated her words: "The other murder?"

"Roach thinks it happened about the same time you were attacked."

"Man or woman?"

"Woman," said Parks. "Small, compact. Brown hair, brown eyes."

"And?" said DuLac, prompting.

Parks scowled, irritated. "She resembled you."

"And?"

"Folks claimed to see a man. Hovering over the body."

"Bold," said DuLac.

"Unrepentant," murmured Marie.

The three were silent, each retreating into themselves. Speculating about the monster.

"What happened, Marie?" asked DuLac.

"Did you learn anything useful?" asked Parks.

She slid down deeper into the bed. The room was spinning; her tongue felt swollen. "It was here. In my bathroom. Or, maybe just in the mirror? I couldn't tell. But it's becoming. Able to walk in daylight."

"Damn," said Parks.

She groaned.

DuLac stroked her hair. "You should be in a hospital."

"No. I'll get up soon." Currents were pulling her down. "Have to get up. Another ceremony."

"Agreed," said DuLac. "But after some healing. Parks did a good job with the binding."

She rallied. "Marie-Clarie?"

"El's watching her. Not to worry." DuLac kissed her brow. "Take care, *chérie*. A man couldn't ask for a better daughter."

She couldn't open her eyes. They were too heavy. She squeezed DuLac's hand.

She felt suspended in air. Then she felt herself falling. Drowning. Falling into sleep, layer by layer, going deeper, deeper, and down. Into an abyss.

✵

She was on the other side of the looking glass. He was the man in the mirror.

She knew his face—from where? He'd been loving once.

She stirred; someone put a compress on her forehead.

Drums sounded from far off. Strains of another sound, too. Some melody. Some echoing cry from the New World.

"You are me."

In the mirror, her twin, dressed in white, barefoot, cradling a snake.

"All things alive. You are me. I am you."

She stretched out her hand. Fingers touched.

She felt power course through her. She could walk on water, pluck the moon. Resurrect.

A shadow cut diagonally between them. Darkness deepening, the shadow grew into a man. Features imprinting on the darkness. High cheekbones. Medium mouth, lips drawn back in a grotesque smile. Eyes that burned.

"Marie. Marie!"

She twisted, flailing, trying to escape its grasp.

"Marie. You're dreaming. Wake up. Just a dream."

She held on to Parks. "Tomorrow," she gasped. "Tomorrow. DuLac's."

"Yes. Yes. Now sleep. I'll watch over you."

"Sleep." She curled on her good side. Exhaled. "*Je suis* Marie. And he is—He is—" She knew his name. Had always known it. "His name is—"

But the name wouldn't animate her tongue. It was just beyond her reach. In her soul's recesses. Hidden by time, history.

Hidden in her blood.

SIXTEEN

DULAC'S HOME

MONDAY EVENING

DuLac's home was a jewel box of a house.

The porch was a deep square with a rocker and a swing. Marie gingerly walked up the steps, holding on to the railing.

After sunset, it had started raining again. A bone-chilling rain. Out of place in New Orleans.

Through the screen door, Marie could see DuLac, in the vestibule, on the phone.

"That you, Marie?"

"*Ici. Moi.*"

Stepping into DuLac's home was like stepping back in time. Everything about the home was plush, sensual, decorated in the belle epoque mode.

Red velvet walls. Plump chairs with clawed feet. Parisian cabinets. Crystal chandeliers. High, arching ceilings trimmed in gold.

Paintings covered the walls: streetscapes of the Quarter at sun-

rise, sunset; reclining nudes, bodies copulating, eating pomegran-
ates. The house had been in DuLac's family for two centuries.
DuLac, the original Frenchman, had gifted the house to his quadroon mistress—DuLac's great-grandmother.

"You shouldn't be out of bed. Does Parks know?"

"He's not my jailer," she countered. "Carlos isn't having any
luck. You?"

"No. But I'm hopeful. That was Alafin. Said there's a man in the
Ninth Ward claiming to know about *wazimamotos*. From his father
before. A Nigerian who immigrated in the twenties. Alafin's going
to record his testimony tonight. We may discover how to destroy
it."

"Good. But I'm not waiting. I want Laveau to possess me."

"It's one thing to call the *loas,* but to call the dead? The Guédé
might not appreciate it."

"I know. Still, I've got to try." *Loas* came and went at will, but
ancestors were honored, prayed to—seldom did they possess. Ancestors could haunt; appear in visions; even speak in dreams, but,
rarely, possess the host.

"Agwé can be the intermediary," she said. "The river is swelling.
Don't you think that's a good sign?"

"It's still dangerous."

"You think the great Laveau would care?"

"It's only been a few years since you've been developing your
powers."

"You're doubting me?"

"No. But I think we should wait. Alafin might have news."

"And he might not."

Marie sat on the ottoman before the fire. When he was home,

DuLac always had a fire. Even when it was ninety degrees. She felt overheated, dizzy. "Another woman's dead."

"Parks wasn't supposed—"

"You think I didn't know? JT. Rudy. Sarah. Haunting. Two more women. Both young. Both resembling me."

"Are they here?"

Marie looked about the room. She'd grown used to the spirits. Lying in bed, trying to dream, she'd open her eyes and see JT sitting on the edge of her bed. Or Sarah staring at herself in the mirror, seeming to wonder how she ended up a prostitute, how she ended up dead. Another girl, newly dead, wept, her voice whining like honeybees.

Kind Dog always knew when the spirits were present. He'd stare, sniff the air, his tail drooping low.

"I don't see anyone," she said. "Six dead. Including the priest. I should be doing something."

"You're too hard on yourself."

"More people dying. The *wazimamoto* growing stronger. What would you have me do, DuLac? What are my gifts for? Aren't you always telling me this is my *fa*? My destiny?"

"Agreed. But I love you and I'm frightened for you. Spiritually, physically, you've taken a beating."

"I'm strong enough. Help me do this."

"Come."

She followed DuLac down a narrow hallway to his altar room. It had been a small bedroom, perhaps for a maid, tucked in the farthest southeast corner of the house. Crossing the threshold, Marie could feel the room's power.

The altar honored Damballah, the father to all the gods. Catholic and voodoo gods coexisted in the New World. Acculturation. The Virgin statue stood beside Ezili. St. Peter and Legba were both painted in oil. Candles—red, white, and black—glowed, their flames licking toward the ceiling.

Moonlight streamed through two windows. Enough light, yet light that blurred dimensions, without the sharp clarity of manu-factured bulbs.

DuLac gathered Agwé's possessions. His sword and admiral's hat. With chalk, he drew a large circle around them. "Inside here," he said, "will be a sacred space. Inside here, you'll be safe.

"I've had dreams, too, Marie. I know Laveau is the one to help. Agwé's sails point toward Damballah. The snake eating its own tail. I've seen it, in dreams. The gods are affronted by this monster. Only their cherished daughters—the Maries—can help."

He opened a cabinet. "*Tafia*, rum and molasses, to appease the Guédé." He poured the brew into three cups. One for each of the death gods who dressed in top hats and tails. "Perhaps they'll for-give our excursion into their realm."

"You think I'm right then." It was a statement, not a question.

"Yes."

"Two nights ago, I had an urge—no, a compulsion—to bring the painting in here. There," he pointed.

Marie turned. On the wall was the painting, normally kept in DuLac's parlor. Marie dressed in white, in all her glory, was pos-sessed, conducting a ceremony in Cathedral Square. The St. Louis Cathedral was behind her, its crucifix outlined against the skyline.

Marie touched her ancestress's face. It was young, ecstatic, self-aware. She stroked the oil, feeling that the streams of color were vi-brant and alive.

"She'll come, DuLac. I know she will."

"I'll play the drum."

Marie selected two small bags of rice and beans from the altar. She stepped inside the chalk circle, stroked Agwé's sword.

"Ready?"

She nodded. DuLac's palms tapped the drums; the rhythm filled her with ease. Drumbeats resounded, as they had in Africa, across the continents, the Atlantic sea. Into the Gulf of Mexico, merging with the Mississippi.

She sprinkled beans and rice along the outline of the circle. Then sat, centered in the circle, facing the altar. Legs crossed, her hands resting on her knees, she closed her eyes.

Marie was too sore to dance; nonetheless, every sinew responded to the rhythm. The tap-tapping. Soft, then loud beats. Fingers stroking, palms snapping down on animal skins.

"I haven't purified myself."

"I don't think it'll matter."

"Are you sure?"

"Just make your prayer heartfelt. Here." DuLac handed her *tafia*. She drank deeply.

"More," she said.

DuLac refilled the cup. She drank, reclosed her eyes, focusing on the drums. The rhythm's power to call the gods.

"Help me," she murmured. "Marie Laveau, help."

DuLac drummed insistently, chanting, "Not all accept the glory of the Maries. Not all accept that women hand sight down through the generations."

"I do," said Marie. "I do."

Inhale, exhale.

"Women hand sight down through the generations," she repeated.

Release self, inhibitions. Believe. Have faith. This was her
mantra.

"I believe," she murmured. "I believe in the power of me. The
power of Voudu gods gathering from Haiti, Africa, all the Americas."

Behind her eyelids, she could see another darkness. Gathering
itself, readying to tunnel into her soul.

The drums echoed, the sound rising, falling, like water upon a
shore.

Briefly, Marie opened her eyes. She could see DuLac, opening
himself to glory, pounding the drums, calling with his hands and
heart.

They were a pair. Outrageous in their power. And faith.

"I believe," she whispered, closing her eyes again. *There was a*
continent inside the darkness. "I believe.

"Legba, open the spirit gate." *She saw the spirit, bent, crippled,*
like an old man.

She heard Agwé: "Blood blends with water."

She could feel his spirit filling her body. She took the point of
Agwé's sword, slicing his symbol into her palm. A line for a ship's
mast, another for a sail, another for the boat slicing the water.

"I am yours," she whispered.

Blood drained down her wrist, between her fingers, onto the
floor. Drums resounded.

Blood speckled the floor.

"Agwé? Come."

Blood rushed through her body. Her heart's rhythm pumping

blood like water crashing against the shore. A shore swirling with blue-green currents, seaweed, and fish.

She was in a ship—reaching out of the water were skeletal hands, hands of the bones of people, Africans, who died during the Middle Passage. Agwé brandished his sword. Slicing through waves, thrusting at sea foam and kelp.

A shape rose from the water—not bone, not flesh—a plume of smoke. Smoke that dispersed in the air, reassembled. Shaping its self into a man.

Agwé stomped, his sword flailing.

The shadow man grew taller, like a giant, until it seemed to walk on water, until it blocked Agwé's ship from view. Blocked the full moon.

"The *wazimamoto*. It comes from the sea," Marie murmured.

"We'll send it back." DuLac intensified his drumming. *Boudom.*

Candle flames flickered high, elongating, sending up smoke, mimicking Marie's spirit vision. The shadow figure grew, threatening to overtake the entire ocean, the horizon, the sky. Agwé had disappeared.

"Say your name," said DuLac.

"Marie."

She pressed her bloodied hand to her heart. "Marie." *She felt an overwhelming desire to feed. She studied her palm. The wound was still bleeding. Her tongue flicked the salty blood. She sucked her palm as hard as a child at her mother's breast. Like waves, the blood flowed out and back into her body. An endless loop, like the sea's pulse.*

She heard Agwé: "Blood blends with water." *Heard another voice, more feminine: "Blood trumps water. Bloodlines. Nothing stronger. Je suis Marie."*

And she knew in her soul it was Marie from the painting speaking. Marie, the feared and most revered Voodoo Queen. The great, most famous, infamous Marie.

She felt her body tilting sideways. Some force gently pressing until her cheek rested on the floor. She focused on her open hand, bleeding, glowing with Agwé's ship, drawn in blood. She could see all the other Maries. Her mother; Marie Laveau's daughter; Marie Laveau. Laveau's mother, grandmother, and great-grandmother, Membe, the African slave. A line of women stretching back to Eve.

But Marie Laveau shone brighter than all the others—the New World voodooienne, healing, in touch with her feminine power. Doing good in the world. This was her mother—more than all the others. More than her birth mother. This Marie—the healer. Her truest ancestor.

"Ask," said DuLac. "Ask who, what it is."

The vision was fading.

"No, don't go. Please. I'm a healer, too."

The room became colder. Marie's breath was smoke. The candles flamed higher.

Marie Laveau's spirit entered her, possessing.

She remembered: dancing in Congo Square; walking on the waters of Lake Pontchartrain. Healing, ministering to the ill, the poor. Intimidating cruel masters, aiding escaped slaves. "Je suis Marie." Haughty, arrogant, when she needed to be. Joyful in her power.

"It's here," shouted DuLac. "The *wazimamoto.*"

Marie stood, staring down the thing in the corner. Protecting her blood, bloodlines.

The wazimamoto *had cheekbones, brown eyes, hands that tapered from wrist to fingers. It wore clothes: a black suit and a cravat, sparkling black boots.*

"Hello, John," Marie Laveau said.

The shadow man opened its mouth and wailed. A sound between pain and rage.

Marie Laveau stuck her bloodied hand, Agwé's sign, where John's heart should be. She felt the evil, yet she also felt how he was made evil. There was a rapid fluttering of images: a ship; slave shackles; branding; a ruthless whipping. Then John's evil: strangling a free colored for money; beating a mulatto until she submitted to rape.

"I killed you before, John. Do you remember my serpent?

"Damballah," she murmured.

Conjured out of air, Damballah, a rainbow-colored snake, circled John, tightening, choking, until he began to disintegrate, losing clothes, features, torso, limbs. Until he disappeared.

Marie Laveau stretched her arms wide. Relishing sensation, being inside a body. She swayed to the drums.

"You are me, child," she whispered inside Marie's head. "Find John's gris-gris, his secret of youth. The emblem from his tribe.

"You are me. A woman of power. You can defeat John, as I did.

"Look to the painting. It holds the blood tale."

Marie collapsed. DuLac cradled her. She felt she was drowning, pulled by an undertow of emotions emptying her out.

"You're safe. You're safe," DuLac kept repeating.

The doorbell jangled. There was pounding on the door. "Doc? DuLac!"

"Here, Parks," shouted DuLac, helping Marie to sit.

Parks was on the threshold, chest heaving. "Doc, you all right?"
She nodded.

"I found you gone," he said, exasperated. "Roach called. I got
here as soon as I could. Thought you'd want to know."

"What?" asked DuLac. "Another murder?"

"Alafin's dead. Another man, too."

DuLac sat back on his heels, his face drained. "I just spoke with
him."

"Someone reported a murder. Officers found an old man dead.
Professor Alafin, less than an hour ago. Bloodless.

"I came looking for you and Marie, first at the apartment. Then
here."

"DuLac, I think we could use a drink," said Marie. "Plain rum."

"You're hurt." Parks took out his handkerchief, wrapping it
around Marie's hand. A bruise flowered on her face.

"Let me get some ice," said Parks.

"No, stay. The *wazimamoto* was here. Must've come after the
murders. It was more alive than ever."

"Here." DuLac handed glasses all around. "It wore clothes. It
must have some kind of lair. I wouldn't have believed it if I hadn't
seen it. A barely visible mist, now almost a man."

"It drew on the organic substance we have in the lab. Feeding
would have accelerated its growth."

"You did a ceremony," said Parks, softly accusing.

"Yes. Just me and DuLac," said Marie. "I needed to understand
a few things."

"Do you? Understand?"

"Some. Look." Marie drew Parks and DuLac to the painting.
"This Marie, my anscestor, conducted ceremonies, blending

Catholicism and voodoo into a powerful force against oppression. In the painting, hundreds—rich and poor, slave and free, black and white—watched Marie dancing with a snake, before a bonfire.

"See that figure there?" In the background, the painting's far-left corner, Marie pointed at an alleyway beside St. Louis Cathedral. "You almost don't notice him." An indistinct figure stood in the shadows watching Marie Laveau conduct her ceremony.

"This is John. He discovered Marie Laveau. Wooed her from her grandmère. Introduced her to voodoo."

"I don't understand," said Parks.

DuLac poured more rum for each of them. "Laveau's mother was crucified. John did nothing to save her. The grandmother escaped, hiding her infant granddaughter in the bayou. Raising her Catholic.

"Marie Laveau knew nothing about who she was.

"When Marie reached puberty," DuLac continued, "John seduced her away from her grandmother. Heritage and sex—a powerful combination."

"He manipulated her. Misused her power. Eventually, she killed him. Strangled him with a snake." Marie shivered.

"You're cold," said Parks, wrapping his coat around her.

"Marie loved him. Hated him. He fathered her child," said Marie.

"That means," said DuLac, draining his rum. "John is also your ancestor."

"Great-great-grandfather."

"I don't get it," said Parks. "Why try to hurt your descendant?"

"Self-hatred," answered DuLac. "Isn't that what Alafin said was key?"

"Jealously, too, at least according to Laveau's journal. He hated his lack of power. Hated the matrilineal line of Maries. In Africa, he was a king's son. Slavery stole his status. Self-respect. Everything."

"Part of the blame for voodoo's poor reputation," said DuLac, "is because of John. Voodoo, for him, meant trouncing enemies. Black, white, it didn't matter.

"He spread the rumor of 'goats without horns'—the supposed sacrifice of white babies. He ran a house of prostitution. Invested in slave ships. Ran auctions. A man who both hated and identified with the colonizers."

"Motive," said Parks. "John used the Maries to serve his ambition."

"Enough motive to resurrect himself as a *wazimamoto*," said DuLac. "Especially when a powerful new Voodoo Queen has been found."

"Do you think John knew Alafin?" asked Parks. "That would mean he has consciousness. Premeditation." Parks swallowed rum. "Fucking bloodsucker."

"Back to its watery grave," said DuLac. He poured more rum. "Bottoms up."

Parks looked around the room. The candles on the altar and floor, the array of black-and white-faced statues on the altar. A drawing of Damballah on the wall. The painting of Marie, her face lit by fire and moonlight.

"John's motive is revenge," Parks said.

"If he feeds on me, he'll have the power he always wanted. Doubling the power generated from hatred."

"He'll become a complete man, haunting the Quarter. Killing," said DuLac.

"Unbelievable," said Parks. "No, I mean, I believe you both. I've just never been involved in something so horrible. I don't know how to solve this. Capture a *wazimamoto.*"

"I do," said Marie. "But I need to find John's gris-gris, his charm. An emblem he had from his tribe."

"How're you going to do that?" asked Parks.

"I don't know yet." She felt an overwhelming desire to see Marie-Claire.

"How much time have we got?" asked DuLac.

"Maybe a few days. If that. He's been killing more frequently."

"Rest, Marie," said DuLac. "Plenty of time to talk tomorrow. You've notified Alafin's family?" he asked Parks.

"Yes."

"Will you be all right, DuLac?"

"I want to drink myself into a stupor. Nine dead. My dear friend."

Sympathetically, Parks offered his hand; DuLac clung to it.

Marie's fingers grazed the painting. Down right, almost as an afterthought, the painter had brushed in musicians. Brass players. Another drummer. A quintet.

Marie crossed the threshold into the hall. She vaguely heard DuLac and Parks whispering.

She felt soul weary. Sorrow for DuLac. All the many people dead.

She walked out of DuLac's ornate home, down the porch steps, to her car.

"Let me drive you."

"No."

"Follow you."

"I'll be fine, Parks. What were you and DuLac talking about?"

"He wanted to know if I found Alafin's tape recorder. I told him no." His irises flared.

"But you did. Find it. I can tell."

Parks grimaced. "No one should have to hear that tape." He kissed her deeply, thoroughly. His hand gently stroked her breast.

Marie sighed. "It feels good when you touch me."

"Let me touch you some more."

She clung to him, letting passion sweep over her. Aroused, Parks kissed her face, her neck. Part of her wanted him now. She'd unzip his pants. Let him enter her. It didn't matter who saw.

She leaned away. "Tomorrow, Parks. Let's talk tomorrow."

"Talk?" He was the surfer boy again. Cocky. Sweet. Nibbling on her ear.

"I want to be with my child tonight."

Instantly, his expression was serious.

"I understand. I'll come by tomorrow, around four. Take you and Marie-Claire to the Riverwalk. Dog, too. We can eat beignets and drink café au lait. Chocolate milk for Marie-Claire. Water for Dog."

"He likes beignets, too."

"Okay. A beignet for Dog. Two. A dozen for me, you, and Marie-Clarie."

Marie laughed. "Thank you, Parks." Then her expression grew grave. She inhaled the damp mist. Rested her head on his chest.

Parks hugged her, his hands sliding to her crotch. "Tomorrow, we can steal an hour? Can't we?"

"Afterward, we've got to get Marie-Claire out of town. Until it's over, I can't be near her. You'll take her to DuLac?"

"Agreed." He kissed her brow. "I'm still going to follow you home."

She slid into her car. She waited a minute, watching through the rearview mirror, Parks getting into his patrol car. He flicked his lights.

Marie turned on the engine. Almost midnight. It felt good. Knowing Parks was following her home.

The "Maries." Everywhere he turned, every attempt to fix his power, there were the Maries. Foolish, naive. And when he made them whole—capable of wielding power—they betrayed him.

Without him, they lacked ambition. With him, they would have ruled the world. The latest incarnation was a backwater healer; protected by the Marie he'd made the most formidable—the Marie who long ago had killed him.

He'd been lost, waiting in the sea for resurrection. Hate was his life's blood. Hate for those who'd enslaved him, sought to castrate him. Colonizing him. Hatred for those people who didn't rebel against slavery. Hatred for the weak women blessed with spiritual power.

Hate kept him alive and now that he had risen, he'd wreak his revenge.

He'd wield power without the Maries. Surviving on the blood-laced evil of men like Rudy, the weakness of a JT, of silly whores.

By blood, he'd live. By blood, he'd rule.

By blood, he'd undo any need for the Maries.

SEVENTEEN

The day was glorious. Bright, sunny. Kind Dog was chasing seagulls. Marie-Claire was squealing. Marie had given her a rainbow lollipop for promising to stay in her stroller.

Parks was lighthearted, happy. He wore a Hawaiian shirt and sandals.

"You look ridiculous," she said.

"Hey. This is my best Hang Ten shirt."

"If your fellow officers saw you, they'd laugh."

Marie slowly pushed the stroller on the boardwalk.

Marie-Claire shouted, "Dog! See gull."

Kind Dog, tail wagging, perked his ears. He made one last dash at a gull, before running back to Marie-Claire.

"Dog! Dog!"

Marie sat on the bench, smiling at Dog licking the sugar from

Marie-Claire's face. Shading her eyes, she watched the steamships churning the Mississippi.

Part of her didn't want to do battle. She wanted to sit here, in the sun, seeing the world as ordinary, *being* ordinary, a woman dating a man. Only ordinary dramas threatening her family.

Kind Dog sat, leaning his body against Marie's knee. Marie-Claire, eyes closing, leaned back in her stroller. Her lollipop rested on her sky blue shirt.

"I'm not sure how much time we have," she said.

Parks dug in his pocket for his cigarettes. "I was trying not to smoke."

"Don't smoke around Marie-Claire."

"All right. Fine." He stuffed the cigarettes back into his pocket. "At least we've got a reprieve. We've got today."

He clasped her face. "You're crying."

Kind Dog started whimpering, empathizing with Marie. His nose nudged her hand.

"I'm not crying."

"Could've fooled me."

Marie studied the passersby. Young couples, strolling, linking arms. Children, wearing Aquarium of the Americas T-shirts, cartwheeling on the grass. An elderly woman fed bread to pigeons; three boys fished off the pier. Families, not partying tourists, were enjoying the day—sunshine, popcorn, and the strains of jazz from tourist ships puttering down the river.

"Laveau said, 'You are me.'"

"Are you?"

"Yes, I think so. Like me, she valued voodoo's healing power—physical and spiritual. It's not an accident that I became a doctor.

Murder isn't something we're good at. Physicians swear, 'Do no harm.'

"Laveau said: 'Find John's gris-gris bag, his secret of youth. The emblem from his tribe.'"

"It's a clue?"

"Yes."

Parks said, "Good. That I can help with." He took his pack of cigarettes out again, frowned, and stuffed it back into his pocket. "You know, I've been thinking about getting the hell out of New Orleans. Bad romance. More murders, more corruption in one year than I've seen in seven years as a cop. Then this bloodsucker. Leckie's death. Roach says the department won't suspend me. They might even give me a medal. Figures." He shaded his eyes.

His tattoo was fully visible. A thin sword covered by briars. Swirls of lightning.

Her fingers stroked the tattoo. "What's this?"

"I had it done when I was fourteen."

"So you were the Eagle Scout. The kid who thought he could slay dragons. Awaken the sleeping beauty."

"Stop it."

"I'm sorry."

"I always wanted to be a cop. For a long while, I've been wearing down. Then I made love to you. I was thinking maybe I could stay. Here. In New Orleans. Maybe I've been looking for the girl who needed me. Depended on me. You're not that woman. Okay, I get that."

She kissed him, letting her mouth linger on his.

"Do you want me to stay?"

Marie held on to him. Her arms circling his waist, feeling the pounding of his heart, the shuddering of his lungs.

She knew the speech had cost Parks. She was beginning to understand more than ever how vulnerable, how sweet he was. He could be tough, hold emotions in check, "protect and serve." In his own way, he was healing, too. Making the world better. A cop and a doctor. Both seeing the worst humanity could do to itself.

"Help me get Marie-Claire and Dog packed. El and DuLac will watch over her. Maybe take her out of New Orleans."

"You're not going to answer me?"

"I can't answer you. We've got a crime to solve."

"Fair enough." Parks stood, offering Marie his hand. Marie took it, rising. He didn't let go. "Afterward?"

"We'll talk afterward."

"So where do we start? Where do we find this gris-gris?"

"I think the answer was in the painting. I think we start at Cathedral Square."

Marie slipped the lollipop from the sleeping Marie-Claire's fist.

Kind Dog panted, licking his mouth.

"Not for you," said Marie, dropping the lollipop into the trash.

"Sun's going down," said Parks.

"I know." The horizon streaked with blood red, like a wounding. "We should hurry."

Kind Dog barked at a man flashing by on Rollerblades.

Marie-Claire, startled, wailed big, wallowing cries.

"Dog. Come!" Marie shouted as Kind Dog made another dash at a gull.

Tail tucked beneath his flanks, Kind Dog followed Parks and Marie, pushing the stroller, to the Riverwalk garage.

⚹

Marie slipped Marie-Claire into her crib. She'd fallen back asleep.

The blackbird mobile was still. Kind Dog stretched out beneath the crib, as if it were his special cave. Marie stooped, rubbing his belly. Dog stretched, rolling onto his back.

"Such a pretty dog. Such a good dog." His fur was so smooth, silky. Dog flipped himself over and licked Marie's face. She patted his head, rubbed his ears. "I'll be back. Watch Marie-Claire."

Dog cocked his head, then licked her again. She closed the bedroom door.

"Parks, did you call DuLac?"

"Just did. Told him we'd be over in less than an hour."

Marie pulled a suitcase from the closet.

"Alafin was cremated today," said Parks.

"A quick burial protects from evil spirits. There probably wasn't an autopsy."

"No, I don't think so."

"Good. I think Alafin would've thought it was a desecration.

"We all need a break from New Orleans," she said, grimly. "Parks, in the kitchen, you'll find Marie-Claire's oatmeal, some jars of food, her favorite biscuits. Bananas. In the refrigerator, there's soy milk. Put it in a bag. I'll pack her clothes. Ten minutes, Parks."

"Ten minutes and we're out of here."

Kind Dog started barking.

Marie ran to the bedroom door. "It's locked. Parks!"

Marie could hear Dog growling, barking; she'd never heard him so fierce. Parks threw his shoulder against the door; the frame splintered but didn't break.

She could hear Dog grunting, growling, as if he was trying to tear something. Marie-Claire's cry became more high pitched.

"I'm coming, baby. I'm coming."

"Stand back." Parks fired two shots at the lock.

Dog was yelping. Snarling. Then, his yelp turned into a whine.

Parks threw himself against the door again. It exploded open.

Marie ran to the crib. Marie-Claire was standing, crying, face red, arms raised, wanting to be held. Marie gathered her up, holding tightly.

Parks, gun drawn, searched the room. "Nothing's here. Is she all right?"

Marie checked Marie-Claire's wrists. "He didn't touch her. Dog?"

"By the window."

Holding Marie-Claire so she couldn't see, Marie saw Dog, his neck twisted, broken. He wasn't drained. Except for the unnatural angle of his neck, Dog appeared asleep.

"Spite," she murmured. "John killed Dog for spite. I should've known better."

"This isn't your fault."

Marie-Claire quieted, her face buried in Marie's neck. Her pudgy fingers wrapped about her mother's neck.

"Reneaux and I rescued him. He was our Dog."

"Come on, Marie." Parks was opening drawers, gathering clothes. "We've got to get out of here."

She'd have to mourn Kind Dog later. "Sleepwear is in the bottom drawer."

"I'll meet you in the car. You and Marie-Clarie. Just get out of here."

Marie turned, forgetting that Marie-Claire could see Dog over her shoulder.

"Dog!" Marie-Claire screamed.

Marie wanted to shelter her child; but she also didn't want to lie to her. "Something came into the house and hurt him, Marie-Claire. We have to get out of here to be safe. Let's go see Uncle DuLac," said Marie, distracting her. "Auntie El."

"Dog, too?"

"No. We'll come back and bury Dog later. We'll find a beautiful spot for him to sleep and we'll plant flowers."

Marie-Claire started to cry.

Marie hurried down the stairs, feathering Marie-Claire's face with kisses; in the car she snapped her into the car seat.

Parks rushed out of the courtyard. He put a bag and a suitcase in the backseat. "Another car ride, Marie-Claire."

"Bye-bye."

"That's right. Going bye-bye." Parks shut the rear door, then moved round to the driver's-seat door. Key in, ignition engaged, he steered into traffic.

Marie peered into the night, a black cloak shrouding New Orleans. Night unleashed all kinds of passion.

Hatred swelled. "I'm going to kill it tonight. John won't hurt another soul. Ever."

EIGHTEEN

Marie and Parks stood before St. Louis Cathedral. Far enough back, they could survey the entire scene. The lawn where Laveau had conducted her ceremony. The street that had once been filled with horses, carriages. Hundreds of people, some worshipping, others indulging in thrill seeking, had created a circle, a perimeter around her.

At DuLac's, Marie had studied the painting, trying to impress the details on her mind. Now at the site, she tried to re-create the painting. Ignoring the tourists, the violinist playing for tips. The shopkeepers and tarot readers.

"In the painting, the bonfire is centered," she said. "The drummers are on the far right. Farther right, the other musicians. The disapproving priest would've been at the door, near the pillar."

"The sky was more overcast," said Parks. "But it must've been hot, like tonight. Many were barefoot; the women didn't wear shawls."

"Laveau wore a white shift." She moved through the flowing crowd to the center of the lawn, in front of the cathedral door, in line with the rooftop crucifix. She imagined the bonfire. Laveau possessed.

John would've been behind her, on the right. In the alley, beside the cathedral. Pirate's Alley. How he must've watched, envied Laveau.

"Come on," she said to Parks. "We should check the alley."

It was dank, dark. Only a block long, extending from Chartres to Royal Street. On one side was the church; on the other, the Cabildo, the old Spanish governor's mansion.

"Legend has it that Pirate Alley's been a hiding place for criminals. Robbers used to attack those leaving Mass," she said. "Or murder a double-dealing pirate. Rape a girl."

The cobblestone path was laid by slaves. Halfway down the alley was a lamppost; its glow weak.

"No doors anywhere," said Parks. "No entry into the church. If you're looking for a hiding place, it's not here."

Marie let her hands roam over the moss-laced bricks. They were solid, cemented with history, blood. "This is a perfect hiding place. A cathedral. A governor's mansion. Crimes might happen in the alley, but who would violate a church, a governor's mansion?"

Parks ran his fingers between bricks, pressing the dirt-and-smoke-stained caulk. "This stuff is solid. Better built than anything in this century."

Marie, her back against the church wall, looked left, right. At the end of both sides of the alley, normal tourist life passed by. Think. Feel.

"What're you doing?"

"Sssh, Parks." Marie looked skyward; the stars were bright, caught in a narrow sliver between the rooftops. All the bricks seemed in place. She closed her eyes, trying to conjure, a past time. What had been? A lost time when slaves, free coloreds, conquerors, and the conquered mixed. Where a Voodoo Queen made an attempt to heal.

Marie shuddered. "Nothing." No visions, no clues from the past.

"John's changed his tactics," said Parks. "He killed Alafin, Dog, without being called. There wasn't any music. No drums."

"He just *was*—present. He's gaining control."

"Have you seen JT, Rudy? Any of the other ghosts?"

"No," Marie pushed off from the wall. "I haven't. They might help."

"Can you call them?"

"Maybe. Before, they just appeared." When did they stop? It upset her that she hadn't missed them.

"JT helped me believe," said Parks.

Marie smiled. "Taking Wire's sticks. He wanted me to solve his murder."

"They all do."

"Let's get to it." Marie moved farther down the alley, where John, shrouded in darkness, had watched Laveau. Marie turned back around. At the alley's east end, people were partying, drifting by, some stumbling, drunk; the silver-painted man was playing statue; a man made music with a washbucket; the river was black, dotted with ships.

"JT? Rudy?" she called softly, like a lover. "I need you. Please. There," she pointed. "Can you see?"

Parks craned his neck. "No. But I never saw Tinkerbell either."

Across the street, near a park bench, beneath a wide willow, JT and Rudy stood, side by side. One by one, the other dead appeared at their side. Sarah, two other women, Alafin, and she guessed the Nigerian Alafin had tried to interview.

People flowed around and through them.

"Do dogs have ghosts?"

"Yes," Marie answered. "Everything alive has spiritual essence." *She saw Kind Dog, sitting, subdued, as he never did while alive.*

"Come on, boy," Marie called.

Dog came at a trot, the others followed, close behind.

"I feel them," said Parks. "It's freezing."

"Dog is nuzzling your hand."

Parks moved his hand up, and away. Then, he let it settle, hovering over air. "Good dog."

Marie swallowed a smile, then looked at all the sad-eyed ghosts. A band of nine. Slack jawed and restless.

"Somewhere, here, is John's gris-gris, a bag filled with all the charmed herbs, soil that protected him, kept him young. Help us."

Alafin stepped close, close enough for Marie's hand to pass through his hand, for her to feel both cold and timeless energy. He moved deliberately down the alley, coming to a stop near a church gutter.

A rat scurried out of a drain, its fur brushing against the brick, its feet tracking dirt from the crease between the cobblestones and the wall. Then it furrowed into a hole nearer the cathedral's southwest corner.

"Parks, come see." At the building's corner, the last foundation brick touching the earth was discolored. Red instead of gray.

Parks pulled out a knife, the tip digging at the earth, the space between dirt and brick.

The ghosts swayed, fingers pointing at the spot. Their expressions feral, as if they, themselves, could be monsters draining blood. Dog snarled, baring gums and teeth.

"Move, Parks." Marie fell to her knees, digging, clawing with her hands. She felt hatred, vengeance rising in her, felt the fury of the ghosts, her own anguish over Dog's loss, Laveau's torment.

She felt such ire. John would destroy her, Marie-Clarie. All the descendants down through the generations. Her nails cracked and chipped.

"Marie," Parks shouted.

She dug, frenzied. John's secrets lay here.

"Marie."

She felt a howl roiling in her belly.

"It's here," she shouted. "I know it's here."

"Let me help."

"It's mine to carry. All of it." Her hands threw up dirt, digging like a rabid dog.

"Marie." Parks gripped her hands. "I believe you. You're bleeding."

Her fingers were red; Agwé's symbol on her palm was speckling. Her rib cage ached.

"Let me help." Parks dug with his knife. Penetrating deep, deeper. "Something hard."

"That's it," said Marie.

Then, all of them—Parks, Marie, Dog, and the ghosts—peered into the hole. Parks lit his lighter.

The small flame shone on a box.

"My god," said Parks.

"Voodoo gods," answered Marie.

She crouched, gently wiping away dirt. The box was small: four by four inches. It had a lock, but time, erosion, had rusted it, broken it in two.

Marie turned to the small band of ghosts. "Thank you."

The ghosts and their cold faded.

"They're gone," said Parks.

"Yes, and I hope this will help destroy John."

She clasped the lid, hesitating.

This was the second time, as a *voodooienne,* she'd been called upon to hurt. Destroy. Was this why her mother had hidden her heritage?

Marie lifted the lid. A blue silk bag, weathered with age. "His gris-gris. Everything inside it made John who he was." She tasted the grains. "Asafatida," she said. "A powerful root." She lifted strands of hair. "John's. Part of his essence." She smelled. "Grave dust, perhaps."

"What does that do?"

"Maybe protected him from the Guédé? I don't know." She fingered a snakeskin. Her lips pursed. "Bones. A cat's femur. A rodent's spine. Predators like him."

"What's that?"

Marie tugged at worn leather, gently pulling it out of the bag. She held it high; a piece of ivory dangled from the bottom. "His family's emblem."

She laid it in Parks's hand.

"Lion marks?"

"I think you're right."

"Cold." *Parks was lifted, tossed brutally across the alley.*

Marie held tightly to the gris-gris. *John lifted her to her feet, shaking her like a rag doll.*

"*Mine.*" His voice was real this time, sounding like rocks falling on stone.

"Parks," she screamed, throwing him the bag. "Hide it. Get it away."

"I can't leave you." He fired his gun. Beyond the alley, tourists screamed.

John's shoulder jerked, the green substance drained.

"Please, Parks. Run," shouted Marie.

"I'll empty it." Parks held the gris-gris bag upside down. "All of it. All I have to do is untie the string."

John roared.

From far off, sirens wailed.

"Let her go," Parks demanded.

Marie dug her nails into John's arm. Beads of green. Sea-based bacteria.

John's face was fully drawn; she could see the marking, three diagonal lines, like the emblem, on his face.

"I'm warning you. Let her go."

Police cars stopped at either end of the alley. Shouts: "Put the gun down. On the ground."

Parks didn't move.

John stared into Marie's eyes; she saw fury, hatred. "You belong to me."

She felt certain he'd kill her. She exhaled, clearing her mind of all thoughts, emotions except love for Marie-Claire. Sweet baby Marie.

The police fired a shot. "On the ground."

John disappeared.

"Put the gun down."

Parks laid the gun on the ground. Held his hands high. "Detective Parks," he called. "Shield 682."

Police slowly moved in from each end of the alley.

"You all right, Parks? Where's the other man?"

Marie slid down the wall, blocking out sounds. Just breathing. Understanding that John would never kill her body, just her soul.

Foreboding washed over her. Vindictive, John wanted control. How better to control her than take away all she loved?

Parks's cell rang. He answered. As he listened, he looked at Marie.

"No," she screamed. "Tell me Marie-Claire's fine."

"I don't know. Come on." Parks grabbed her hand, running to Pirate Alley's end. He commandeered a patrol car. Clicked on the siren. "Move, people!" he shouted, his hand punching the horn. "Move!"

Panic and frustration kept building. The car couldn't move fast enough. Marie prayed. Calling upon Damballah's mercy. Her ancestors. Marie Laveau.

DuLac's house was ominously well lit. Lights blazed from every window.

Marie dashed out of the car.

"Wait," shouted Parks, drawing his gun.

She raced up the porch stairs, bursting inside the house. "DuLac! El."

The telephone was off its hook. Police officers were in the parlor.

"DuLac? Marie-Claire. Is she all right?"

The kitchen was deserted. A butcher knife lay on its side next to raw chicken. A glass of wine had been overturned.

Marie ran down the hall. DuLac lay across the altar, drained; his flesh, crepe paper thin. A forensics expert was powdering the altar for fingerprints.

"Marie-Claire!" she screamed.

"In here, Dr. Laveau. Across the hall." Roach was in the guest bedroom, holding a sleeping Marie-Claire in his arms.

"Let me hold her." Marie kissed her brow, holding tight to her relaxed, chubby limbs.

"El, that's her name, right? Died protecting her," Roach said, his voice low.

El had been thrown onto the bed, her blood drained. Her skin no longer looked young; wrinkles covered her face; her red nails were more witchlike.

"DuLac, too. As far as I can make out, DuLac let himself be bait."

"He gave El time to escape," said Parks.

"She almost made it. Look here." Roach moved to the window. "I almost didn't see it. The curtain was caught by the window frame when El closed it."

A piece of torn lace was caught on the window's metal tracks.

Parks opened the window. "El laid Marie-Claire in the grass. She might've had time to escape, too."

"Maybe," said Roach. "Instead, she bolted the door. See." He pointed at the splintered wood and broken lock. "To buy time."

"Buy time?" whispered Marie.

"DuLac had phoned the police."

Marie shifted Marie-Claire onto her shoulder. She pulled her cell from her jeans pocket. "'Missed call.' He called me, too."

"Let's try and get you and Marie-Claire to a safe place," murmured Parks.

Marie ran her fingers through her daughter's curls.

Parks embraced them both. "Let's get out of here. Another state. New Jersey."

"No. I have to stay. In New Orleans. I won't run as my mother did. Run, and you never stop.

"Roach, when you take," she swallowed, "DuLac and El, will you take Marie-Claire, too?"

"I'll do my best to protect her." The potbellied man blinked.

"Take her to the church priory. Maybe Father Donnelly can look after her better than I can. Just get her safely there."

"I will," said Roach, gathering the lightly snoring Marie-Claire.

Marie kissed her.

Roach signaled the attendants to collect the bodies.

Marie walked out of the room. Parks followed until they reached the parlor.

"You still have the gris-gris, don't you, Parks?" Marie asked.

"Yes. Why can't we just empty it? Won't that kill it?"

"I don't think so. John was threatened, no doubt. The gris-gris represents an important part of his self. Something to conjure with. But I think we'll need more. In Laveau's journal, she said, 'Sorrow comes in threes.'"

She opened her cell phone. She couldn't bring herself to press Voice Mail.

"I'll double-check on Roach, Marie-Claire."

"Thanks, Parks." She went to the hall phone, dialed Charity.

"Carlos Gutierrez. Hospital lab, please."

Roach passed by, a blanket covering Marie-Claire. Behind him came El's body on the gurney. A hand, fingernails painted red, dangled outside the sheet.

Marie turned her back to them. "Yes, Carlos. It's me. Any luck on the cultures? Good. Penicillin it is." The first antibiotic. "Can you make a spray?"

"You should look at this," interrupted Parks, holding the painting of Laveau's ceremony at Cathedral Square.

Laveau's face had been scratched out. The oil scarred and flaked. In blood—DuLac's blood?—the letters J-O-H-N had been scrawled.

"I'm not surprised," she said softly, studying the scene. "It named itself. Not just *wazimamoto*. Also, imitation man. It can be hurt. Your gun wounded it. But we'll need far more."

She spoke breathlessly into the phone. "Carlos, bring the spray to Preservation Hall. Hurry."

The screen door opened; the attendants had returned for DuLac.

"Parks, I need Wire."

"Why?"

"He's the third ingredient."

Marie walked back into the red velvet parlor. "DuLac?" She felt, rather than saw, his presence.

She turned, just in time to see DuLac's body carried from the house.

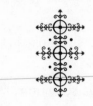

NINETEEN

PRESERVATION HALL

WEDNESDAY, EARLY MORNING

Morning, 2:10 AM. They were in the small dressing room of Preservation Hall. "Bourbon Street Blues" was playing in the club.

Dressed in white, Marie had tried her best to purify herself. She'd taken a milk bath, lit candles to the gods. Made a special offering to Agwé. Part of John was sea organisms, in Agwé's dominion. She'd fixed a platter of rice for Damballah. The snake god had once killed John. She'd prayed, said a rosary. Asked for grace from both Christian and voodoo saints.

Marie looked at the three men: Wire, Carlos, and Parks.

"Thank you for coming. I can't do this without you."

"*De nada*. Anything for the Madonna," said Carlos.

Marie grimaced. "I'm not her."

"Just the New World Voodoo Queen. 'Wicked as a snake, strong as a bear—'"

"Funny, Wire."

"I think he's on to something, Doc," Parks chimed. "A little levity goes a long way."

"I know. Just to be clear," she looked at each man in turn, "we could all die."

Wire shrugged. "Got to go sometime."

Parks's hair was matted to his forehead. His jacket off, you could see the two holsters beneath his arms. "There was another murder tonight. Ten. The papers are filled with vampire tales."

"My girlfriend bought extra crosses. Garlic."

"Dracula didn't birth John," said Parks.

"Too bad," said Carlos.

"No precolonial fix," said Marie. In medicine, she followed her hunches. This was no different. Except in medicine, only the patient died. In this, they all could.

Marie looked at her three champions.

"Did you bring it, Carlos?"

He pulled a small aerosol can from his pocket.

"Test it."

Carlos puffed a spurt of mist.

"Good. Keep it ready."

Carlos made the sign of the cross.

"I call it?" asked Wire. "My drums are the bait?"

"Not entirely, Wire. You've asked some of the musicians to stay?"

"They all want to—the entire band, right after this gig. After the last set, usually it's 'Take the A Train.'"

"We don't need them all. Do we, Doc?" asked Parks. "We're risking enough lives."

"Try and get rid of them," said Wire.

"I could make them," said Parks, his hand on his gun.

"It's okay, Parks."

"You said, 'Not entirely,'" said Wire. "My drums weren't entirely the bait. What else am I supposed to do?"

"Improvise."

"I don't get it."

"Just play, Wire. You and the others, play for all you're worth."

"Agwé's rhythm."

"Any rhythm that moves you. Play your heart and soul."

"What do I do?" asked Parks.

"The gris-gris bag. Empty it. Break the emblem."

Parks nodded.

"If the worst happens, if John drains me, keep Marie-Claire safe." She stretched out her hand to Carlos and Wire. "All three of you. Can you do that? Promise me? Swear?"

"Three musketeers," said Carlos.

"You may need to leave New Orleans," said Marie.

"Since *mi madre* died, I have nothing to keep me here."

"Wire?"

"No one's needed me for anything before. My family believed in voodoo stuff; I play jazz because there's never been a for-real Voodoo Queen until you. I've been waiting for you. Thought I'd die before you came."

"Parks?"

Parks was once again the restrained cop. Stoic. Unreadable. Music wafted into the room; you could hear patrons clapping and stomping after the tenor sax solo.

"Parks, please? I need you to do this for me."

"Water," said Parks. "As long as it's near water."

Marie kissed his cheek.

Wire stood: "I'm going to listen to the last set. Get inspired."

"Time enough to pray to the Madonna. I'll be out back, saying a rosary for us."

"Carlos, keep the canister ready."

"You bet."

Parks gripped Marie's hands, turning her around. Face-to-face, they stood.

"What's in the spray?"

"A scientist's cure, I hope."

Parks brushed his lips against hers. "They're giving us time alone," he whispered.

"Sweet of them," murmured Marie.

Parks embraced her, tight, hard. Still serious, he caressed her cheek. "I didn't take you for a one-night stand."

"I do them all the time," said Marie.

"But not with me."

He sat, pulling her down onto his lap.

"Hey—"

"I know. Let me hold you."

She rested her head on his shoulder, feeling his arms tighten about her waist.

"Your turn to be strong will come soon enough," he said.

"So it's your turn now?"

"No. I'm not being strong. I'm just loving you."

Three thirty AM. Preservation Hall customers had drifted back to their pricey hotels. Waiters and waitresses counted their tips, then went to the Café du Monde for breakfast.

Following Marie's instructions, the musicians had moved nightclub tables and chairs against the wall. There was open space for her to dance.

Dede nodded, and bowed, signaling that all was ready to start. All of them were conspirators. But Marie knew none of them appreciated how dangerous this ceremony would be.

None of them—except, perhaps, Parks—had guessed she wasn't certain of success. Her plan was instinctual. Like a diagnosis for what might heal, there were no guarantees.

She instructed Carlos to place candles at the room's four corners.

Wire whispered to the musicians, inspiring them like a priest his flock.

Parks cleaned his guns.

With chalk, Marie drew Agwé's boat sign, three wavy lines beneath it to indicate the sea. She placed John's gris-gris on the boat; then she drew Damballah's sign. A rainbow arcing over a snake. The rainbow to recall creation. Antithesis to destruction.

Marie looked about the bland hall. Windows were blackened and shuttered. The bar was clean, amber liquid and beer bottles sparkling in the mirror.

None of the ghosts had appeared; but she felt certain DuLac would come.

Between the rainbow and the snake, Marie laid John's emblem, then she chanted, "Honor the tribe. Dishonor John's cruelty."

She looked about the hall. All the musicians, somber, intent, watched her.

She inhaled. "All of us make magic." A murmuring rose from the bandstand.

"Let's begin," she said. "Time to begin."

Wire began on the *djembe*—*boudom,* announcing his presence, the ceremony's start.

"*Je suis* Marie. I am Marie," she said fiercely, with pride.

Wire shifted rhythms, his hands flying across cat skins, syncopated, driving. She recognized Damballah's, then Agwé's rhythm.

"From the heart, Wire. Speak your heart."

He looked at her glassy-eyed, his palms slowing. His head rolled forward; then, gradually, the sound shifted time. A blending of six-eighths and one-sixteenth time. Unique. His palms sliding, snapping, cupping against the *djembe*. A rhythm from Wire's heart.

Marie swayed. Her dress brushed against her legs, her bare feet tapped the rough-hewn floor.

"Mercy," Marie murmured. "Have mercy."

Carlos was on his knees, his crucifix, pressed to his lips. "*Madre,*" "Madonna," fell from his lips.

Parks, a sentinel, was alert.

The other musicians cradled their instruments, expectant. The pianist stroked his ivory keys without making a sound.

The drum was dislodging Marie's present self, connecting her to impulses, drive, desires.

To a time before time.

"Legba, remove the barrier for me. So the spirits will come through."

She felt drumming in her bones; she danced, her body talking to the rhythm. A cold breeze stirred in the closed-window room. The candles flamed higher.

Parks stepped forward, searching. From where the wind blew.

Marie danced before Wire; his heart was in his hands. Sweat streamed down his face.

"Now, Wire. Make your sound. Make a community."

Lips trembling, his entire body engaged in the drumming, the sound filtering through his soul, Wire nodded at the clarinetist.

A sweet tenor rose, in and around the *djembe*'s sound.

Parks paced the room, squaring off the four corners.

DuLac appeared upstage right.

Marie rejoiced. Her plan might work.

She twirled, her arms isolating the drum's rhythm. She murmured, "Come. Legba, come."

Legba arrived, bent over his walking stick. He opened the spirit door.

"Come."

Marie Laveau appeared. Regal, her hair in a chignon, gold hoop earrings, a rainbow-colored skirt shimmering with stars.

Marie opened her arms, embracing her ancestress. Her head jerked back. She was two: herself and Laveau, capable of unending power, clasping the moon, capturing a star, walking on water, delaying death.

Marie thought of all the dead—El, DuLac, Alafin, and all the other victims.

Rage reared. Bitter, encompassing. Marie bent, drawing a chalk line through the middle of the room.

"Come, John. I demand it."

Wire renewed his efforts; a sax added its voice, seductive, lamenting, to the drum and clarinet.

"Come, damn you."

The hall darkened; candles stopped burning.

She heard fearful voices. Feet stumbling in the darkness. Then Dede shouting, "Courage. What a woman stands, a man can stand. Play."

A trumpet blared bright, like Gabriel's horn.

The candles relit, shining brightly. A freezing wind swept through the room.

Parks undid his gun's safety.

The wazimamoto—*John—solid, seemingly human and alive, stood on the other side of the line. Cravat; black vest; form-fitting pants; elegance from another age. His hair was closely cropped; the scars on his face now like black worms. His eyes were midnight, not dilated, neither absorbing nor reflecting light.*

"Do you think you can destroy me?" John stepped forward; his strength seemed boundless.

"I did it once before," answered Marie.

John started forward, then stopped, looking about the room. "This is a trap."

"Is it? Are you afraid of me?"

John hissed.

"Women hand sight down through the generations. Mother to daughter," she murmured.

"No," John raged. "Why should that be? What have any of the Laveaus accomplished? Sniveling. Weak. For generations."

"But not me, John." She stepped backward. "Twenty-first-century women are stronger than you can imagine.

John stepped closer. "Then join me."

"Why should I? What have you to offer?"

"Power. People are controlled by fear."

"Like you, John? What do you fear?"

"Nothing."

"Liar." Marie motioned to Parks.

Parks picked up the emblem.

John's arm struck out.

Parks dodged him, swinging the emblem beyond John's reach.

"I should destroy him," said John.

"But you won't." Marie held her breath, knowing she needed to taunt John, dare him to make a mistake.

John's shoes touched the line. He pushed his face forward, drawing close. Closer.

Marie could smell rotting sea life and blood. She refused to flinch.

"You're not afraid of me," John said approvingly.

This close, John was unsettling. Marie felt his seductive power—what he was, had been, intoxicating, like wine. Her ancestor had once thought she'd loved him.

She looked at Carlos, signaling him to be ready.

"Join me," she said.

John reached for her.

Marie didn't move quickly enough. She gasped as her throat constricted, gagged.

Parks fired his gun. "Let her go."

Green liquid poured from John's leg. "You won't kill me."

Carlos inched closer, his voice chanting, "Hail Mary, full of grace . . ."

John snarled, "Stop it."

Carlos pressed, spraying the antibiotic into John's face.

John staggered back, his hands covering his eyes. "What've you done?" His face distorted, shedding cells, definition.

Marie gasped, "Play, Wire, play."

Wire played a rhythm—echoing the capture of slaves, the Middle Passage. Syncopation sounded like tears and the auction block. Sax and clarinet added their voices, a sound recalling pain, heartbreak; then a trumpet sounded, heralding, demanding witness. Another trumpet and another. The piano entered the improvised song. Then all the sounds soared; the dozen musicians inspired. Dede slapped a tambourine.

Rudy blew his horn—a sound that seemed infinite, reaching between life and death.

"Stop it," shouted John. His hands covering his ears.

All the musicians played as if their lives depended upon it, their spirits speaking of their pains, hurts, joys, and triumphs. Speaking to their ancestors. Traditions. Overcoming. Music consoling. Sound bearing witness to survival.

Oppressed slaves, colonized free coloreds, had triumphed by evolving, creating new traditions, blending African and Catholic faiths. Blending music, creating a new music. Jazz to herald their becoming, their new identity.

Not assimilating; instead, triumphing. Becoming a new people.

"Louder," shouted Marie. "Play louder."

Carlos sprayed John again.

John screamed, collapsing.

"Louder."

There was no space other than the space between notes, sound. Rhythm.

Marie bent over John. "I rule here. Always have. Always will."

Carlos sprayed his limbs.

John—flesh dissolving, less a man, still shadow and substance— jerked Marie's skirt, tilting her off balance.

"Marie," screamed Parks.

Snarling, feral, a shadow mouth punctured Marie's wrist.

Locked in the embrace, Marie could feel her life, her memories draining. Feel John growing in substance, reviving; she tried to pull away, his grip, crushing.

The music grew louder; a community of brothers, exorcising. Good over evil.

Marie took strength from the music, but it wasn't enough.

John kept draining her blood.

"No," Parks raged, lifting the gris-gris bag, scattering its contents. The centuries-old dust, hair, the insect bones.

John roared, shifting focus enough for Marie to crawl backward and away. Blood dripped from her arm.

"Agwé. Damballah. I call upon your power."

Agwé appeared, rattling his sabre, slicing at the green-tinged darkness; Damballah, a spirit snake, tightened about John's torso.

John was losing form, substance.

"The emblem," Marie shouted. "Give it to me, Parks. Play, Wire. Play. All of you."

Parks dragged her farther away, handed her the emblem.

Marie yelled, "You've dishonored your tribe. Your people. You rule from hate. Not love."

Rudy's trumpet trilled, soaring up. DuLac pressed inward. So, too, Alafin, Sarah, JT, and the ghosts of all John's other dead.

"See them?" Marie shouted. "You've done no good. You don't deserve life." She held the emblem high, then let it fall.

The shadow that was John screamed: "I loved you."

"Liar." Marie raised her foot high, then stomped, cracking the emblem.

John howled.

Carlos sprayed the last of the penicillin. *Green, organic matter, separated from darkness, becoming inert. Intangible.*

Rudy blew a note—so piercing, both sweet and sharp. The note held for a minute, two. Held all the pain of a people transported to America.

Wire shouted and the other musicians followed suit. Shouting, playing, hollering . . . a cacophony of unscripted power. Improvisation based on their souls' celebration. Tapping feet, music soaring. A shout-out for a community's glory.

Marie stood over the contracting dark green mass becoming ever smaller.

"'Back to the sea,' says Agwé," she murmured. "'Back to your grave,' says Damballah. Science says you'll never rise again. The bacterium is dying. Back to an unforgiving past."

One by one, the musicians silenced themselves until only Wire was drumming.

Carlos stood over the fading mass.

Dede stood next to him. "I believe."

Arms upraised, Marie turned to the musicians. "Together, we did this."

Wire stopped drumming. Laboring to breathe, his shirt soaked with sweat, his expression was ecstatic.

"It's gone," said Marie.

On the floor, there was no substance. No evidence that a *wazimamoto*—that John—had ever existed.

"Will it come back?" asked Parks.

"No," said Marie.

Parks embraced her tightly. "I will."

Marie relaxed, her head resting against Parks's chest.

"You need rest," said Carlos.

Parks lifted Marie into his arms, cradling her like a bride.

"We did it, people. The vampire is gone," shouted Parks.

The musicians nodded, appearing cool. Wire slumped onto the floor.

Carlos said, "Take her home. I'll watch here. Make sure it's dead."

Dede volunteered. "I'll clean up. Make sure no one knows what happened here. Just another gig. Right?"

The musicians lit cigarettes, weed. Heavy eyed, they prepared to go home. Sleep.

The piano player helped Wire to stand. "Time for bed."

Parks looked at all the black and brown men. "You are all amazing," he said. "I can't thank you enough."

He looked at the men in turn—the trumpet and saxophone players, the piano player, Wire, the clarinet players, Dede. Finally, Carlos.

"Sure, Detective." Carlos waved his hand.

"Anytime," said Wire. "For Miz Marie."

Parks nodded. "No need to call the station. Our secret. They wouldn't believe us anyway."

"Play it as it lays," said Dede. "Tomorrow night. Full house. Arrive early."

The musicians grumbled. Carlos sat, his legs crossed Indian style, guarding against John resurrecting.

"Put me down, Parks."

"You sure?"

"I'm strong enough."

Marie stood—still—her arms at her side. Gradually, others stopped moving, too. Stopped packing a sax, lighting a cigarette, walking out the door. All the men were motionless, focused on Marie.

"My people," she whispered. One by one, the musicians bowed. Until all their heads bowed in respect. Marie bowed back.

"Jazz is voodoo made secular. Alive. An African-American triumph. Oppression overcome with song. We were all *loas* tonight. Miraculous."

Dede shouted, "Amen." Wire pressed his hands together in prayer, then stretched them high, as if gathering the heavens. The others grinned, knowing their music transformed. Wielded power.

Head erect, carriage tall, Marie walked from Preservation Hall.

Once outside, Parks offered his arm and an exhausted Marie leaned into him, letting him help her into his car.

"Water."

Parks pulled a bottle from the backseat.

She drank like there was no tomorrow; Parks turned the car onto the road. Slipped his siren on top of the roof; the light swirled, his siren whooped, as he drove himself and Marie home. The rain had become a soft drizzle.

"Tomorrow, the sky will be clear," Marie said.

"Tomorrow, we'll pick up Marie-Claire."

"We?"

Park's, one hand on the steering wheel, reached out with his other hand, clasping Marie's hand. "I'm not going to have you unsafe. You and Marie-Claire need a guardian. Champion."

"I thought I was the one who destroyed John."

Parks jerked the car to the curb; street hustlers scattered. A streetlight cast an eerie shadow in the car. Neon streaks swirled on the car's hood, the street. "If you don't want me, say so."

"I thought you were going back to Jersey."

His blue eyes looked straight ahead. "Jersey doesn't have you."

She cupped his cheek, turning his face toward hers. "You'll be strong when I'm not?"

"Sure. The rare times when you can't destroy a demon from the sea. A *wazimamoto*. A vampire."

She kissed him, long, lingering. Then, embracing, she could see, over his shoulder, all the ghosts. John's victims.

"Drive," she said.

"Where to?"

"Your apartment."

She turned around on the seat, watching through the rearview mirror: *DuLac, El, Kind Dog—a small band, a family—*as the car pulled away.

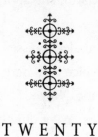

TWENTY

Marie lay naked in bed; Parks's arm was about her waist. His head was buried in the pillow.

The phone rang. Parks didn't stir.

Marie slipped from beneath his arm.

The answering machine clicked on.

"No deaths last night." It was Roach. "Parks, wake up. Tell the doc that Marie-Claire is safe. She's charmed all the priests. Parks, are you there? Wake up. You and the doc, all right?"

She heard a sound, as if Roach was blowing his nose.

"It's a good day. Sunny. No rain. See you at the station. Parks, don't mess with me if you're there. Shit." The phone clicked.

Parks breathed deeply. Sound asleep.

Marie slipped out of the bed. Picked up her jeans where she'd let them fall—or more to the point, where Parks had removed them. She'd known last night that Marie-Claire was safe.

She'd felt it in her bones. Still, she appreciated Roach's thought-fulness.

She opened her cell. Inhaled. Pressed Voice Mail.

Static. Then DuLac's voice. "It's here. Can't stop . . . at an end." Then, "I believe." More static. "In you."

Marie covered her eyes. Wept quietly, then crawled back into bed. Wrapped her brown legs about Parks's white legs. She kissed his nose. His eyelids. Kissed him awake.

"Good morning," he said.

"Marie-Claire's fine."

"DuLac told you?"

Marie laughed. "No. Roach."

"What's so funny?"

"The skeptical cop has become a believer." She closed her eyes, snuggling into the crook of his arm and chest.

"Doesn't mean I understand what happened. You going to ex-plain it to me?"

"Mainly it was instinct. Trying to deduce what could triumph over a colonial? Over the self-hatred of a *wazimamoto*? Music was the common thread—moving from calling the gods to a transfor-mative power when humans became as gods."

"I don't understand."

"Not Christian gods. Perfect on a pedestal. But living, breath-ing, hurting gods like all the voodoo gods. Reflective of pain and sorrow. Joy and hope. Good and evil."

"And the music?"

"The secular transformation of a people. Voodoo, unjustly, became disrespected. Thanks to such men as John. Charlatans intent on a dollar. Jazz became the triumphant sound, the acculturation of a people redeemed through art. Through Wire's artistry and the other musicians. I provided the spirit. Carlos, the science."

"And me? The useless dumb brute force?"

Marie kissed him. "Never dumb."

"Definitely not. Let me show you how smart I am."

Marie lay on her back, looking up at the ceiling. Her body arched as Parks kissed her neck, the hollow between her breasts. His hand stroked her clitoris; she shuddered.

He was kissing her. There and there. One-night stands were over.

She reached down, pulling him upward. Kissing him.

"You and me," he said.

"You. Me. And Marie-Claire."

He stopped kissing her, raising himself onto his elbows. Looking into her eyes, her heart. "Marie-Claire. Marie-Claire and her beautiful mother." Then, his mouth lowered on hers, licking her tongue. His hand, stroking her breasts, thighs, and vagina. Marie squirmed, touching him back. Measure for measure.

Suddenly, she stopped. "Go 'way, ghosts. You, too, DuLac."

Parks sat up, the sheet falling to his waist. "They're here?"

Marie smiled, tugging Parks back into her arms. Kissing him with passion. For the moment, all was right with the world. Her child was safe. She was a doctor, a voodoo practitioner.

"And very much a woman," murmured Parks.

Startled, she blinked at Parks. "You sure you're not psychic? Some Celtic gift?" Parks tickled her; giggling, she slapped his fingers away. "Let's put some music on. Spend the whole morning in bed."

Parks nibbled her ear. "Then, we'll take Marie-Claire for beignets."

"Precisely," she said, touching him, lower and lower, until he groaned.

AUTHOR'S NOTE

For decades I've been haunted by rumors of African vampires; it's especially apt since across diverse regions in Africa, vampires were the product of rumor. Responding to colonization, Africans told tales of white vampires, authorities who caused blacks to disappear. Vampire, fluid in its meaning, became associated with policemen, game rangers, many other authority figures whose jobs involved killing and blood. It was commonly understood, rumored, that often the blood on their weapons and uniforms belonged to humans. Just as it was understood that these authorities, if not white, were Africans who acted as instruments of colonial power.

Blood in all cultures is precious, and to see it drained from a body is abhorrent. In Swahili, the word *wazimamoto* literally means "men who extinguish fire." Even before there was such a profession as that of a fireman, this name—*wazimamoto*—became metaphorically linked to vampires. Some speculate that it's based upon rumors of men carrying buckets of blood, men who in bloodletting, literally drained the fire of human life.

Wazimamoto, bazimamoto in Luganda, eventually extended to the slavers who raided the African continent of humanity. Enslavers, colonizers, believed Africans to be superstitious barbarians. Yet through oral storytelling, Africans were indeed spreading necessary tales about the cultural vampirism of Portuguese, British, and French colonialism and the American slave trade. Africans, and later, American slaves, used narrative power as a transgressive and defensive response to colonization.

The *wazimamoto* is not a western vampire. The *wazimamoto* is a response and a warning about racist brutality, not a species preying on people and killing to survive.

I recommend Luise Walker's wonderful book, *Speaking With Vampires: Rumor and History in East and Central Africa*, published by the University of California Press, 2000.

The *wazimamoto* vampire spirit gave me the opportunity to bring back Marie Laveau's nineteenth-century nemesis—John—from my first novel, *Voodoo Dreams: A Novel of Marie Laveau*. I still feel sympathy for John, whose life and character were corrupted by slavery, the ultimate colonization. Yet, if any character would be strong enough to resurrect as a *wazimamoto*, it would be John, resentful of women and their spiritual power.

Integrating the *wazimamoto* with the power of jazz seemed both natural and logical to me. Studying voodoo decades ago, many writers, most notably Imamu Amiri Baraka, theorized about the importance of voodoo ceremonies in Congo Square and how it encouraged the development of jazz. Music in America has remained integral to black religion and life. It is a cultural foundation—healing, transformative, and, when necessary, transgressive against racist ills. The *wazimamoto* is and yet isn't out of place in twenty-first-century America. I tried to capture that even though the Civil Rights era brought increased black political power, educational and social opportunities for African Americans, and negated the partriarchal and subversive relations between white men and women of color (most notably, the laws and social institutions banning miscegenation), racism and the aftereffects of colonialism still have resonance and echoes in New Orleans.

I've enjoyed writing about Laveau's descendant in the twenty-first century—Dr. Marie Laveau. The first novel in this contemporary trilogy is *Voodoo Season*. *Yellow Moon* is the second. *Hurricane Levee Blues* will be the third, and, in this novel, I hope to explore the devastation of Hurricane Katrina and the subsequent abandonment of New Orleans.

African-based spirituality never died in the Americas—whether in secular or religious manifestations, the Africans carted to the New World were not blank slates but people who influenced and imprinted American culture.

Marie Laveau—the great nineteenth-century Voodoo Queen of New Orleans who was a great gift to America—is the woman who healed, nurtured a community, owned her sexuality, communed with spirits, and, some say, walked on water.

In an era when racial and sexual biases demeaned black life, black women in particular, she was a woman who rose up and said, "I *am*. I am Marie Laveau."

May we all celebrate our beings and our names.

Sincerely,
Jewell